APRIL'S BURDEN

DAVID J. HULL

WAMPAHOOFUS LLC

For My Children

Thanks also to Helen Baggot, Robert Kirk Moore, Sarily Ryea, and Kelly Sayre for their extremely valuable feedback and encouragement. Thank you.

PROLOGUE

Things aren't adding up. Something's wrong. These were Leena's thoughts on her drive back from her mother's house on Clover Drive. Leena was closer to her mother than her brother Derek, she always had been. Still, based on what she was seeing, it was time to involve him.

Leena just had one of the most puzzling visits with her recently retired mother. Leena's husband Eli stayed home with Everly that Saturday morning. She felt compelled to see her mom without the distraction that a five-year-old brings. Leena sought some meaningful adult conversation with her mother based on some suspicion that was mounting in their last few interactions. The last time she spoke with her mom earlier in the week, things felt *off*, as if she weren't fully present. She seemed only half engaged in the conversation which was atypical of her mother. April Densmore was always on her game; driven by time and schedules, driven by work, by her children, and now a grandchild. Leena's mother was one of those people who was perpetually focused if not consumed by daily tasks—as if she had to complete a certain number of actions on her to-do list—before allowing herself the luxury of a good night's sleep.

At the moment, Leena wasn't *overly* concerned. It takes more than one irregularity before there is a trend, she thought. Everyone can become distracted, and her mother was human after all. At thirty-one, it was probably time to admit that her mother was human. April had always been such an incredible mother and a propelling force for Leena and Derek that it was hard to wrap her mind around that she had frailties like the rest of us.

Leena disguised her visit as a drop by—out on a shopping trip without her daughter so that she could have a few minutes of alone time with her mom and sneak in a peaceful trip to the grocery store. While at her mother's house, their conversation was superficial, polite, but mostly just *off.* She seemed fidgety and remote, pleased to see Leena, but also sending her a vibe that she could leave anytime. For thirty minutes, they talked about everything from the spring crocus and hyacinth flowers that were emerging, to Everly's most recent tooth fairy visit. From there, they discussed the price of produce at their local supermarket and then on to Derek's lack of a love life. It was all on the surface— every facet of their conversation. It was as if Leena was speaking to someone who only half cared to understand. Leena did virtually all of the talking and what she got back in return were yes or no answers, or an occasional brief comment. April never took the bait to expound upon the conversation, and so it fizzled into a one-way dialogue. Her mom always had a point of view and was full of advice for her children. Her opinions weren't overbearing, she was simply assertive in things that mattered to her. And her mother was consistently open to the other sides of a conversation, with her peers, her sister, and her children. She was respectful of all parties, even if she didn't agree. This attribute made it easy to have a conversation with her, but that was not happening now. Try as she might, Leena could not get a fluid discussion going with her mother. It was clear to see that it wouldn't have mattered if she brought Everly along.

Twice, she processed the entire scene that had just unfolded with her mother on her drive back to her house, seeking clarity from introspection. When she arrived home, there was now enough reinforcement in her mind on the decision to bring in her brother Derek; to alert him that something wasn't right.

Derek sat in the parking lot, his arms resting upon the steering wheel, and started to wonder what was so important that Leena asked to see him today. When they got together, they planned well ahead. Leena's voice was approaching urgent last night, and so Derek complied. The way she was acting, it had something to do with their mom.

It was a rainy morning in April. One of those damp, pervasively gray, bone chilling spring days. The month was doing what it did best, and in doing so, it was paving the way for what May did best. The parking lot was approaching half full at 11:30AM. Derek's thoughts turned to the restaurant in front of him, thinking how strange it is that the sun can make something that appears dreary, much less so. Stranger still, that a layer of low hanging thick and smothering clouds can make something bleak appear even more melancholy. The restaurant's appearance did not benefit from the cloudy, chilly day.

The eatery did its best for what it was designed for;

good food—and larger than needed servings—for not a lot of money. The ability to feed a family without breaking the bank and to afford the opportunity for a family to experience a meal outside the home was its true design. Still, Derek observed the puddles in the parking lot, the dingy exterior walls, the weeping paint on the exterior sign, and the lackluster landscaping—it all created a venue that screamed mediocrity—and he knew just by observation, that the establishment had already seen its best days.

The rain necessitated a quick jog from his car into the glass vestibule. After a hurried escort to his table by a gum chewing host, he removed his raincoat and sat down to take in his surroundings. He sat patiently. It was a family style restaurant—no frills, no fancy, no extra flair. Yet there was a lot to look at in terms of people watching. Arriving fifteen minutes early, it allowed him time to get acclimated with all of the people at the beginning, middle, and end stages of their meals. He became most enamored by two sets of people. One pair was a quiet couple somewhere in their seventies. The other, a family of four, on an outing where it was obvious neither parent wanted to cook and then deal with the epic undertaking of the post meal clean-up adventure. As Derek had observed by watching his niece, when the meal is done, a hefty load of after dinner work begins, removing the plates from the table, cleaning faces, scraping partially dried food remnants off the table, sweeping the floor. From that point, the vacuum comes out and then finally the kitchen work begins. But for now, he observed plenty of fries on the floor, forming an almost perfect circle of repurposed potatoes around a two-year-old's highchair. She started to stare at Derek.

Why do children stare? he thought, while taking a sip of

the perspiring water the server had set in front of him moments ago. He paused and answered his own question with another question. *I guess the real question is, what are you doing right now, only slightly less discernible?* Feeling embarrassed, he took a deeper draught of the aggressively chlorinated water. He knew better but felt compelled to draw out a giggle from the French fry girl. And with one more sip, he sat his heavy glass down, raised his eyebrows, opened his mouth, and as best he could, distorted his features into the best *just-walked-into-a-surprise-party* facial contortion he could muster. The girl's first reaction was shock, then after a pause, she burst into a set of scales-on-the-piano giggles; up and down. And loud. So loud they disturbed the quiet couple in the corner. Derek looked over to her mother and father, he had already been caught as the instigator of the mischief. He just smiled and shrugged his shoulders. Each of them flashed back a quick smile that demonstrated that they were fine with his taunting and appreciated the interaction.

The restaurant was called *Unwind*. He believed Leena had picked this spot because it was where their mother took them periodically as children. It was a rare occasion when he and his sister were treated to a meal outside their home. Dinner was even more rare, being three times more expensive than breakfast. While his mom could have afforded an outside meal more, she was good with her finances and saved where she could. Three owner changes and one name change later, the bones of the place still looked the same as he remembered, just more tired. The fare was the only thing that seemed completely unchanged over time, as was apparent by the children's menu, a sophisticated line-up of chicken nuggets, fries, hot dogs, and macaroni and cheese.

Derek turned his focus on the graying couple in the corner. They were the opposite of the little girl; they ate their meal in quiet, in a sort of silent torpor. Their eyes only focused on their food, and then the fork, and then into their mouth. Repeat. Not once did Derek observe any other pattern. There were no looks at one another, no eye contact whatsoever. They were there physically together, but they were both alone. They sent no glances to the server, nor did they have any desire to take in their surroundings. Rather than reading the room, they were content with being read. They were in a food-to-mouth trance, and the only thing that broke the spell was the snickering girl's outburst. *Yes, I'm the guilty one. I am responsible for activating the lungs of the fry eating munchkin'*, Derek thought.

A text appeared on his phone that he had placed next to his fork. It was from Leena. *Just parking now.* Derek picked up his shoulders with a shrug. He was not sure why people had to announce themselves just before they arrive. Derek wondered again why Leena wanted to meet today and took another chug of water.

Leena was wearing dark blue jeans and a light blue top. At two years younger, their age difference was imperceptible. She looked healthy and vibrant. Her life was good, and stable; marriage, house, child, it was all becoming on her. She was a great sister, and his only one. She was there for him when he stumbled a few times, and he was there for her. He was mostly just an ear for her to bounce thoughts upon, but that was enough for Leena. Their relationship was closer than some sister brother scenarios, yet they weren't as close as some either. Derek longed to be emotionally closer to Leena and her family—to his entire family. He had seen some friends where their families were so tight that siblings hardly went a day not speaking to each other. *I just don't know how to get there,* was his last thought before Leena arrived at his table.

A customary quick hug, and Leena and Derek sat face to face. "Right on time," Leena proudly stated. Derek bowed his head with a yes.

"I'm good, Leena Pielski, how are you?" Derek responded sarcastically to her introduction.

"I'm good, Derek Densmore. Remember when we used to come here with Mom?" Leena asked. She was adjusting her full size blue and white swirly umbrella, propping it against the table; the rain had intensified outside. She then turned to her hair and made the motions of patting it down; an attempt without a mirror, to bring it back to how it looked prior to the rain.

"Yes," Derek replied. "It seemed, what's the word I'm looking for, more magnificent when we were children." Derek brought his eyes once again to the nearby family. Leena's eyes followed his. They both focused their gaze on the two-year-old who was calling for an encore. "Through the eyes of children, magic is everywhere, and all things are new," Derek finished his thought.

"*Hea-vy,*" Leena said, emphasizing both syllables with equal weight. "Did you think of that while waiting?" She smiled at him with genuine warmth.

"No, but look over in the corner," he instructed his sister. Leena, creating a diversion by adjusting her umbrella again, glanced over to the couple in the corner peacefully eating their early midday repast. "OK," she responded. "Are they famous? Should I recognize them?"

"They don't talk. They don't look at each other. It is as if they are alone, yet they sit facing each other. It makes me sad. I don't want to become like that. What happens? Do you just run out of feelings, thoughts, and things to talk about?"

"First off, *judge* much?" Leena retorted. "Secondly, I can see myself and Eli becoming like that, and it doesn't bother me," Leena went on, "my take—they've lived so much of their life, and they are still together. Can you imagine the experiences they've shared together? More than likely, they've watched children grow, watched them stumble, watched them thrive. They've fought with each other, and through their own hopes and desires, as individuals, and yet made it as a pair. They've toiled at jobs, and they've done housework. The joys, the sorrows, the ups, the downs. The blah days—like today's weather. The holidays that have come and gone. And yet, they're out as a couple today, enjoying a meal. It breaks up a day where they would be having a meal at home. It's something different. And they are doing it together after all that roller-coaster life stuff. I think it's wonderful."

"Touché," Derek said. "I've got no reply to that. I almost want to go over, shake their hands and pay for their meal." His tone was sarcastic, yet he fully understood the point Leena was making. In the grand scheme of things, the couple had a calmness about them and there was certainly an aura of enduring love that resided in the corner that you could not deny.

"Besides," Leena started. "You'll never have a chance to be that couple, because by definition, a couple is two and you are only one. Any dates lately?" The conversation shifted to the inevitable. It was an unwritten rule that when Leena and Derek got together, Leena would ask about Derek's relationship status. It was more upfront in this conversation than usual. And today, Derek had come to the conversation with his normal blank relationship canvas.

"I gawk at work," Derek began, "but, that's it." He paused a moment. The server appeared and poured a glass of water for Leena and handed her a menu. After a nice welcome, he disappeared to another table to provide them with a few more minutes before taking their order. "Most of the women are already in a relationship, or married, or many of them I have no idea—because it's none of my business—because it's work."

"There are other venues for meeting women," replied Leena, now sipping her available water. "Be bold at the grocery store in the produce section. Nothing screams love like hot peppers. Here's one, start up a conversation when you're on a walk. You know, when you see someone interesting out for a stroll with her dog, stop and talk to her. She won't bite, and the dog shouldn't either. Or, and this is mind bending, they have these things called dating apps. You would not believe it, but there are others out there right now that want to meet you, Derek. Yes, you."

Derek rolled his eyes at the mention of dating sites. "Nope," Derek retaliated. "Not that desperate." It was not that he was vehemently opposed to the idea, it just felt forced. He was at peace with being an idealistic romantic, and that one-day, love would walk into his life, and it would become *The Notebook*, part two. This time, he'd make Nicholas Sparks cry.

"I know I'm thinking way ahead, but bring someone to our place for Thanksgiving," Leena said. "OK? I only want you to be happy." She could detect his level of happiness; they were siblings after all. Before Derek could interject, she finished with, "Just to level-set, I *know* you're happy. I know. I know that you are content. But there is still a piece of empty that I feel. The right person can bring a lot of joy."

"What are you ordering?" Derek asked, as if the last few words never materialized from Leena's mouth.

"I see," said Leena, "time to change the subject."

"I hear the fried clams are good, and we have a critic raving about the fries over there," Derek's head pointed over again to the little girl. Her father started to put on her yellow raincoat. She was still sending glances to him after their bond earlier. Derek gave a tiny wave. The girl did so in kind and gifted him with a beautiful smile that can only come from a happy two-year-old.

"A salad for me," Leena went on after noticing the interaction. "I see a family in your future. Eli is grilling for us tonight, so a lighter lunch is in order."

"Nice," Derek replied, "you're quick on your feet today, weaving in multiple subjects at the same time."

After the girl and her family headed to the exit, for a brief moment, the restaurant became a few decibels quieter. "How's Everly?" Derek asked.

"She's great. Still queen of all she surveys and of all she surrounds." Leena picked up her phone, went into her photos and scrolled through a few recent pictures of her five-year-old. Derek observed a photo with Everly under the kitchen table, trying inconspicuously not to be seen.

"She's a peach," Derek said shaking his head, "what a little ham."

"In that one, she's trying to be low-profile. She said she was being a spy, watching my every movement and would report me to the authorities if I didn't behave. Can you actually believe she said 'authorities', this is coming from a five-year-old? And I'm still not sure where she picked up on espionage being a thing, let alone wanting to aspire to the occupation. I must be slipping as a parent. Influences, they are all around us and not all of them good." Leena finished her statement just as a busboy hurriedly began to address the table where the family had been. He had his work cut out for him and his face didn't hide his displeasure. "Hey, let's get you over soon. You can only be a hero uncle for so long before the magic wears off."

Derek paused for a moment and thought on that. Five years for him seemed to blur; the same job, the same small house. The routine of get up, go to work, go home, go to bed with eating and a little exercise in the mix created a ceaseless timeline of a predictable humdrum. But Leena and Eli's life in the past five years was vastly different than his. Everly came on the scene like all newborns, then proceeded to roll, crawl, walk, and talk and now had the audacity to enter kindergarten this year. All Leena had to do is mention Derek's name and Everly would go into a rant about the last time he came over and would regurgitate every minuscule detail of their previous visit.

"I will," Derek said, "you are right. This stage is so fun and in a blink of an eye, I'll just be a run of the mill uncle, or worse, some guy that shows up from time to time to visit her mom. I have to say, I do enjoy my current rock star status. And all rock stars fade, well not all. There is Adam Levine."

The server took their orders. More lunch traffic appeared. It was evident that Sundays were good for business. Tables filled with three generations in a booth at a time.

It was as if they subconsciously waited until their order was taken before they were in a mindset to tackle the subject matter that brought them here in the first place. They paused and looked around the room. Going from talking about Everly into a deeper subject was a shift and it was worth a mental breather. Their smiles faded.

"Time to talk shop? What's going on?" Derek started.

"I'm not sure if Mom is really shop talk," replied Leena, "but yes, I wanted to get us together to have a conversation." It was as if the clouds outside suddenly appeared inside, above their table, and the aching gray dullness blanketed them. When a sister and a brother have *a conversation* about a parent, it was sure to be heavy.

2

"**S**he's basically stopped talking. When she does talk, it's about the mundane; little logistical things, like getting something from the grocery store. When I went over yesterday, she didn't even ask how Everly was, let alone you. I had to bring up everything in conversation. And she's agitated. You know Mom, she's always had a touch of sad, but she's always projected some joy for life. It's gone, Derek. She's turning inside herself and is in a place of mental fidgety."

"Mental fidgety? Is that a psychological term?"

"You know what I mean," Leena replied and in no mood for her conversational partner to bring in deflection as a tactic. "I think she's been slowly withdrawing for some time. I've been noticing it. That's why I went over without Everly. She's alive, but in no way living. Derek, when is the last time you went over to see her?"

"I'm due for a visit. I went and saw her two weeks ago—I go over rain or shine every two weeks for a small visit. I make sure everything is in order, there are no major to-dos for the house, you know, I check-in. I check-in regularly to see if she's OK."

The server returned and poured more water. At this point, the restaurant was approaching full capacity. The server was burning a copious number of calories today, flittering about from table to table. "Do you ever have meaningful conversations with her?" Leena asked. "Like, asking how she is, beyond getting enough to eat or the quality of her sleep?"

"Not really. It's usually on the surface stuff. Come to think of it, I haven't fully engaged in a meaningful conversation with Mom in a while, I'm ashamed to say. I don't know what to say, I'm not sure if it's her or me, or both of us. I want to be closer, but there seems like there's," he paused, "a divide." Derek tried to suppress what was bubbling up in his mind relative to his relationship with his mother. They were closer when he was younger—at least to some degree, but when he became an adult, their relationship didn't seem to evolve. Mom was always just Mom, but not Mom as a friend or confidant. He wished he graduated into this next stage with her. But as in all relationships, things don't get addressed if you don't address them. And as time wears on, you accept the status quo and find ways to convince yourself that this is the way it is—without doing anything about it.

"I know. It's OK. I'm guilty too, and I'm not judging you. I just need you to understand and believe me that we're dealing with something different now. Her mind seems elsewhere—I want to say always. And since you challenged me, let me define mental fidgety. She seems restless and anxious. She's disturbed in some way, and I don't know how to get at it. I even asked her straight up if something was bothering her."

Several more tables filled with hungry customers. Reluctantly, they had to start to speak louder on a subject that the two fundamentally introverted people didn't want to discuss at all. The din of all the conversations and off-rhythm drumbeats of forks on plates made it necessary to turn up their own volume, making things more uncomfortable. They both shifted in their seats.

"I should have got us a booth," Derek said. "I feel like we're on display." Booths lined three of the four walls at *Unwind*. Tables were sprinkled about in the center.

"My point is," Leena began again, "I don't know what to do. She didn't even really respond to my question about her being OK. Her eyes just gallivanted around the room in a disconcerted way. Her mind is restless, Derek; that's the only way I can put it. Ergo, mental fidgety. I'm worried for her, and I think we need to address it. She's not eating much. Mom has always eaten healthy and exercised. I don't think she's doing much of either. And not to weird you out or anything, but I don't think hygiene is at the top of her list either. Don't get me wrong, she's clean, I mean, but you know Mom... a shower every single day, and sometimes, two. But now, it's more like when she gets around to it."

With that last statement, as if on cue, their meals came. A salad for Leena and soup and sandwich for Derek. He tried to wrap his head around Leena's last point; their mom did everything within an extreme cycle of regimen—house cleaning, exercise, planning the day ahead, and certainly hygiene. To Derek, denial felt like a good place to go. Mom not talking was one thing, but behaviors not being consistently like Mom was ...other. Not only did the clouds from outside feel wrapped around them, but the spring's dampness began to enshroud them.

Out of habit and not hunger, Derek and Leena took a few bites of their meal, providing a much-needed moment to reflect. For whatever reason, Derek thought of an algebra problem; solve for x. He liked solving for x because it was solve-able. If you knew the rules of mathematics and all of the tips and tricks of algebra, then x was a moment away. It was just a little puzzle, and then all of x's and y's shifted into numbers and then you were done with the problem.

"I don't know how to solve for x," Derek whispered, barely loud enough for Leena to hear.

"What? What do you mean?" Leena replied, putting down her fork and reaching for her napkin.

"I mean, I have no idea where to start on this, this thing, this situation, Leena." Leena knew Derek had shifted to a new place in his mind. He rarely used her name while conversing. By using it, they entered an unfamiliar area together into the subject of their mother and a vast new space of seriousness and discomfort.

"Go seem Mom. Tonight, or tomorrow," Leena told Derek. "That's the first step. For all I know it's some sort of mid-life crisis. Or something could be seriously wrong, maybe with her health."

Derek thought for a moment. His mind went everywhere at once. He even wondered if this was the beginning of the end of a certain normalcy in the relationship he and Leena had with their mother. Change was part of life, and he felt comfortable with change in most aspects in his life. At work, if there was a new process or new business application, he was all about it; he prided himself on his adaptability. Yet, if there was a change to the family dynamic with his mother, Leena, and himself, it seemed to disturb him far more than he imagined.

"I'll call her this afternoon. Like I said, I'm due for a visit. Maybe bring over some take-out for us. One further, I'll report back to you this evening after my reconnaissance." Everly's espionage picture popped into Derek's mind.

"Now that's what I call sibling responsibility," Leena said with a speck of lettuce in her teeth, "but seriously, thank you. I think you'll find it disturbing. I know nothing of this sort of thing; however, I cannot stop wondering if it's some sort of nervous breakdown."

More things to consider. Derek did his best to look on the bright side of things. Despite his efforts to find an optimistic angle, there was a churning in his stomach, and it was not the fault of his lunch.

They did the best they could with their meal, trying not to waste it. Considering the topic, it was not exactly an appetite aphrodisiac. They both ate roughly half of what was in front of them. The server appeared and asked if everything was OK with their food. Both Leena and Derek flashed obligatory smiles and expressed how everything was fine. Leena even finished with a "My eyes were larger than my stomach." This seemed to please the server, now understanding his tip was not in jeopardy.

As several minutes passed without conversation, they looked at each other. And as only two people that share the same childhood beliefs and conditions can, their feelings were entirely in the same pensive place.

They waited for the check to arrive. "Anyway," Leena

did her best to find a way out of the conversation they were just in, "I'll set another plate at Thanksgiving. That's over seven months to find a girlfriend." Her statement slightly lessened their somber state. Maybe they weren't the closest siblings, but their relationship was a caring one. He took solace from that thought.

3

After a quick hug and another recap of Derek's newly formed itinerary for the remainder of the day, they both found their way to their vehicles.

"Sugar, Honey, Iced Tea," Derek said aloud in his car, in a deep sigh, thinking about their conversation just a few minutes ago. The rain had subsided, at least temporarily, but the clouds and cold dampness had no desire to leave. Before he and Leena met, Derek had planned a day of laundry, tidying the house, and trying to deflect the Sunday night blues with a beer and getting lost in a ball game. It was spring and baseball was just starting. If he couldn't find a Phillies game, it didn't matter with baseball. Most times, he could care less about the teams involved; Derek was fascinated with baseball for two reasons. It was a sport that had no hardcore time boundaries. Baseball had no division of a quarter or a period which contained a clock ticking down the time. And it was a sport where the foundation of the game all started with a dad and a son tossing a ball, together in the backyard. Those were romantic thoughts, and the latter of the two fascinations had eluded Derek. He had no father growing up. Between watching the family in the restaurant and talking about his spirited niece, he started to wonder if having a toss with a son or daughter was in his future. It started to sprinkle again, and the water droplets were enough to drag his thoughts away from baseball. He wondered if he should go back to his house or if he should call his mother from the car. Laundry was a must though and with that, he started the car.

At home, Derek threw his keys upon his dining room table. They say location is everything in real estate. Not so, it is really about what is available when you are looking to purchase a home. When you are ready to purchase, you have only certain options—buying a home is all about timing. He would have preferred a bit more privacy than having neighboring houses to his left and to his right. But, nevertheless, his crisp white two-bedroom bungalow was on a coveted cul-de-sac, and that meant not a lot of traffic. It was small and it needed quite a bit of attention when he purchased it, but not much traffic —tradeoffs.

Derek and Leena's mom did the best that she could. Derek, as a child, was hard on his mother. As an adult, he realized all of the sacrifices she made. Raising two kids on your own and choosing not to bring someone else into the family dynamic; he respected fully. His mother was a beautiful woman, and still was. She had aged gracefully and the gray in her hair seemed to accentuate her features in a manner that was complementary. She certainly could have landed someone in a heartbeat, and he often wondered why she didn't date, or why no stepfather or even a stepfather figure entered the picture.

It seemed never an option in his mother's eyes. As much as he respected her now, he remembered times when he was a boy and was relentlessly unforgiving. In hindsight, he was jealous of his friends with fathers. And jealousy is a strange thing where your own hurt soaks in a marinade. After saturating, it then manifests itself into a grotesque lash-out towards the person you love. It is a bizarre recipe. Take one-part envy, blend in self torment, mix it, and stir it some more, and then throw the dripping concoction of loathsome at someone else—in all cases, the person you care most about. *What a strange human thing*, Derek thought. He supposed he pushed her away, year after year, and that was the reason why they weren't close. He took full accountability in this, after all, why would his mother have an issue with him—preventing her to be close with him?

He crammed all of his laundry into one load, not bothering to separate the colors. There wasn't time today for two loads.

Derek grabbed his phone and plopped down on the couch. He then proceeded to let out a deep sigh; first developing in his toes, radiating through the legs, into the lungs and then the mass of air rushed from his lips—half breath, half moan. Instead of asking, he decided he would just tell his mother he was coming over for a visit. A direct approach seemed the best path today.

"Hullo, Mom," Derek spoke, "how are you?" There was a delay in the response. "Fine," there was another long pause. "I'm OK. What's going on?" Already, Derek thought that things might not be the picture that Leena had painted—she was speaking to him clearly—at least for now.

"Thought I'd bring over some take-out later this afternoon and have a visit. Chinese food sounds yummy.

What can I put you down for?" Derek added enthusiasm to his voice. He had already mentally wrapped his head around an afternoon with his mom. He never dreaded visiting Mom. Although, it did seem more like something you did, like laundry, versus something you looked forward to. He wondered if that was normal at all and felt a pang of guilt for even having these thoughts.

"Not all that hungry. Whatever you think is best," his mother responded. At least there were words coming out of her mouth and she was answering his questions coherently and appropriately. Derek's next thought was that she could just be in a funk. Everyone gets down— funks come and go. The best of us gets knocked down. A Japanese expression he heard one time came to his mind, *seven times I fall, eight times I rise.* Certainly, Derek thought, if she were depressed, she would find her way back out. Mom was more of a seventy-nine-times-I-fall eighty-times-I-rise, type of person.

"You *will* be hungry—later on. It's from *Wok-To-Me*. They have the best Singapore Mei Fun, and their eggrolls aren't greasy," he continued, "they are crisp and golden, gettin' hungry yet? Am I selling you up?"

"Sure, that'd be fine." The tone of her response couldn't have been more neutral. It wasn't cold, yet the warmest it could ever be called was tepid.

Casting aside her tone, as he wasn't seeing her body language, he let it go. "Give me some time, I've got to finish up laundry and Leena and I just ate a bit ago." He waited for some sort of an acknowledgement from his last statement. At least this is how the conversations had always gone in the past. When you have a relationship with someone, albeit friend, mother, father, partner, over time, the dialogue seems to develop a foreseeable pattern. You can predict when and how they will respond, with tone and meaning, the pauses, the mood, the expression. His mom would typically confirm his last statement, yet he continued to wait. Awkward silence continued. "Mom?"

"I'm here." Her response finally came.

"I'm going to be a few hours, and then I'll come over, OK?" This time Derek emphasized things with an unmistakable question, seeking a response in the affirmative.

"Sounds fine. Bye." Derek's mom ended the call. *Since when does Mom end our calls like that?* thought Derek. They usually ended a phone call by letting each other know that they had run out of things to say. Or, even for a quick call like this, they would align their good-byes together. Today, his mother had rewired all of their years of unspoken rules of phone call etiquette.

"Sounds fine. Bye?" Derek said it out loud and stared at the phone. He was glad that Leena called a lunch for them to discuss their mother's current state. It was puzzling. While listening to the usual whirling of the washer and the spinning and clunking of the dryer, Derek spent time thinking. What was causing his mother not to act like his mother; depression, a major health issue, was she not adapting to retirement, did she bet it all on a horse and lose it? The only thing that took his mind off his mother was taking stock of his laundry supplies. He was low on dryer sheets; static electricity was an unwelcomed guest.

4

April Densmore resided in a development carved out in the late twentieth century. She lived in the same town as her daughter, Leena Pielski, and the town over from her son, Derek Densmore. At the genesis of the development in which she lived, the houses were built by the same developer and as was customary at the time, the houses looked almost identical to each other. Cookie Cutter Drive, or so goes the cliché. Over time, the residents had done their best to distinguish their homes from their neighbors'. A mudroom addition here, updating siding there, dormers on this house, a bay window on that house—but all still held the same basic DNA; a small Cape Cod with two bedrooms upstairs and a half bath, one bedroom downstairs, a full bathroom, a combo kitchen dining space, and a modest living room. It was a sea of middle class. The kind of middle class where everyone had enough to eat. The kind, where you were warm in the winter and cool in the summer. It was, however, the same middle class where you dreaded the next visit to the grocery store and wondered if you would have enough left over for the power bill. It was the middle class where you got by with a roof over your head but going on a vacation was usually a fantasy. Here, you added shrubs and perennial gardens for a front lawn face lift, not to look better than your neighbor, and not just to make things more aesthetically appealing. Here, in this neighborhood, you leveled up on your landscaping simply to feel an ounce of control in the constant struggle to make ends meet.

April bought the fourth sage green house on the left of Clover Drive twenty-nine years ago. And like her son, she realized well before him that it was less about location, location, location. Real estate is about what is available and what is affordable—at least to a first-time home buyer with two small children who is desperately seeking a way out of a dingy apartment. And while most of the homes had some degree of plastic surgery, 23 Clover Drive, other than being painted twice, looked the same as it had when the last nail was pounded into its frame. There were two trees out in front that were not native to the original grounds. When Derek and Leena were young, they got to choose and plant their own tree. Leena had proceeded to pick out a Crimson Red Maple, and Derek selected an American Beech. Both trees, now well over twenty years old, provided so much shade to the little house that the roof displayed more moss than it did shingles.

While raising her children, April had worked in customer service for a local energy company. They delivered oil, propane, and kerosene and were the ones to call if your furnace decided to take a winter vacation. Because April was so competent, she inherently received more responsibility than just customer service. April became the office manager and kept the office running well. She made sure all appointments were met and the company's delivery workers and technicians fulfilled all their obligations. More than once, when a delivery driver had the flu, April would think nothing of grabbing the keys to the truck to deliver fuel to those in need.

With a small pension, the innate ability to stretch a dollar, and putting a little extra each month to every mortgage payment, April retired at the age of fifty-six—with the option of returning part-time. That was less than a year ago. Retirement sounded wonderful at first. For the first few months after not having to get up before dawn every day, she took advantage of sleeping late in the morning. On her first day of retirement, she spent the entire day in her sleep attire. But for April, a woman who was born into rising and shining each day of life, to get up and be productive, there was no real satisfaction that came from being lazy on a Monday morning. The more she slept late and put on the television for company, the more restless she became. As the head of customer service and being the office manager, her expertise was solving problems; how do you contend with an employee that wasn't making the grade? Or finding more customers? Sometimes she had to deliver bad news to the owner. She even convinced the CEO to expand into solar. Whatever the reason, she solved problems in her sleep. Now as she slept, there were no more work problems to solve. But her subconscious began to turn to other uninvited matters.

5

Derek was pulling his mixed load out of the dryer and began folding the warm, dried clothes. Wanting to be in the moment of folding his clean clothes, he did his best to concentrate on his hands and to feel the warmth in his shirts while placing them in a neat pile. Try as he might, his thoughts rolled back to the earlier conversation he had with this mother.

He and his mother always stayed in regular contact through the years. Even seeing each other every few weeks, and living in the next town, he recognized more than ever that they were not emotionally close. With no father, Derek was both hard on her and over-protective as well. He thought of a time when he relentlessly begged his mom to take them camping. After giving in one summer, sitting by the campfire, she was into a glass of wine, and Derek was into a roasted marshmallow. Leena had already gone to bed. He remembered this moment well, because it was the first time his mom had ever spoken to him, the way she did. The stars were out, the mosquitoes kept at bay by the smoke, the fire was warm and glowing, and captured their gaze as fires do. "I'm doing the best I can, Derek." At ten years old, you are running fast at becoming a teenager. But at ten, like most boys, your thoughts still focus more on Legos and less about legs; you're still very much a child. His memory allowed him to see him finishing the perfectly toasted marshmallow. He turned to his mother and looked deeply into her eyes. The light of the fire allowed for only a small portion of her face to be revealed, but he was certain that he saw her eyes begin to water. What was a wonderful memory ended as a regret—as too often a vivid memory can. The ten-year-old Derek responded with something different than what he wanted to—even at the time. "I know," was all that Derek had said. But what he genuinely wanted to say was, "You are the best mom in the world, and I can't thank you enough for all you do." And perhaps that is what irked him so; for the first time, he was being talked to as an adult rather than as a child. Instead of responding like he wanted to, he chose marshmallow avenue. Many regrets are about what you say at a particular time in life—nasty things, hateful things. Yet some regrets, Derek realized, were about what you don't say.

Wok-To-Me wasn't anything like a dive. He forgave the pun that the owner used for its name, for in fact, the restaurant received a considerable amount of foot traffic. There was a lot of thought that went into the business; they knew the secret sauce of execution—make every detail count. Their entrance was welcoming, and the lobby was immaculately clean. Always, without fail, you would receive a top-notch welcome when you arrived and you were offered a genuine smile; not an obligatory upward turn of the lip, but an authentic, great-to-see-you expression of joy. When you left after procuring your brown paper bag filled with your order, you received the most genuine thank you from the owners and everyone on their staff. The food was always fresh, delicious, and the prices were beyond fair. Every detail of the experience gave you the feeling like you belonged, and the final product—it left you warm inside—guaranteeing a return customer. Derek tried not to be a frequent flyer, but still ordered there about once a week. For him, running solo had its perks.

He could feel the heft of the Singapore Mei-Fun, seaweed salad, and two jumbo eggrolls as he walked across the parking lot. Derek's car soon began to smell like the establishment he just left. He immediately thought that this was the best way to get his mom to eat. Resisting this trifecta from *Wok-To-Me* would take some real discipline. Twenty minutes later, Derek took a left down Clover Drive and then another left, into the driveway of the sage green cape with two large, yet quite different varieties of trees; the crimson maple already starting to leaf out. His beech, he knew from experience, was one of the last deciduous trees to believe that spring would arrive. The April rain still lingered. Derek shut off the car and headed to the front door holding their dinner in a brown paper bag, now covered with raindrops.

6

"Hi Mom," Derek knocked and entered at the same time. "I've brought dinner!" No response initially came. Louder this time, Derek increased his decibels. Another pause came, and then he heard the light tread of his mother coming down the stairs.

"Mom?" Derek's question was a hello and an *are you alright* at the same time.

"Hi Derek," his mother responded in an expressionless voice, "to be honest I couldn't remember if you called earlier, or if it was a dream. I napped a bit ago."

"Well, if it was a dream, this is the best dream—*ever*." Derek held up the bag of takeout and brought forward a smile. "If you're not hungry, this will *make* you hungry. I don't have the 'best customer' parking space out front yet, but I'm working on it." More attempts at humor to see if he could spark some sort of emotional response from his mom. Her face remained stoic.

So far Leena's story had checked out. His mother's

hair laid flat and was two shades darker and slightly glossy. She and a showerhead had not had relations in at least a day.

April Densmore strolled over to her television watching chair, or so she called it. Derek followed his mother into the living room and sat upon the nearby green loveseat that was a spot-on match to the exterior color of the house.

April had always kept the house tidy and clean. Always. She ran her house like she did the office she managed. Through all the years, Derek and Leena had never known an object out of place. Leena had said one time to Derek that she learned the term 'Dust-Bunny' in college because such corner loving little fuzzballs had no place in April Densmore's house. The floor was swept daily and the few rugs they had were vacuumed weekly. It wasn't an operating room, but growing up, Derek and Leena had learned the core belief that a house was to be neat and clean, at the expense of sleep if so required.

On the coffee table was mail from what looked like weeks ago. Derek had glanced into the kitchen and spotted dishes in the sink. There, he saw a few combinations of dirty forks, bowls, and plates—the biggest sin of the house. *Crap, Leena,* Derek thought and shook his head. Rome *was* burning.

"Are the Navarros back from their trip yet?" Derek was doing his best to entice any conversation he could from his mother. While he didn't know the next-door neighbors well, they seemed like good people. Although reserved, they were always pleasant in every interaction he had. As April's next-door neighbors, the Navarros moved into the third house on the left on Clover Drive well over ten years ago. While he had good experiences with them thus far, to this day, there was some sadness he felt when asking about them. It wasn't that the Navarros moved in next door to their mother; it was who moved out. The Vaughns moved to Ohio three months before Jan and Petra Navarro moved in. All this meant that Cynthia Vaughn, the strawberry blonde, one grade below Derek and one ahead of Leena, childhood friend never came back during the holidays. For Derek, it created an unfillable emptiness. If ever there was an analogy from a caterpillar to butterfly, Cyndi was it. Cynthia Vaughn and all her pimples, braces, blushing face, beanpole body, and the observable social awkwardness of an introvert at a cocktail party crawled into a chrysalis in the summer between her freshman and sophomore year of high school. Upon the moment she broke free of the cocoon, Derek could never talk to her the same. He found it difficult to make decipherable words form whenever she was around. She emerged as a woman as graceful and confident as anyone he knew. From that point on, he would glance as much as he could, trying to avoid staring; the confidence and elegance amplified her natural beauty and curving physique. He wondered how long it had been since he had seen Cyndi.

"No, I don't think so," his mom said with little to no enthusiasm. "We don't talk too much." For Derek's mother, good neighbors were cordial but kept to themselves; so, for April, the Navarros were perfect neighbors.

It was then that Leena's final point from their earlier conversation that day checked out. While Leena had coined it a sort of mental fidgety, it was obvious that his mother was in a low-grade agitated state that was accompanied by a pinch of irritation. While seated, her right knee bobbed up and down in fifth gear. Her shoulders looked tight, and her neck appeared stiff. Derek's eyes finally took in his mother's face. While he had seen her just two weeks ago, her face looked as if she was much older in half a month's time. Her eyes were sunken, wrinkles that seemed small were now in crisis mode. Her thinning face pronounced her cheekbones and not with a healthy sort of enunciation. An intense pang in his stomach brought reality front and center. His mom looked old, at least to him, for the first time in his life. He was glad to be sitting down. The solid rock that was his mother through all of his life now sat before him diminished, frail, and noticeably distraught. It was like seeing the day that inevitably comes when you have a bouquet of flowers in a vase on your dining room table. The flowers stand proud and boastful until finally that one morning arrives, and it changes from full on beauty to wilting frailty. His mother, for the first time, appeared fragile, and she also exuded a thick and palpable tension.

"Mom," Derek was going straight in, "are you OK?"

"I'm fine, I'm just not that hungry," she replied with eyes shifting up to the bookcase to her left. It was not the first time Derek caught her gaze launching towards it. Upon the bookshelf were a myriad of neatly displayed souvenirs, a small eclectic assortment of hardbound books, and an old goldfish bowl—void of any fish— holding only its neon pink gravel and fake green plants as its residents. Way back, Leena had a goldfish that lived for at least a decade. Locks was its name, short for Goldilocks. But Locks was long gone, yet her bowl of a home remained on April's bookshelf. Derek suspected that it reminded his mother of a time when Leena and Derek were younger, a time when they always ate as a family together and talked about their day. Now, they ate together mostly just during holidays—just a few times a year. Sometimes you need to hold onto memories of the past and you need physical, real-world reminders of how things were to have those memories endure. With those good and pure memories, you need to hold down and hold on to how things were at a certain time in this ever-moving continuum of life. Derek believed Leena's, rather Locks' fishbowl to be that memory anchor for his mother.

"I know you're not hungry, Mom," Derek started again. "Let's at least have an eggroll." He unfolded the paper bag and reached in for the still warm eggrolls and dug deep for the napkins and duck sauce. April was going through the motions for her son and started to nibble on what Derek sat on a napkin in front of her. All the while, she seemed distracted and distant. Again, her eyes darted up onto the bookcase. "Fine as in, good fine? Fine as in, great fine? Fine as in, just leave me the Hell alone fine?" Derek threw out this last salvo; trying his best to get any sort of clarification around her current disposition.

"I'm going to stay with Aunt Eileen for a bit of time. And I'm fine, fine—really, Derek." The way she concluded the statement with Derek's name was her way of saying that she was done talking about it.

Leena was named after their aunt, but Leena chose never to use Eileen formally; in all aspects of her life other than on her birth certificate, she was known to the outside world as Leena. To this day Derek still wondered if her husband Eli even knew her real birthname. While more times than not, Aunt Eileen would come up to his mother's place to visit, it wasn't unusual for her to go down and see her sister every so often. The drive was about two hours and easy traffic. Derek felt a relief. If she were going to see her sister, it meant that things weren't completely unraveled—some time with family is a good thing—and this would certainly be good for both of them. Derek's appetite started to kick in with this news and took an enormous bite out of his handheld eggroll. After some more chewing he swallowed his bite. "When are you leaving? Do you want me to keep an eye on the house?" Derek was licking his lips; *Wok-To-Me* outdid themselves again.

"Tomorrow. I'm playing the trip by ear and am not sure how long I'll be. Don't feel you have to, but maybe you could get the mail a few times. That would be nice." And with that, Derek could feel that his mother was done talking and had produced as much information as she was going to. Simply relieved that she would go for a visit to her sister's, Derek backed off.

"Of course," Derek replied. He had been wanting to patch a small hole in the sheetrock of her downstairs bathroom. The doorstop had been stepped on, came off, and failed to perform its job. The effect resulted in the doorknob having a rough fight with the drywall. The wall had lost the fight—badly, and a doorknob shaped circular hole now resided in the sheetrock. In addition to fixing the wall, he thought he would surprise his mother by filling up her grill's propane tank and buying a new cover for it. The current cover, besides being unsightly, was sun bleached, weather cracked, and could no longer perform its function of keeping the grill dry and protected. With his mom going for an out-of-town family visit, it would give him the time he needed. And then coming home to a few loving acts of service, Derek thought her spirits would rise and she would find a way out of the funk she was in.

Derek stayed to watch his mother finish her eggroll. It was an obligatory snack, and she only did it so that her son would actually find himself on his way. "I see you have a hyacinth," Derek said while leaning over to pick up what had to be a newly purchased flower—probably from the local grocery store. It was a grouping of three hyacinths, snugly fitted into a small plant pot with glossy purple wrapping. The flowers were not quite ready to reveal their color. But judging from the packaging, it was obvious they would soon explode with vibrant purple. "Want me to plant it for you?" Derek asked.

"No!" his mother's reaction was strong, and it took him aback. "I mean, no, I'm going to bring it down with me."

"Oh, a gift for Eileen. That's nice, she'll like that. Please say hi to her and Uncle Bo for me," Derek finished.

Derek issued a quick, one arm hug to his mother, as she continued to sit in her armchair. As they exchanged good-byes, Derek headed for the front door. He gave one more glance back towards his mother. While he didn't necessarily want to take in her image again, he felt the pull to do so. It was still there; a feeling of agitation and weariness that hung all around her, and he swore that he caught her again, looking up at the bookcase, moreover, directly at the fishbowl.

7

After retirement, April expected her dreams to flow into a more peaceful rhythm without anything nagging them. She had raised two wonderful children. For all practical purposes, she ran a local business and saved it from bad times on more than one occasion by helping the owner change and adapt to the evolving competition in the next town. She found a way to pay off the mortgage and own her small home. She had overcome many obstacles in her life and was proud of never falling on victim status. April took charge of her span of control. Countless times, to herself and to her children, she would say that life was a shuffled deck of cards. Each day you were dealt cards. It was up to you to play those cards to the best degree you could. Sometimes you got a great hand, sometimes you got a poor hand. When the dealer slapped down crappy cards, you could cry unfair or even try to quit; but each would drag you down. However, if you played each hand with a smile on your face, you would learn to live in an uncertain world—making the best out of any situation.

It was this poker analogy that propelled April in many facets of her life.

Yet, April's sleep became anything but restful. A darkness, which she at first attempted to deflect, began to invade her nighttime dreams. An invasion of marauding thoughts became impossible to ignore and haunted her sleep without forbearance. Most nights, when she turned out the light, her body tossed and turned, directed by her overactive mind. Things, shrouded with darkness, long buried, seemed to surface; some things which April had commanded to disappear long ago. The conscious mind can be tamed. But at night, when the mind tiptoes away from the awake and slips into the crevices of sleep, it reveals what it must—and you have no choice in the matter. The subconscious mind has its own cards to deal.

Not long into this new stage of being retired, after the sleep-late-and-be-lazy option lost its thrill, April started to journal her thoughts. She began to get up early again, five minutes earlier than the time she awoke while working full-time. She vowed never to sleep past this time on weekdays. At first, the journaling became therapeutic; letting things out onto paper she had never let out, and she found that the writings were quick to compound upon each other. She likened it to a computer that was in desperate need of defragging its disk space. She began to reach into places of her mind where doors were closed—and in some cases—bolted with a myriad of padlocks. She sifted through her life of memories; the good, the mundane, and then onto the darker, more painful accounts of her life. April found two old spiral bound notebooks, unused from her children's school years. She filled these two notebooks with any random thought that entered her mind. The notebooks filled up with names of people she worked with, funny anecdotes of customers, a time the pipes froze in her house, a time when she patched the ceiling after Derek played lightsaber with a golf club, a time when they ate a Thanksgiving meal without saying a word to each other, a time when she and her children went for ice cream after they finished up a school year and they sang and laughed all the way home in the car. She wrote about a time when she had no money left over to buy birthday presents for Leena. She wrote about a time when she was harder on Derek than she should have been—something that happened all too often. She wrote about a time when she cried herself to sleep, feeling completely alone in the world when her children were still toddlers. April wrote about the time when she cried with happiness seeing her granddaughter for the first time.

The first notebook was the easiest to fill. Every memory that surfaced, she let flow out from her pen. It seemed as if the first notebook was an exercise that made her mind and hands develop a natural state of flow. She was awakening the mental muscles in which to transform memories into words that now lived in a college ruled notebook. The second notebook, especially the second half, is where April began to struggle. Her dreams turned more ominous and pushed April towards a decision. There comes a time where you must choose; let things that you have intentionally buried stay where they are, and never confront them, or to turn on the light and examine what has been buried in the basement, in the dark and unpleasant corners. For April, up until now, casting light upon everything in her past made no sense. But for some memories, even if you actively choose to discard them, they still exist, and they ceaselessly nag you over a lifetime. Like something you throw away, it still lingers, in some landfill, somewhere. Such it is with certain haunting memories that you choose to treat as refuse. After years of telling herself to let go, April—without the distraction of work—had the time to relinquish everything entrapped in her mind and filled the pages on which she wrote.

When the second notebook was complete, April began on a third book. For this, she bought a black, hard cover journal, one worthy of accepting her organized composition. But instead of this book being random contemplations of unorganized thoughts, her prose was structured and methodical. In this book, April wrote of three well composed life secrets that could only have come from the depths of her mind—protected and guarded confidences from times long ago.

For over two months, she poured out her thoughts in her hardbound journal—line by line, word by word, meticulously organizing each passage. And when she was finished, she read it aloud to herself. April spent much of her life letting the past be the past. Now, with her words on the pages, they reopened vaults that her younger self swore would never be opened. It was one thing to bury your secrets. It is another, to confront them all on paper in your own handwriting. The attempt to reach closure is different in all of us; that relentless desire to find the release of all your emotional entanglements. April now faced another dilemma. As a step towards closure, she now had to decide how she would act on these demons —written with ink, now down on paper in the hardcover journal.

8

That night, Derek texted Lenna with the new information about their mom going to see Aunt Eileen. Hearing from him that he was in alignment with her assessment was important for her. Leena also took it as good news that she was going to visit Eileen—it might be exactly what she needed, to escape from whatever place of mental abandon she was presently in.

As a seasoned financial analyst, Derek liked where he found himself in his career. He enjoyed working forty hours, except for the four times a year where quarter ends required more effort. While he wasn't ever going to be spotted in an article as one of the world's richest, he was comfortable. He lived in a warm house, and he drove a car that pleased him; a gently used all-wheel drive BMW, of which, Leena gave him a significant hard time about. She constantly poked fun at him about his vehicle, and the rest of the driving populace not being good enough for him. For Derek, it wasn't about prestige, or ego. It was because, to him, the vehicle received an enormous amount of engineering. He ignored Leena's teasing, for it had no shimmy in the steering wheel—regardless of speed—even with snow tires. The cradling leather seats with warmers and the gripping all-wheel drive fit hand in hand with his driving prerequisites.

Two times, Derek was offered a promotion to oversee the entire financial roll up of the company; a twenty-six store, locally owned—but becoming more national—home improvement entity. They had not only survived in a world of larger competitors, but also thrived. Their competitive advantage was created by strategically placing stores in locations well outside the radius of one of the larger box stores, but also in areas where multiple townships would find it nearer to their homes. Secondly, similar to the Chinese restaurant Derek frequented, his employer concentrated on the small details of conducting business. Many of the staff were long time employees and the business had a strong family feel. A visit into one of their stores meant that you received exceptional service, and you left feeling like a human being. The founder and founder's daughter who recently became the CEO, would consistently say, *there's nothing better than being treated with kindness; more so when you are parting with your hard-earned money*. Employees bought into it. Beyond treating customers with kindness, the culture defined treating employees with kindness, too. Derek knew it came at a cost. They paid more for their employees, in some cases much more, than the competitors. But over time, keeping good people who genuinely cared, brought in more customers—and more profit. He also felt like a part of the family and was respected at all levels of the organization. When the CEO asked him the second time to take the promotion, he was tempted. He declined only because he was not quite ready to relinquish the benefit of being out by 5PM each day. She had told him in a half joking, half serious manner that she would only ask him three times. *Maybe in a few years*, Derek thought. He wondered how many people say that to themselves every day. And a few years go by, and then the time cumulates into decades, leaving an opportunity forever in the past.

It was after work on Wednesday that he decided to go to his mother's. Derek's office was on the second floor of their flagship location; their largest store and being the headquarters, it contained more fanfare than other satellite locations. Because it was their headquarters, the CEO saw fit that it would reflect everything and more about what the business stood for. Derek headed downstairs at lunch and joined other customers shopping for items to fix and improve. He purchased some spackle, a quart of primer, and some fine grit sandpaper with his employee discount. He also remembered to pick up a grill cover and a new propane cylinder. When he visited his mother, he often used the grill. One thing she really liked using the grill for was fish. Not only does grilled fish taste better, but it also meant that you spared the inside of your home of the unmistakable pong of fish-for-dinner.

As planned, after work, he drove to his mother's, retrieved her mail, and set down a few bills and advertisements on the kitchen counter. There were still dishes in the sink. He tried again to comprehend this new and troubling anomaly. He could not fathom his mother having dirty dishes in her sink, let alone leaving them when taking a trip out of town. Quickly, he washed the few plates and cups and carefully stacked them on the drying rack.

It was time to attend to the bathroom wall's injury.

Derek calculated that it would take him three trips to complete it. The first coat of spackle, then a good sanding if he waited long enough for the spackling to dry. The second would be dedicated to another spackle treatment—lastly, sanding and after that, if he found where her residual paint cans were stashed, he could finish the job. Voila, a bathroom wall sans doorknob hole. He left the spackle and other sundries on the bathroom vanity for his return trip.

Derek then moved to his next task and headed outside to the deck. He removed the old, rusted gas cylinder and reattached the new one, now full of liquid propane. He proceeded to remove the old cover and was just about to place the new one on top when he decided to peek under the hood to assess if it needed scraping or other cleaning. Inside, he was expecting to find the small remnants of the last time she grilled fish. What he found was more perplexing than his mother's untidy kitchen sink. Instead of finding remnants of his mother's last meal, his eyes took in what looked to be fragments of burnt paper. If he didn't know better, it looked as if someone tried to burn one or more notebooks. The final clue confirming this were two metal spirals, the kind you find on a college ruled notebook, traditionally used for school.

9

I t was late Saturday morning before Derek returned to Clover Drive, once again to pick up the mail and then also to attend to the second phase of his bathroom wall patching project. With the help of a box fan, Derek thought he could speed up the drying process enough to finish a little later that day. Perhaps he wouldn't need three trips. In-between steps, he paused to raid the refrigerator—there wasn't much of interest. He did spy a jar of raspberry jam in the door. *PB&J, why not?* Derek thought. He wondered how many thousands of peanut butter and jelly sandwiches Leena and he consumed under the roof of this house. His memory flashed to a time when he pretended to be a chef for Leena and Cyndi Vaughn. All he had in his repertoire were PB&Js; with the key variable of offering three different types of preserves or mixing all the jams and jellies together—that's how Cyndi liked it. Why he remembered, after all this time, how she liked her peanut butter and jelly sandwiches, he had no idea. His other honed culinary skill was being able to cut the crust off the bread—something that his mother would never tolerate. Wasting food, even bread crust, was on par with wickedness. Leena and Derek had no idea that one could eat a sandwich without crust; something unimaginable until Cyndi brought this new age concept into the Densmore household. Derek made sure he always balled the crust up after cutting it off and threw it outside in the backyard, where the woods bordered their lawn. Throwing it in the garbage can was far too risky. His mom would have grounded him for a week if she saw this sort of waste. "Again, with the Cyndi," Derek spoke the thought out loud while raising his eyebrows. He wasn't much into social media and actively avoided it. For the platform he used, he seldom spent time peering into the facades of others. Derek knew he was old fashioned when it came to social media. On the inside, he was proud to shun what he felt were platforms of narcissistic amplification. He saw too many acquaintances pretend to have a perfect life, which in turn incited envy and jealously in other acquaintances. Sadly, in turn, they retaliated with their own facades. To Derek, it was a self-absorbed arms race with no winner. And then there was the addiction part of it. But there was also the shame of not embracing it. He felt left out and almost shunned because he didn't use it much and was probably talked about as an outcast. His view was that the friends he wished to stay close with, he did; he texted, emailed, or one better, saw them in person when their schedules allowed. Not using social media regularly, or hardly at all, had its disadvantages. His sister was the social media user, and he thought that the next time he spoke to Leena, he would ask how Cyndi was. He was sure they stayed in touch. In Derek's head, he had already constructed a picture of Cyndi's life; a successful veterinarian, married to an investment banker, once in professional minor league baseball. His imagination continued to embellish Cyndi's achievements. There was likely an indoor pool and a 5,000 square foot house that abutted the links; a large boat sat in the third bay of their garage. At least that's what his thoughts crafted when thinking of Cyndi's life. She was going to be successful. Cyndi always loved animals and as childhood friends, her kindness to all living things rubbed off on Derek. To this day, if he found an uninvited spider crawling up his wall, he gingerly plucked it with his fingers and brought it outside to carry on. Such can be the impact of one person on another.

He chose to eat his freshly made sandwich—this time with crust to honor his mother—in the living room. In the bathroom, the box fan was humming on the highest speed, drying his attempt at a patch. He chose his mother's chair; unthinkable if she was there with him. It wasn't taboo to sit in his mom's chair, however, if they were both there together, he would be on the couch, and she would be in her chair—it was just the way it was. It was a comfortable chair and a fine place to eat a peanut butter and jelly sandwich.

His favored ratio of raspberry jam to peanut butter was 60:40. Derek was pleased with his impromptu lunch and sat back in the chair for another bite as he chased it down with a sip of tap water. He had another realization. Other than Wednesday night and this moment, he hadn't been alone in the house for years. After leaving his childhood home for college, he returned for visits and holidays. But his mom was always here when he came over to visit. In fact, he tried to think of the last time he was alone in the house. With another bite of his sandwich, he chewed and thought, and chewed and thought some more. He was certain that the last time he was here alone was over a decade ago when he was back from college one summer. How strange it seemed to Derek to be alone at this moment in the home of his childhood. There was almost a deep loneliness to it, and he found no other way to describe it other than it made him miss his mom. The pang of missing her surfaced as the quiet of the house screeched with the sounds of emptiness. For a quick moment, his thoughts turned from missing his mom to a genuine sorrow. There was never a truer cliché—time flies. Time was fleeting, he was in his thirties now. He thought of Everly, he thought of his mom already retiring. He thought of turning down a promotion. *Why? To go home to an empty house and watch a game on TV?* Time was moving too fast for his taste.

Finishing his last bite of PB&J, he wondered if his mom missed Derek and Leena—when she sat alone in her TV watching chair. "Heavy thoughts, heavy thoughts," Derek said it out loud with his mouth still full of sandwich. His eyes glanced around the room. He thrust himself out of the chair and was about to check the status of the bathroom wall when his eyes caught something bright in the pink gravel of the empty goldfish bowl. He didn't recall the gravel being multicolor, but he swore he saw a speck of silver in the sea of pink.

Derek reached for his glass of water and gulped down three more swallows to wash down his lunch. His attention now shifted to the fishbowl—a standard, two-gallon glass bowl with a sturdy round lip at the top for reinforcement. He couldn't remember a time when the bowl wasn't in its place on the bookcase—with or without a goldfish inside. But it had been many a year since Locks had her time in the bowl. Derek paused a moment to think back on the only pet Leena and Derek had as children. They were never sure if Goldilocks was a girl or a boy fish, and it didn't really matter. Leena wanted a dog or a cat so badly that the nagging wore down their mother like an eroding beach. She eventually compromised on having a pet—if a goldfish can be considered a compromise. Derek smiled a moment wondering if his mother ever dreamed that Locks would have had the life force stamina she had. Unsure of the world's record for longest lifespan of a goldfish, Derek was fairly certain that Locks had a legitimate shot.

His curiosity had taken over. At first, Derek tipped the bowl slightly to see if it would dislodge whatever he thought he saw and enable a better view. This didn't work as the florescent pink stones at the bottom did their best not to reveal anything. About to give up, he decided to give it one final try and launched his right hand into the pebbles, grasping for anything that didn't feel like pet store aquarium gravel. Then, in the mix of stone, he felt something cold and metallic. In disbelief, Derek pulled out a metal key. It was quite easy to identify what type of key it was, for at the top, it was round and had a black plastic casing over the metal; in the middle of the top circle of the key was the classic VW branded design—with the V on top and the W on the bottom. The key was worn and obviously had been used for many years; both the teeth and the key's head were considerably worn down. The plastic head displayed nicks and scratches as if being inside a pocket or a purse over a long period of time. It was also clear, that this was an older key; certainly not a modern fob, and it was apparent that the head contained no security chip. Derek scratched his head in a display of bewilderment. It was perplexing; he had just fished out an old Volkswagen key from a fishbowl that had no fish.

He put the key on the table by his mother's mounting advertisement collection of mail for now, choosing not to focus his thoughts on the bizarre find. More than likely, he thought, it somehow got tossed in there by accident at one time. And over the years, found its way deep into the pink gravel. He returned to the bathroom for the last sanding and primer application. With the help of the box fan on the jet engine setting, he also applied two quick coats of the *Soft Sunshine* yellow wall paint. He resecured the door stopper at the base of the wall so that the offense would be prevented from happening again. Examining his handiwork, he thought it wasn't bad for an amateur, certainly not bad for a financial analyst.

Derek swept the floor of the bathroom, cleaning up the mess he had made when sanding the spackle and proceeded to put the remainder of the primer and paint cans back in the basement where he originally located his mother's stash of residual house paint. The basement sparked another childhood memory. Being alone in the house seemed to generate a multitude of recollections, one after another. Without his mother here, his thoughts were his own. Because he wasn't actively engaged in conversation with her, it allowed his mind to wander just as he wandered through the quiet house. This place had witnessed almost all his childhood experiences outside of school. Derek paused to reflect on the power that an inanimate object has on a human being. He wondered if this shelter, his home while growing up, had a memory. After all, it knew Derek as a child as well as anyone. As a boy, he had no thoughts about it other than it was their family home. Today, alone in the house, seeing it as a man, it appeared lonely. At that moment he felt a tinge of sorrow. Perhaps that was the lifecycle of almost all homes; it holds a family through the years and then launches out the children to be free independent adults. Later on, it would turn itself over to a new family to repeat the exercise for as long as it still possessed the ability to be a shelter, a house, a home.

The basement at 23 Clover Drive was one hundred percent unfinished. In-between the freezer and the washing machine was enough space for a few children to fit perfectly. He recalled that space being everything from a jail to a taxi, and many times, a home. In this memory, Derek focused in on a time where he parked his tricycle in the space, pretending to arrive home after work and he shouted to his make-believe family— "I'm home!" He loved playing this role and did it often, by himself, and with Leena and Cyndi. An epiphany jolted him after thirty-three years; he was acting out what he genuinely wanted as a child—for his father to return home after a day at work. In his fantasy, he would drop everything and shout "Daddy!" and run to him with a large welcoming embrace and he would receive one in return. Chills creeped quickly up and down the spine of his back. The vivid childhood memory was eye opening, and it was sobering. And it sparked Derek's mind to slip more into a trance of reminiscences.

His only memory of his father was nothing more than a shadowy blur in his mind's eye. He was somewhere around the age of two and at that time his mother was pregnant with Leena. He tried many times growing up, to focus on that time in his life. All that he could ever recall was a time when he remembered a man dressed in a khaki-colored coat, talking with his mother in the kitchen. In reality, it could have been any man. His facial features were a complete blur. The man stormed off after a disagreement between he and his mother. There was no yelling, just two sets of voices entangled in anger and emotional pain—that is the best he could do to describe it. The man in the khaki coat paused and looked back at Derek and then hurriedly departed out the front door. It had to be his father; there was no one else it could have been. His mother, he recalled, was distraught just after the man left. Very few times had he ever seen her not completely in control. Her face was red, and it matched the color of her eyes. It was at that time that she approached him, knelt down, and hugged him—he remembered how hard she squeezed with her big belly pressing up against him. And that was all that Derek had of his father; a tiny three second sequence of a visceral video reel tucked in the corner of his brain. At two years old, that was as much as he could piece together. Of all the memories he had, for better or worse, it surfaced more often than any other. Another realization began to emerge for Derek. Anytime he had this memory, it seemed that he pushed his mother a little further away from him.

Returning upstairs, he continued his clean-up. He had used the entire plastic cannister of spackling; any residual he wiped out with a paper towel and tossed the empty container into the recycling bin, which was now a half full collection of empty seltzer cans. He was pleased with himself. His mother would be delighted when she discovered her bathroom was now blemish free. Deep down, he felt good for having performed this chore for his mom and looked forward to her returning to stumble upon his handiwork, as well as noticing the new grill cover. Thinking of the grill, his mind jumped directly to his last interaction with it. *What the Hell was on that grill?* Derek thought. As he thought this, he did one last look around before heading out. His eyes found the dining room table, the stack of mail, and the VW key. *And what is that key all about?* Derek said to himself. He went to the table, grabbed the key, and put it in his pocket. He headed out the door and told himself that he'd call Leena shortly. Scorched notebooks on the grill, a VW key, and a mother that seemed not herself. Clues that were worthy of a bona fide mystery. Perhaps Leena could put all this together.

10

After his drive home, Derek put on some music and lay down on his leather couch. Like usual, he grabbed the decorative pillow on the matching chair that juxtaposed the couch and rested his head upon it. Derek's taste in music was broad and eclectic; he shunned very few genres. Yet, when he was in such a mood that he was now, he had only one cure for his ears and that was clear flowing classical music in the Baroque style. Today he craved Samuel Barber's opus as the fix. "Adagio for Strings," Derek called out. The music's soothing melancholy began.

As with most people, Derek found music to be an emotional outlet. If you are happy, you have happy music. If you are angry, you have angry music. If you are troubled, you have troubling music. And so on. He was fascinated by music in that it could perform a dual role. First, music kept him company. Often, he invited music in as a guest, freely listening to what it had to say, and he opened his heart to the artist's emotional release—either through the melody, or lyrics, or both. But not only was music a companion, for Derek, it provided the means to unlock his thoughts, especially with classical music. Most classical music, having no lyrics, suppresses the part of the mind that tries to focus on words and the mind is free to be captured by a stream of musical notes, set together into a string of harmony, kept in motion by precise timing. And as sure as "Adagio for Strings" will produce a surge of goosebumps up and down your arms, your ears are rewarded with poetic decibels. And so, it was for Derek, that if he needed to think deep thoughts, violins and cellos unlocked his capacity to do so.

Relaxed on the couch, he allowed his thoughts to unfold. He never remembered a Volkswagen from his childhood. After some internal deliberation, he pinpointed a memory when he was between two and three—and it was not long after the vague memory he had of his father. It was dinner time and he and his mom were sitting at the table; his mother asked him to touch her enormously large belly. It was the sibling talk. The exact words, he didn't remember, but Derek got the key take-away—sister, soon, baby, Leena. Then he shifted through memories of he, his sister, and mother, trying to connect them to vehicles—rides they took together. This was a harder task. After all, how often when you are a small child do you pay attention to the make and model of a vehicle? When you're little, a car is just a thing to get into and it magically takes you to the store where there is candy and sometimes toys. When you're a child, you accept things as they are. As a child, you have not developed, nor refined your judging skills—for better or worse. At that time in life, everyone from your perspective could or should be driving the same vehicle as your mom; it's all you know.

And then it came to him. When he was somewhere

around five, his mom picked he and Leena up from daycare in a different colored car than what she dropped them off in. This new vehicle would be the family car for years to come. It was a red Ford Taurus and he remembered being hauled to elementary through middle school in it—he eventually learned to drive in it. Derek smiled, remembering his first kiss in it, and a fumbled attempt to get to second base. He could not isolate what came before the Taurus. For the life of him, he could now only remember two things. The prior car wasn't red. There was a contrast—so it wasn't red, but he could not remember anything else about the color. His second conclusion was that the prior vehicle was also a sedan as was the Taurus. There was an engine in the front, four doors, a seating capacity of roughly five people, and a trunk in the back. He recalled a prior vehicle before the Ford, but just couldn't identify it. It was frustrating, and he crossed his legs on the couch. The caressing waves of Barber's opus washed over him. *What is this car, what is this key, what were those burnt papers in the grill? Why did she seem so agitated? How was her visit going?* It was time to call Leena. She would have checked in with their mom once already. It was time to let his sister in on his enigmatic discoveries. While the music did not solve his riddles, it stirred the right thoughts and heightened his need to get to the bottom of all of this. Derek turned off the music and reached for his phone.

11

Leena's weekend was comprised of a mixture of chores of all things Everly. She, like her husband Eli, were baffled by the amount of work a single child could generate. From the very start, there was always another room to attend to, the same room that before, stood vacant and days would go by without either of them setting a foot in it. Once Everly arrived, laundry exploded and the toys started to multiply; many of them found ways to cleverly reproduce on the floor at night, ready to lay claim to human feet the next morning. Leena, like her brother Derek, held the belief of having a neat house, instilled in them by their mother. Eli bought into this as well, so the two of them appeared like two Zambonis in-between periods of Everly's downtime. Naptime became one of the largest pick-up times as it was a rare ninety-minute opportunity for them to tiptoe around the house while quietly tidying. Each of them had their own jobs that developed organically without creating verbal plans, and it became a rhythmic order to the weekend afternoon. If they did things right, and Everly slept for the full hour and a half, they each were gifted thirty minutes of downtime with a completely quiet and straightened house. Both Leena and Eli sat in peace in the living room after their cyclone cleaning event. Leena's phone started to vibrate.

"Hi Derek," Leena's tone was somewhere between whisper and her normal voice. She glanced at her husband and her body language informed Eli that she was heading down to their finished basement to have a conversation with her brother.

"Hi Leena," Derek whispered back, mocking her with overcompensation. "Naptime, huh?"

Leena responded with a "You got it." Her voice now louder upon shutting the basement door, heading down the stairs.

"Do you want to be Daphne or Velma?" Derek asked, trying to keep things light, at least at first.

"Daphne, always, without question—and what are you talking about?"

Before launching into his recent discoveries at their mother's house, he posed Leena an upfront question. "How is Mom, have you spoken to her?"

"Yes, twice. She's maybe slightly less weird, *maybe*. It's hard to tell. She and Eileen have been visiting, watching movies, going for walks."

"I owe her a call, too. Are you still concerned? About her current state, I mean?"

"Well, I'm not if she is headed in a better direction, which I'm hopeful for," Leena paused, "when she gets back and is still on edge, I think we should get her into the doctor."

Leena explained to Derek that their mom wasn't giving any indication of when she would be returning home, which was out of character. But she was retired and didn't have obligations to return home for—so long as Derek got the mail and checked in on the house from time to time.

"So, what's up with the *Scooby Doo* reference?" Leena asked. It was Derek's turn. He started at the beginning, discussing everything from fixing the bathroom wall to what he found in the gas grill.

"Do you have any memories of what Mom drove before the red car?" Derek asked. "Before the Taurus, there was another car, for the life of me, I can't remember what it was."

"You're *older* than me. If you can't remember it, I certainly can't. This is a very strange conversation, I'm just going to say it," Leena responded. "Are any of these things related?"

"It's a mystery—I also found an old car key. It obviously goes to a Volkswagen. And guess where I found said key?"

"In the freezer?" It was the only obscure place that Leena could think of, off the cuff. "I have no idea."

"Even weirder," Derek responded. "Locks might have had a roommate." Derek thought for a moment how bizarre his comments were. He thought that Leena might be thinking he was losing his mind. Leena didn't bite. Either she was awestruck by his last statement or was losing her patience.

"The key was in the fishbowl, at the bottom, mixed in with all of the pink gravel. I saw just a glimpse of something metallic—I went in with my hand and pulled out an old VW car key." There was more silence on the other end of his phone, Derek decided that it was time to pose a different question. "Who puts a key in the bottom of a fishbowl? Heck, who has a fishbowl still on display on a bookcase if there are no fish?"

It then became a two-way conversation again. "She was obviously hiding it from us," Leena said. "What's your hypothesis?" Derek went on about how he couldn't put any of it together and was hopeful that she might have an inkling.

Derek asked, "Do you think it was a stolen car?"

"Now that is funny," Leena replied. "Mom and *Grand Theft Auto*, I don't think so. She's going to be out of town for a while. I say you either call her and ask her straight up, or you snoop a little more."

Derek was taken aback. Slightly offended, Derek responded with, "I'm not a snooper. I stumbled upon both the key and the burnt notebooks on the grill, none of it snooping and all done fairly and squarely." His mind flashed back to his mother sitting on her chair and glancing up at the bookcase, now presumably at the fishbowl and the key therein. Her agitation seemed connected to it. "I don't think the time is right to ask her about the key, or whatever I found in the grill," Derek paused. "I think Mom's going through something—what, I have no idea—but I believe there is some sort of linkage."

Derek tried different angles with Leena. He was positive that she would be as into the puzzling clues as he was. But no matter how he pitched things, Leena seemed disenchanted with the new developments. The best he could do for now was getting a promise from Leena—that she wouldn't talk to their mother in their next conversation about any of it. Leena agreed. Derek thought that if she were terribly interested in his new findings that she would want to ask their mother in her next call. Leena seemed fine with not bringing them up.

But again, Leena had not been sitting with him and his mom, the day he visited. She had not witnessed how his mother acted, peering up at the bookcase, at the fishbowl. "I guess I'm going to have to be the entire Mystery Machine gang on this one," Derek said, attempting to get off the topic by applying a pinch of frail humor.

"I will let you know how the next call with Mom goes. And it wouldn't kill you to reach out to her—other than a text, you know," Leena replied. "Hey, guess who reached out to me. Actually, one better, guess who is moving *back* to the area—next town over?"

Derek was still a few sentences in the past, trying to catch up and grasp his sister's inattentive interest in everything that he just brought up. After registering her question, he replied, "No one is famous from here that I know of—who?" Derek wasn't up for playing a guessing game with Leena.

"Cyndi Vaughn," Leena replied, "she's landed a job in the area. Says she really misses the community and her old friends, even the hills—she still loves the outdoors, and of course animals." Leena could have gone on about what she knew about Cyndi but waited for Derek to reenter the dialogue. She and Cyndi grew up playing everything from charades to video games. She also found Cyndi the best of her friends to talk about boys with. She was that person you trusted, and you just knew she wouldn't spill secrets to anyone. A secret was safe with Cyndi, and that level of trust made them tight friends, moreover, friends for life. Leena was as saddened as Derek when Cyndi and her family moved to Ohio. She was *framily*, as Derek and Leena called her. Closer than a friend—an adopted family member through earned trust and time. Leena also knew of Derek's infatuation with Cyndi later in high school. He did what he could to hide it, but strong connections through years of togetherness, emotional attraction, and a pinch of teenage lust, are nearly impossible to conceal.

"*Really?*" Derek asked, spending significant energy on the one-word question. He wanted additional substantiation.

"Yes, she is," said Leena, "isn't that great?"

Derek's mood, a few minutes ago, dejected by his sister not picking up what he was putting down, was fully reversed by the news of Cynthia Vaughn moving back. "Is she married?" Derek asked, and then regretted his question immediately as if revealing more than he wanted to reveal.

"I already did the reconnaissance work for you, Derek," Leena responded, enjoying this immensely, "she's not married, and she broke off her engagement. She not only has a new job, but I think she's looking for a fresh start. Oh, and the engagement has been off for over for six months."

Derek's mind was everywhere. Excited just to see his friend, he could not contain the growing emotional exuberance that was becoming a fountain of dopamine. "It will be so great to see her," Derek could only find this understatement as a retort. "When? Can I see her, I mean we, you and me?" he continued.

"Why Derek, your voice sounds different all of a sudden," Leena said, playing coy. In the recent communication that Cyndi and Leena had, she noticed that Cyndi did as much asking about Derek as she did about Leena and her family. "Want her cell number?"

"Yeah, if you have it," Derek said as nonchalantly as he could.

"I'll send it to you in a text," Leena replied.

"Thank you," Derek said, still high off this new development. "Alright, if I find any more Mom clues, I'll bring you back into the fray. Let me know how Mom is doing?" With that, he handed off the baton, putting the ball in Leena's court to contact their mother.

"Sounds like a plan. And remember, Everly is asking about you. Capitalize on this time, Derek—come over soon."

"I will, promise. Talk soon," Derek agreed in his good-bye.

Derek's mind was stirring. He had the mystery of his mother taking shape and brand-new news of his high school crush returning from Ohio. "How about them apples?" Derek said out loud and slowly, unsure where to place his mental energy.

The fact remained that he was not a snooper; he had legitimately stumbled upon both the key and the burned remains within his mother's grill without intention. If you had the intention to inquire and intrude, well, that was by the definition, snooping. A question started to nag at him. What if his mother was in some sort of real trouble? What if there were connections between this key, the burned notebooks, his mother's current mental state, even the visit to her sister? Perhaps he had read too many mysteries, or Hollywood had laid claim to his subconscious over time, but he was being nagged by this enigma and he wanted answers.

Tonight, already being Sunday, meant work tomorrow. But tomorrow after work he decided he was going to his mother's place again. No game plan yet, but there was time for his mind to create a strategy. He grabbed a beer from his depleted refrigerator—overdue for a visit to the grocery store. He sat on the couch and reached for the remote control. Derek was craving some time to decompress from all this. Halfway into the beer and on the third commercial in a row of a baseball game, his phone indicated he had a text—three quick tap vibrations. He picked up the phone from the coffee table with one hand while using the other he took another sip of his beer. The text read, *Brother of mine, here you go...* It was Cynthia Vaughn's phone number. With a deep smiling breath, Derek realized that in no way, would there be any Sunday night blues tonight.

12

Monday during lunch, Derek texted his mother. *Hi Mom, how are you doing?* He admitted to himself that it was banal and set his mom up for the short response that would surely follow. *I'm doing fine. Are you OK?* And that's exactly the next text message that manifested on his screen three minutes later. At least he was attempting to stay in contact; he knew that she wouldn't reveal much via text. But he was making an effort and letting her know he cared. He responded, *Yes, I'm fine. Work is work*—he resisted inserting a frowning emoji—*and it is Monday.* He thought for a moment about letting her know that their childhood friend was moving back into the area but decided against it. Besides, it was more than likely that Leena would have already informed her. At least his mom was responding, and she was responding in a manner that seemed appropriate. Then again, even if she wasn't in a great place, what mom is going to tell her son that she's *not* OK? Especially via a text message. His mind further cemented his decision to go over to his mom's that evening and see what he could see; not by snooping but by observing. He refused to rummage through his mom's personal effects.

It was the kind of spring day that showed promise of warmer times ahead. Spring, especially the month of April, was a season of tension; winter had no desire to leave and did whatever it could do to enforce its distaste for being driven to abandon what it so loved doing; blanketing the ground with snowflakes and filling the air with see-your-breath skies. But today, a warmer southerly breeze dared to take a step forward. As Derek left work and made his way to his car, he breathed in the air and felt a sense of optimism—the trees that were still unsure if they could unfurl their leaves would soon have the right to do so.

After getting the mail from his mother's mailbox, Derek unlocked the front door and set the mail down on the dining room table as he usually did. He could always just look and see what kind of mail she was getting. And with that thought, he ferreted through the collection of mail on the table that had been acquired the last several trips. Advertisements for internet service providers, local supermarket flyers, a ski resort brochure from Killington. Most of her bills she paid online, so it was infrequent to see something in the form of an invoice arrive by way of the US Mail. At the bottom of the stack was the local newspaper—still in publication. He wondered how much longer the *Three Town Surround* would continue in this digital age. *How many people read newspapers anymore?* A few more articles of mail, but there was nothing of interest. Sometimes his mother would keep the important things that came in the mail and place them in a bill holder that hung on the kitchen wall—like a tax bill or a town water bill—those municipal one offs that did not believe in electronic billing of any kind. *Why not, it's just a bill holder*, Derek thought to himself, and he stepped into the kitchen preparing to investigate.

As expected, his mother did sort the mail, discharging advertisements and placing anything remotely important or interesting into the wooden bill holder which contained three slots. The first and lowest of the slots looked to be where bills would go that needed more immediate attending. This is where the water bill was—due in three weeks. The second slot appeared to be reserved for charity; a local museum was asking for pledges in its annual fund-raising campaign. There was also a solicitation from the local food shelf centering on *Fifty Feeds* and went on to explain how far a $50 donation would go on the local war against food insecurity. The last slot, located at the top of the bill holder, was apparently the miscellaneous section. Here, Derek found everything from a two-year-old postcard from friends who went to Mexico for vacation, to a coupon for $10 off a tune-up at a local mechanic. At the very back, Derek's eyes were finally rewarded with something out of the ordinary. The very last article of mail was addressed to his mother, April Densmore. But much more interesting than who it was addressed to, was where it was addressed from; *Twigg's Enterprises*, Galeton PA. Now Derek's mind began to wage a war with itself. Was he observing? Or was this straight up snooping? The battle raged in his mind for another minute. There was no stopping him now. He plucked the envelope from the holder and withdrew the paper within—as it had already been opened. At the top, printed in the identical font and size on the exterior of the envelope read *Twigg's Auto Storage*. Just below the company name, the word *invoice*, was stamped in bold red ink. Then just below that, in the body of the document was a handwritten statement. "Annual automobile storage for (1) one vehicle for April Densmore" and to the right of that was an amount due for $900. Far below that, in blue ink, in what Derek was certain was his mother's handwriting were the words Paid, Check #2106 – March 11th.

Derek, just days before, who had made snarky *Scooby Doo* mystery remarks to himself and his sister, now found himself a step deeper into what appeared to be a genuine mystery. At the very least, it was mysterious. But what was initially light-hearted now seemed more real, for whatever was going on involved *his* mom. If this was an Algebra problem, his mother's recent mental state, trek to see his aunt, the grill, and the car key were all indecipherable variables. And now an invoice for a car she kept in storage surfaced. Never had he felt what he was feeling at this moment, and it was hard for him to interpret. Concern for his mother was the top layer. Below that was the unknown coupled with plenty of denial; that his mother could be bound up in anything that he was not aware of—was mind blowing. The last stratum of his feelings was intrigue. He did not want to admit it, but there was some level of excitement to all of this. The blend of all of these feelings combined, was something that Derek had no experience with. He was having a hard time processing any of it. *Time*, he thought to himself, *I need some time to sort all of this out, to unravel things.* It very well could be that nothing was going on. He may have simply inserted himself into finding things that really weren't a big deal. Whatever was going on, it was too much for him to take in all at once.

Upon returning home, Derek thought that the best thing to do was to sleep on it and to allow his subconsciousness to sort things out. He might just be seeing things in the dark, and his imagination could be playing tricks on him. For now, he got in bed, and he chose to put his imagination on Cyndi, his entire imagination.

13

April Densmore was finishing her coffee with her sister Eileen; her visit, just shy of a two week stay. April notified her host the night before that it was time for her to depart. "It was a great visit, thank you for coming down. Binge watching *Golden Girls* solo isn't as much fun," Eileen said with a smile.

"Thank you for having me, and for me to interrupt you and Bo's routine," April responded. "I feel a bit more centered after our visit—now that I have more time on my hands—I start to think, well, about everything and anything."

"I completely understand," Eileen said, "thank you for coming. Next time I'll come up for a visit and see that beautiful granddaughter of yours?"

April paused and then nodded her head up and down. "Yes of course, Eileen. Love you tons."

"Are you straight lining it, or taking the backway home?" Eileen asked the question as they walked out of the house before April was about to open the driver's side door of her Ford Escape.

"The back way, without a doubt. I'm in no hurry at all. In fact, I might make some detours, just take my time."

They exchanged one more hug before April departed. She backed out of the driveway and traveled in a westerly direction. Eileen waved and thought to herself that it was going to be very much a detoured approach; she knew of no major routes, interstates, or state highways, that she could readily catch in that direction that would lead April back to her home. Eileen, who was also retired, could relate. Sometimes you started to do new things after enough time passes when you retire. Why hurry home after all. Work didn't beckon you on Monday morning and there were no children to attend to anymore. And with April, no husband or significant other. "Sounds good, April, drive safely," Eileen said out loud, although April didn't hear her; she was well on her way.

April drove for only a few minutes, until she knew she was out of sight of her sister's house. On the passenger seat, positioned on the top, was her black leatherbound notebook she had reread daily over the last few days. Unlike the other *preliminary journals*—April started calling them—this collection of thoughts, memories, and feelings were spared the incineration of the gas grill. She leafed through a few pages until she came to the page she was looking for. Her index finger on her right hand followed along, while her left hand keyed an address into her phone. Once the coordinates were locked in by the GPS and the verbal commands commenced, she shut her notebook and repositioned her phone onto the suctioned cup holder at the base of the windshield. With a full body sigh, she placed the car into drive and got ready to obey the first direction—a right-hand turn. Next to the notebook was her purse. Only one thing remained on the passenger's seat which lay just below her purse. The notebook and purse were positioned in such a manner where it looked to be hiding something, however it was too long for it to be completely obscured by what April classified as a medium sized purse. Below the purse, protruding out several centimeters, was an old weathered and time worn knife that lived in its equally tattered brown leather sheath. April noticed it out of the corner of her eye and while still driving, did her best to reposition her notebook and purse in such a manner that the knife could not be observed. April issued another large and lengthy sigh. She had never thought she would be doing what she was about to do. Yet her mind was clear on her next steps, no more hesitation. After so much rumination—she had entered into a new phase. She was now in a state of mind whereby there was only one path forward. Before arriving at Eileen's, April wondered if the time she spent with her sister might change her mind, that it would alter what she had planned to do over the last several weeks. But her time with her sister only cemented her course of action. April's thoughts now turned to the next stop on her journey, creating in her mind scenarios on how it could play out. Her heart started to pound, and there was a gripping queasiness in her abdomen. The reality of what she was about to do had set in and her body tensed; she observed her fingers gripping the steering wheel as if the road were covered in ice. The car sped up and took a right-hand turn as instructed to do so. She had some driving ahead of her.

Eileen, once back inside the house, ran the

dishwasher and did a load of laundry. There in the combination laundry room-bathroom, she spotted an off-white sweater hanging on a hook that April accidently left behind.

14

Derek awoke when his phone alarm pulled him from a looping dream state. Try as he could, he could not solve a problem. In his dream, even when he thought he had solved the issue, the problem either grew in size, or his solution wasn't the remedy. He was glad for his alarm to take him from his slumber—it was more troublesome than his real-life dilemma. At least being conscious, he could choose his next step. He was also glad to have been woken up by his phone for another reason. While he slept, he kept the phone silent to prevent a call or a text from waking him. He rubbed his eyes, then discovered there were two texts from two different people. He must have received them just after turning out the light. The first one was from Leena. *I gave Cyndi your number. Just in case you're too lame to reach out—which I'd put money on.*

The second text was from a number he didn't recognize.

Hi Derek, It's Cyndi Vaughn. I know it's late, but while I was thinking about it, I wanted to let you know that I've moved back into the area. I know it's been a long time, but I would like to meet up with you and your sister sometime. No rush, and I know you're busy. Be well.

Derek sprang gleefully from bed. On a typical workday, he usually fought off morning sleepiness as he struggled out of bed to head to the shower. Not today. For a guy where nothing much out of the ordinary happened day in and day out, suddenly, all sorts of things were happening. He had a mystery with his mother and now, Cyndi reached out to him. It was now Tuesday, and he already knew it was going to be particularly hard to concentrate today. Between his mother's breadcrumb trail and out of nowhere, Cyndi moving back, he concluded that his head wasn't going to be in the work game today. On most days, examining inventories and profit margins was something he actually enjoyed, but today he wondered how he was going to be able to work at all. He reread the text from Cyndi for the fifth time. After the sixth time, he started to second guess everything about he and Cynthia Vaughn. He and his sister shared so many memories together with her. They had snowball fights and made snow angels together. At Halloween, every year until she moved, they carved pumpkins together—it was tradition. Even during Thanksgiving, after the feast was over at their respective homes, they found their way together to play Monopoly or video games. Sometimes the three of them didn't have to be doing anything. They simply enjoyed being together. Cyndi and Leena were his two best friends growing up. One was a sister, the other felt like a sister, but yet wasn't at the same time. He prayed that she didn't think of him as a brother—at least now. Puberty, like it does, changes everything, and so it did for Cyndi and Derek. One day you're playing on the floor with toys, and the next, you wonder where all the pimples came from and how you can hide them all before your sister's friend visits the house. The irony, he thought. There were times in high school where Derek actively avoided Cyndi because he didn't want her or anyone to think that he was infatuated by her. And for Derek, it was spellbinding enchantment, or allure, or attraction, or fascination, or perhaps all of those adjectives mixed together. Maybe it was because Cyndi felt so much like his sister, that he felt he had a duty to treat her as his family. He must have hurt her, keeping his distance in high school after years of spending almost all of their time together. "I was a fool," Derek said out loud after a sip of piping hot coffee.

Derek had what he classified as two serious girlfriends. Serious by his standards anyway. If he were serious enough, he would bring his girlfriend to meet his mom. And so far, that was two different women. His longest relationship lasted just shy of three years. But all relationships must evolve and adapt, just as change must touch all things. His last girlfriend, he knew, wanted more from him than he could give. They were good friends and enjoyed each other's company and there were elements of love. He loved her for taking such good care of him, for thinking of him often, for the way she held his legs on her lap on the couch while they watched a movie. And as time wore on in the relationship, she dropped subtle hints of marriage, children, and family. Derek did his best to deflect her suggestions, but as time wore on, she pressed him more assertively. He knew he wanted a wife and a family one day, there was no question. There is love, and there is love. And he knew he had a form of love for her. Yet there are many levels of this word, love. In his heart, he tried to picture them together, but your heart can only deliver what it feels—it cannot manufacture something that isn't there. And one day, two or so years ago, she asked to talk after work. Whenever someone writes in a text, *we need to talk*, the outcome is all but certain. And like all things that begin, it ended. He was hurt, but he knew he had hurt her, too. He was simply incapable of taking the next step in their relationship. And for the last two years, not being in a relationship or seeking one out, he wondered about something. His ex-girlfriend was a beautiful, caring, and an intelligent woman. But he wanted to feel a sense of connection to another human being in a way he didn't feel with her. Derek began to question if this feeling really existed; perhaps he got sucked into the fairytale of true love. He started to wonder if he had done something stupid by not taking the next logical step with her. But at this moment, his mind wasn't on his ex-girlfriend.

He examined Cyndi's text one more time, and then the second guessing became third guessing. Did she mean that she only wanted to get together with Leena and him, at the same time? Did her text end the way it did because she was excited to meet up with him but didn't want to be overtly obvious? Why was the text so late at night—could he have been in her thoughts late at night and she couldn't wait any longer? Or could she have been so busy unpacking and getting situated in her new place that the only time she had was at night? Derek brushed it all aside because he couldn't stop smiling. After all, he got a text from Cyndi Vaughn, and she wanted to meet up, and this was good on all levels. After some internal deliberation, he decided that he would put his crush aside and embrace the deep friendship he had with his childhood friend. Childhood friends are the best friends, he thought; you've exposed your soul to them already. Adults learn to protect who they are, our shortcomings, our vulnerabilities. But as children, our closest friends during those years get to see us for who we are, and who we aren't. We aren't ashamed of all the things that make us who we are; the bad, the good, and everything in the middle that make us, us. Cyndi, albeit many years ago, had seen all of Derek—at least as a child and teenager. She had seen him cry from both physical and emotional pain. Other than his mother and Leena, there was no one, guy friends or otherwise, who he showed these levels of vulnerability to—including his ex-girlfriend. And perhaps this was a major reason why he was so over the top excited to see her. The three of them had a deep bond, cultivated from a meaningful childhood friendship. Oddly, once Cyndi moved away, he and Leena grew apart and he wished for that level of closeness once again. One further, he felt closer to his mother before Cyndi moved away.

Derek had banked a lot of personal time-off. It always felt like it was period or quarter end, and for that reason, he accrued weeks of vacation time. He'd take an occasional Friday off to play golf or tennis with his friends, even go to a ball game. But other than that, he rarely took a block of time off. Before his commute to work, he decided that this Tuesday would be his Friday. And, it was only mid-April, he had just closed the first quarter last week. His mind switched gears, back to his mother and the things that weren't adding up. He knew he needed to talk to Leena again. This time, he was hopeful that she would be more engaged after having some time to think about everything that he threw at her. And he hadn't yet told her about the car storage invoice.

Maybe that would be the final straw to get her engaged into this—whatever was going on—thing.

As soon as he found his third and final cup of coffee for the day, Derek submitted for his time off. Unofficially, this meant popping into his manager's office and asking. Officially, he also had to submit something formally in their archaic Human Resources system. Other than being surprised that he was asking for the remainder of the week off, his manager gave the green light and murmured something that sounded like "about time." After his time off was secured, he pulled his phone out of his pocket. He needed to text Leena. But he wanted to text Cyndi. For a moment, the worlds of need and want collided in his brain, until naturally, as it always does when there is a choice, want prevailed. With a rationalization of it being late enough in the morning to text her without seeming too eager, Derek began to construct a text to Cyndi.

Wow is it good to hear from you Cyndi. He was mapping out the next thing to write. That was a good first line after all. The *wow* made it show he was excited, but he didn't want to seem over the top. Now he would move to the second sentence. *It will be great to see you.* Now she would know that he—without Leena—was elated to see her. But he also needed to parley the text he received from her; it needed to be coy. *Shall I coordinate something with Leena, and we can all have dinner together?* He had outdone himself; this way, he put it back on her. Was she interested in seeing him, Leena, or both of them? Then he kicked himself, he just led the witness. How could she respond now without the only answer being yes to meeting up with he and his sister? *I'm overthinking this*, he thought. He put down the phone and started up his work for the day—powering through Tuesday was important if he was going to take the rest of the week off. With all the resolve he could find, he switched off the phone and put it in his pocket to resist the temptation if it vibrated with an incoming text. During lunch he would pick it back up and he would also call Leena and ask about their mom.

Work is a great place to be when one is mentally *at* work. And for someone like Derek, he saw his career as a reflection of himself. But today, Derek wasn't in the game. In fact, he wasn't even at the game. Metaphorically, he felt he didn't even have a ticket to enter the game.

By 11AM, Derek admitted defeat. You can only feign reading and rereading numbers within reports so many times. He got up from his desk and decided to stretch his legs. His office window overlooked the parking lot of the store. Here he could see the comings and goings of store customers; a couple was loading up their pickup with two-by-fours, sheetrock, mud, and paint. It looked like they had a busy few days ahead of them. Continuing to stare out the window, he habitually placed his hands in his front pockets and by doing so, assured his next move. Out from his pocket, he withdrew his phone and turned it back on. Derek's stomach started to churn—legitimate butterflies stirred within his gut. With major anticipation, he watched as the phone activated, waiting for any text messages to appear.

There, on his screen, came a reply text from Cyndi. *Hi Derek! So good to hear from you!* Then followed a grinning smiley emoji. *My hope is to meet up with you and Leena individually, and you and Leena together sometime. You let me know when you can find time. I have the rest of this week off. Next week I start my new job in Taylor. Talk soon?* Another grinning smiley face completed her text. The emoji could have been a mirror. Derek was smiling and he could feel a wave of dopamine cresting, generated from flowing, gushing joy. While Derek considered himself a genuinely happy person, it had been a long time since he felt this sensation—as if he had just opened a brand-new box of sixty-four brightly colored crayons and he had all the time and paper in the world to construct a masterpiece, worthy of the front of the refrigerator.

He reread the text, and reread it again, soaking it in. *Let's not get ahead of yourself*, Derek thought. It was more than possible that they had grown apart from that childhood friendship bond, and this would simply be a meeting of old acquaintances from the past; one where you talk about old times, get caught up and then not see each other for another three years. But Derek realized that he wanted more than that. He knew deep down that his feelings for Cyndi were always there, and he had been suppressing them for years after she moved away. Even during his time with his ex-girlfriend, Cyndi was never far away in his thoughts.

But first, Leena, Derek thought, feeling the need to check in with her to see if she had talked with their mother. Something was going on here, and he needed a sense of understanding rather than just puzzle pieces. Instead of texting, he went straight for a call.

15

Derek found a way through Tuesday and wrapped up as many loose ends as he could. He followed up on every email in his inbox and pro-actively sent several more emails to a few store managers, requesting a status on how their process improvements were developing, procedures they all had aligned to in their last annual store managers' meeting. He tried to cut the store managers some slack. They were after all, overseeing an entire business unto itself. They were responsible for everything, from hiring staff to securing snowplowing in the winter. And there was this thing called profit margin which was the main reason Derek had to be up in their faces. He was certain that his emails would land lowest on their to-do lists. Yet he was able to put himself in their shoes, a core belief that his mother had taught him. After all, when someone called in sick, it was on the manager to fill the shift. And if you've ever worked in retail, you wonder how we're not all in the hospital, all of the time. Retail sickness was a real thing. And like the common cold, there is no cure.

He shut down his laptop and placed it into his work bag. He switched off his light and said a few good-byes to his colleagues who he passed by on his way out the door.

"Free," Derek blew out a sigh. Getting into his car, he moved into autopilot mode for his ride home, his thoughts turned to his conversation with Leena earlier in the day. Leena's interest was piqued when he brought up the car storage invoice, but she still didn't seem invested in unraveling things.

Leena mentioned that their mom was wrapping up her visit with their aunt and would most likely be back in the next few days. Derek pressured Leena on this. Their mom was always precise when it came to these things. While growing up, everything had its place, and everything had its time. April Densmore was in all things punctual and was first in line for the creed of *if you're not early, you're late*. Leena shrugged it off, partially because Everly was demanding her attention, but she also swept it aside because their mom didn't have an obligation to return home for. Leena argued that their mom wasn't bound to the same time constraints that had previously ruled her life for the last thirty-five years. Leena, it seemed, wasn't going to bite on the puzzle pieces. She wanted to see their mom get home first, after her visit to her sister's, before passing judgement on things.

Derek and Leena finished their conversation on the topic of their friend, Cyndi, and he asked if Cyndi had talked to Leena about getting together. Leena indicated that she hadn't, but she was going to send her a text today. When Derek informed Leena, that Cyndi had already reached out to him, she ribbed him with an "umm, hmmm." Finishing up his drive, Derek's joy could no longer be contained. He started to whistle; he was off for the next few days, and he would see Cyndi soon, *hopefully very soon*, he thought. His whistle contained no particular notes of any song he knew—it was a self-fabricated whistle and extruded from his heart, a Derek original, and he blew out notes both high and low. He remembered a comment about whistling from his favorite, most optimistic teacher he had in middle school. When he was in eighth grade, he heard his teacher whistling to herself in the hallway. He stopped and stared at her. She glared back to him and asked with a smile, "Well, have you ever heard an unhappy person whistle?"

Once home, Derek's optimistic outlook was amplified by the sunny and warm southerly breeze that hit him as he exited his car. April was still in a battle with the vestiges of winter, but today the outlook was promising. That hard to identify smell of spring hit him—the combination of wet ground, decaying leaves, and a pinch of warmth that made this fragrance, undeniably vernal. Putting his keys away and changing into comfortable clothes, he mapped his night out. It was Friday on a Tuesday, and with that he grabbed a beer. While he enjoyed cooking, he only found it truly satisfying when he had people to perform for in the kitchen. He had virtually no desire to invest any time in the kitchen for meals for himself. Complimenting yourself on a deliciously prepared dinner only goes so far. He likened it to preparing an elaborate picnic and going on the picnic by yourself; wine, cheese, a fresh baguette, and the pièce de résistance, a red and white checkered tablecloth to set upon the ground. It was painfully anticlimactic to cook for yourself. And so more times than not, he settled into a rhythm of quick and easy meals that paid the bill of sustenance. With a sip of his beer, he peered into the freezer and grabbed a burrito, unwrapped the packaging and placed it in the microwave. For a vegetable, he stared into his produce drawer. Things were low; shopping was required. Over to the cupboard where he kept canned goods, he spotted a can of green beans that ogled back at him. "Boring is, as boring does," Derek mumbled while taking it out. Hot sauce was the cure for any culinary deficiencies. Soon both the burrito and the green beans —freshly microwaved—found themselves drenched with the liquid tangy zip of habanero and garlic.

Derek turned on the television to keep him company. On came the car insurance and credit card commercials. It was time to get back to Cyndi's text. With this thought, butterflies returned. The thing with butterflies, Derek realized long ago, was that there are two types—good ones and bad ones. There are butterflies in your stomach that are activated when you are nervous about doing something you don't want to do, and there are butterflies circulating in your abdomen when you're anxious about something you really want to do, but don't want to mess it up. It was easy to discern that these were the friendly sort of butterflies, there simply to propel him forward versus holding him back with paralysis.

Here goes, he thought to himself after shutting off the television, this time cutting short an announcer describing how much better their warranty was over competitors. *Hi Cyndi, believe it or not, I have Wednesday through Friday off. No real plans. Let me know what works for you. Coffee at Caffeine Nation?* He was pleased with his text. It wasn't over the top in any direction but allowed for them to see each other as soon as she could fit him into her schedule.

Thinking about what he should do next, a returned text appeared. "That was fast," Derek said aloud.

Hi Derek! Out with a friend. She and I are having dinner so I can't talk. Coffee sounds wonderful. Tomorrow morning at 10AM, Caffeine Nation. Meet you there. Derek's dopamine levels gushed once again; soon things would be at flood stage.

Yes, sounds great. I'll be the one wearing a sombrero, tie-dye shirt, Birkenstock sandals and Elton John sunglasses. He couldn't resist; joy makes you joyous after all.

After another minute, he saw the bubbles appear— she was texting back. *I'll be the one doing my best not to laugh at you. I can't wait!* Again, the grinning smiley face, but this time there were two of them. It was going to be a restless night's sleep, which would be steered this way and that way by compassionate butterflies.

16

As anticipated, a restless night of sleep was in store for Derek. Despite a finite amount of rest, he bounded out of bed at 6:30AM. No alarm was needed. He usually slept later on the weekends, but his body wouldn't permit it today. He contemplated what was better on a typical weekend— was it sweeter knowing that you didn't have to get up in the morning, or was it sweeter to actually sleep late? In Derek's mind, both the anticipation of sleeping in and the actual doing so were win-wins. But there was simply no option of sleeping in today because his mind commanded him to waken and prepare. Usually Wednesdays were just another step towards Friday. Today, he thought, could change his entire outlook on Wednesdays.

Derek showered and doubled down on his normal hygiene ritual. After swabbing his ears and applying a concealer on a renegade pimple, he took in his image in the mirror. At thirty-three, he was either at or approaching his mid-thirties, depending upon one's half full or half empty frame of reference. For the first time in a long time, Derek stared back hard at his reflection. Small but in no way subtle lines were etched in his forehead. He noticed that his face was less chiseled, and perhaps a hint rounder than his last long look in the mirror. Everywhere he looked, including his sideburns where he picked out one single gray hair this morning during his shaving routine, his late twenties were nowhere to be seen. He assessed his hair, still full and at least at the moment, it didn't appear to be thinning or receding. "That has to account for something," he said to his reflection, looking straight into his eyes. It's a sobering thing being honest with yourself; coming to terms with the shifts that have occurred within you. Once garbed in an everything-is-possible bulletproof vest of your twenties, you begin to catch glimmers of what is to come. Sobering but grounding; coming to terms with aging is a thing that we don't like to dwell on.

Today, for the first time, getting older greeted Derek's reflection. He shivered in front of himself. His thoughts started to shift; instead of taking today for granted, he was going to take on today for all it had to offer. *Today I'm going to drive fast and take chances*, Derek told himself in jest. He smiled at himself, trying to recover from the heaviness he had just experienced.

By 8:45AM, he was bursting inside. He had another hour to wait before driving to the local café. He sat down for a moment with his phone. Having time, he felt compelled to text his mother to find out when she would be home. While Leena did not seem concerned about her nonchalant timing for returning home, he was. Even though her retirement unlocked a degree of freedom with her relationship with time, she was still his mom. She was as time based, and as time focused, as anyone he knew. She had drilled the concept of punctuality above everything into Leena and Derek, forcing them into the category of Type-A.

Hi Mom. Hope you're enjoying your time with Aunt Eileen. Do you know when you'll be home? His text was short and to the point. Knowing when she would be coming home would start to put his mind at ease. When she got home, his plan was to go over and assess her condition. A visit to her sister had to do wonders, and she was coming home to a repaired bathroom wall. When she was home, he would think of ways to ask her about the key he stumbled upon. Assuring himself again that he wasn't snooping in any capacity; the silver contrast against the neon pink fish gravel created legitimate non-nosy curiosity.

His attention turned back to his impending date. *Is this a date?* Derek asked himself. A part of his mind said that it wasn't a date at all, this would simply be time spent catching up with a dear childhood friend. The other side of his mind responded much differently. This side of his brain said that he was going out for coffee with a woman that he was highly attracted to. Compounded with these mixed thoughts, he couldn't remember spending so much time in the bathroom getting ready.

Date or no date, he vowed to have a good time. He thanked the fluttering butterflies for being so helpful in getting him out of bed and motivating him. As was his custom before leaving each morning, he circled about the house, straightening up anything not in its place. Today he only found a cupboard that was cracked open.

Satisfied that everything was in order, he picked up his keys and headed out the door. Another impromptu whistle began to spout from his lips. His middle school teacher was right, unhappy people don't whistle.

17

It was only about a seven-minute drive to *Caffeine Nation*. Derek gave himself thirty. He wanted to be there early and grab a good seat for them. If he could get it, he wanted to get the most private table he could find. Similar to his recent meeting with his sister at *Unwind*, he disliked it when he overheard conversations. When this happened, he felt uncomfortable hearing about the business of strangers. And so, predicated on that logic, he didn't want others to overhear their conversation.

Caffeine Nation was a hybrid of an old school donut shop and new age hipster seventh or eighth wave—or whatever wave we were on—*Arabicafé*. The seating offered mahogany leather-esque high backed booths with dim lighting and an urban flair. Paradoxically, at the counter were swiveling metal stools with bright red seats, lined up in a row at the coffee bar—round stools with footrests, right out of the mid-twentieth century. It was a perfect blend of vintage and contemporary. The owner's eclectic creativity resonated with a diverse clientele. People who didn't consider themselves either java snobs or coffee afficionados could fast track their way to a simple cup of joe and gulp down their cup of energy on an old-fashioned round stool. The more adventurous could find any style milk for their latte propelled by Fair Trade, organic beans from Sumatra— which included a picture of the coffee farmer on a high-definition video screen juxtaposing the daily changing chalk board menu. Old school and new school can co-exist in harmony, and it was because of this that it was Derek's favorite place around to enjoy the art of taking your time to sip and contemplate over a good cup of coffee.

Derek landed the furthest booth he could find, away from the busy counter, where baristas and customers exchanged greetings and orders. He sat facing the door so that he could see Cyndi arrive. He marveled at the array of ages of the customers; some just able to drive, and some at the counter, obviously retired, discussing lawn mower brands. They all came for one purpose, the splendid awakening stimulus we know as coffee. Regardless of how you preferred it, iced, espresso, Americano, and everything in-between; it brought in every type of person who needed to shake off the morning of every morning.

Nervous excitement didn't begin to describe his state of mind and he noticed that his hands were shaking slightly. Perhaps he didn't need much more caffeine this morning. Attempting to assuage his anxiety, he reached for his phone and to the outside world, tried to cast the image of calm and collected, for inside he was anything but. Perhaps his mother responded to him, or one of his friends. He really wanted to know when his mother was returning home, which would help his current state of mixed-up emotions. Derek did receive a text, but it was not from his mom or a friend.

Hi Derek, it's Aunt Eileen. I also texted your mom, but just in case you talk to her, could you let her know that she forgot one of her sweaters? It was just after Derek started to digest these words, when Cynthia Vaughn entered the café and Derek Densmore's mind went completely blank, the awe he was experiencing as he watched Cyndi enter the coffee bar temporarily prohibited meaningful patterns of thought from developing in his mind.

She wore a soft pink oxford style shirt and semi-faded form fitting jeans with brown boots that ran up close to the knee. Her hair was medium length, dirty blonde and wavy, just the color Derek remembered. And while her hair style had probably changed many times, the color, a dirty blonde with strong hints of strawberry, was unmistakably Cyndi. Perhaps she could have looked better at some time in her life, but he was confident in his own biased mind that she had never looked better than today. Never better than on this particular Wednesday, in the late morning, in this light, at this café.

Boldly, Derek stood up from his booth, flashed a wave to her and the two smiled with locked eyes. Derek wished he could have a photograph of that moment; the instant their eyes connected and with smiles that were wide and genuine. For those few brief seconds, no one existed in the café but the two of them. While many of the memories of life are created without consciously knowing that a memory is captured forever in your mind, today, Derek was fully aware that this moment in time was endlessly going to be in his future; a woven tapestry of warmth and joy permanently deposited into the storage of his forever memory. This memory was guaranteed. It would benefit from years of compounding interest linked to the elation that is created when true friendship and real chemistry dwell at the same place and at the same time.

"It's you," Cyndi said with exultation. "It's really you, Derek G. Densmore," she repeated while they hugged and squeezed each other. He had underestimated how excited he was to see her. Derek was still in a state of hyper stimulation, at the crossroads of nervous joy and anxious jubilation.

"I totally forgot the sombrero," were the first words he could find.

Perma-grin can be a real affliction, and this Wednesday, both Derek and Cyndi had a severe case of the condition. "Your hair looks great, I'm glad you didn't wear a hat," Cyndi responded. Derek thought back to this morning's episode in the mirror and mentally scored one point for a full head of hair.

"Your hair looks wonderful, too," Derek fired back, unsure if it was the best retort, but it was an honest one. And it wasn't just how it looked. During their embrace, he took in a deep inhalation of the top of her head. He was already falling victim to the intersection of where pleasing fragrance and optical beauty collide.

"What would you like, my treat," Derek asked Cyndi.

"I had a cup of coffee this morning. Habit. But I would love a green tea."

"Green tea it is," he responded. After ordering, he came back with their beverages and they both shifted their positions gearing up for some ultra-smiley conversation. Not exactly knowing where to start, Derek proceeded.

"Really, how are you?"

"I'm doing quite well," Cyndi began. "New job, new apartment, new town, new life. I'm excited about all of it." Derek was torn between letting things alone, and desperately wanting to understand her relationship status. He decided that playing dumb is often the best card to play.

"Is your fiancé here already?" He was surprised how forward this was after it fell out of his mouth. And for the first time today, Cyndi's smile vanished.

"Ken and I aren't together anymore," Cyndi responded. "And don't say you're sorry. I'm happy and he's happy. Let's just say that sometimes things don't work out."

"You can tell me anything," Derek said, "I don't judge." Cyndi's smile returned to her face; it was as if it was exactly what she needed to hear from her old friend.

"Tell me about your new job," Derek asked, sensing it was time to move far away from the topic of her broken engagement.

"You always knew my love for animals," Cyndi examined his face for confirmation, and she received it with his gentle nod. "I went to college thinking I wanted to be a veterinarian. And while I could have done it, I also realized how hard it was going to be on so many levels. Lots and lots of school. And I guess one day I woke up and had a deep realization. If I became a vet, I didn't want to be saddled in debt and then have to charge obscene amounts for an annual checkup for a cat or a dog."

"I can't argue with that," Derek responded.

"So, with a change of plans I got my Bachelor's in business," Cyndi continued, "and wouldn't you know where I ended up," she paused for a moment. "I'm now the Director of Marketing for *Vet Med*." Derek learned that *Vet Med* was a growing business of six, soon to be seven, full care veterinary offices, offering services way beyond a typical animal hospital. Dog grooming, a full line of supplements, even doggy-day care was offered; highly coveted for those over-the-top dog owners who want the peace of mind knowing their fur baby is pampered, plus the added bonus of having a doctor in the house. "I get to grow this business," Cyndi said, "the other revenue streams generate enough to help offset costs of the traditional vet side of the business. Ergo, free spaying and neutering. Pet owners are so grateful for this, they become life-long *Vet Med* members—*not customers* mind you."

"I can see you're in marketing," Derek flashed a smile. "I'll buy two of whatever you are selling." They laughed and in a synchronized way, sipped at their beverages.

It was evident that Cyndi was more than a little excited to start her new position. And from what Derek could tell, she was in a good place in terms of her prior relationship. She had used the phrase, *new life*, and Derek construed that she wanted a fresh start in all facets of her life. If there was anything Derek knew he didn't want, it was to be a rebound to Cyndi. But as they spoke more freely, it was obvious to Derek that she had fully moved on from Ken. She went through the feelings stage that we all must go through to move on; to know it will be OK without this person that was once weaved into every aspect of your life.

We all deserve happiness and meaningful purpose in our life, Derek thought. Life brought ups and downs. For Cyndi to sit across from him now, she must have gone through quite a down period; letting go of her old home, her old job, and a relationship that was supposed to be forever. As painful as that must have been, Derek was grateful she was smiling back at him on this Wednesday.

The sun was shining in their booth and her left side was swallowed up by sunshine. Just as light carries the symbolism of optimism and hope, the glare on the left side of her face brimmed with courage and positivity. They were both squinting all the while sipping and smiling.

Derek's mood started to shift away from nerved-up angst, and he began to transition to what could only be described as captivation. Cyndi sat upright; her posture carried confidence but serenity. Her voice was clean, soft, and kind, and it projected clearly. For a moment, his concentration was being put on trial. He was trapped in between listening and processing her words, and at the same time, he became aware of just how awestruck he was by her. Cynthia Vaughn was in front of him now. Little Cyndi who he taught to tie her shoes, who taught him patience, who would tag along behind him on their bikes, little Cyndi who made him feel better when he got a bad grade on a test. But Cyndi was no longer little in any capacity; sitting before him was a fully educated, a fully developed, a fully magnificent, fully courageous Cyndi. He forced his ears back onto her words, so as not to miss an important part of her story. Even how she held her mug placed a spell on Derek. She cycled through a sip, first placing both hands upon the mug and hugged it for warmth. Then one hand would move away, while she picked it up with her right hand, she would then take a small sip. After some more conversation, both hands would again wrap around the mug, perfectly cradling it. But then she would rotate, this time picking it up with her left hand—bringing it to her lips for another sip. And this identical process repeated until she finished. It was so perfectly balanced, this simple rhythm of enjoying her cup of tea. He wondered how much else in her life was blessed with this form of balance—if something as trivial as drinking a cup of tea for Cyndi screamed Zen and universal equilibrium. For Derek, it wasn't long before captivation graduated to the level of pure enchantment.

The conversation turned to Derek and his work, then to Leena and her family and of course to Everly, Derek's niece. Without having anywhere to be, they allowed time to melt away, permitting it to dissolve into nothing and everything, as if clocks and the passing of time were never invented.

But the movement of time is always tracked. The fastest two hours of Derek's life vanished and the oversized, mammoth blue and white analog clock on the wall indicated that it was already noon. He realized he deflected any meaningful conversation about his mother, and he was also cognizant of the time and didn't want to consume all of Cyndi's day—she was kind enough to come for a visit—she most likely had things to do.

"Are you all settled in your new place?" Derek asked, continuing to avoid speaking about his mother's predicament—or whatever the current state with his mother was.

"All I need are some groceries," Cyndi responded. "I have some curtains I ordered online and some new silverware coming, too. The fridge is pretty bare, and so is the spice rack. It is, after all, customary to cook with spices and herbs. You know, flavor." Another larger-than-life smile erupted and appeared on Derek's face. She was humorous without any exertion.

"I don't want to keep you, if you need to go shopping," Derek responded. "I think the store I'll be doing my shopping at is open twenty-four hours. And besides, you're not *keeping me* at all. Unless you would like to keep me?" And it was at that moment that his head spun with a wash cycle of naturally produced feel-good chemicals that inundated his bloodstream. Derek's need to keep up appearances started to fade. As friends growing up, he always felt that he could tell Cyndi anything. And this conversation made him revisit this feeling—there was this level of trust—at a level so high it cannot be described.

"I have an idea," Cyndi said. "What if we go shopping *together*? We can continue to get caught up, and here's the best part of this offer, Derek G. Densmore," she glared at him intently wanting to observe his next move, "I'll make you dinner—that is, if I'm not *keeping you*."

18

She spent the majority of the day at a small reservoir that had been turned into a town park. There, three unique parking areas all equidistant from each other, offered ample parking, each parking lot near a cluster of picnic tables situated in the shade, afforded by timeworn hemlocks. Several communities surrounded the 75-acre body of water which was more the size of a large a pond, yet it held the name of Lake Pincer. It was sunny and while the chill of April continued to cling to the air, there was no wind, at least for today. This weather made it a perfect day for walking. Around the reservoir, the municipality had paved a walking path—later they had widened it to clearly delineate a separate bike lane. Walking is exactly what April did. She lost count for how many times she completed the lap around the lake. Her legs physically walked her body around the path, but her mind was nowhere near the reservoir.

The enormity of self-reflection; it is overpowering after spending a life doing everything to prevent it. Once your mind opens the doors of past feelings, the inevitable becomes fruition. Your self-reflection converts itself into self-realization, and your awareness grows. No matter how many times the earth circles the sun, no matter how much you pretend things didn't happen, no matter how far you dig to bury the pain, the law of motion prevails; you cannot escape the inevitable truth that with every action, there is an equal and opposite reaction. More than ever, April's mind was consumed with events she had long ago left in the past. Many of these memories she had thought were permanently discarded. But the mind is not a landfill, and while things can be temporarily buried, they will eventually find a way back and be unearthed.

April's phone indicated that she walked over twenty-three thousand steps. She usually never checked her phone for this purpose, but her feet were hurting. Blisters developed on both feet, and she hobbled back to her car. The physical discomfort of the moment forced her back into the present.

Tired and sore, she entered her car and sat behind the steering wheel, taking off her shoes, she let out a sigh. In sock feet, she picked up her phone again and started to search for a place to spend the night. She was in the right area now. Tomorrow she would take care of the first thing on her list, the first promise of three she made to herself. Anger, sadness, and grief bubbled to the surface again. For now, she put it aside; the pain from her feet was a welcome change over the blanket of emotional anguish she was wrapped in.

After making a reservation for a one night at a local, average as you can find motel, April picked up her journal and flipped yet again to the last page where she wrote out three numbered tasks. Her mind flashed back to the other notebooks that she burned on her grill. It took all of those many hours of writing to get to this— these three things on her list. In reality, they were not things, rather three names. Names of people. Three names that could only come from April's focused and besieged mind. Three names which were ensnared into the journey she was now on.

In the car, she read the header of the last page to herself, yet again. At the top of the page, the subject line was boldly written, and April had gone over it with several different colored pens. The subject line contained only three words: *Making Things Right*. She put down the notebook, laying it down on the passenger side seat, carefully doing her best to conceal the distressed hunting knife in its tattered sheath, something she required to complete her task.

19

For his life, Derek could not remember a more fun time in the produce section of a grocery store. Most times, picking out broccoli and lettuce always seemed mundane in every sense of the word, but just being at a grocery store with Cyndi with a single shopping cart—together—was euphoric. Periodically he would go fetch something she needed and navigate his way back to her. After he went for a run to retrieve a clove of garlic that they had forgotten earlier, he approached her from behind. The way she walked and pushed the grocery cart stirred Derek in a way he couldn't really explain. To him it was like he was watching someone superhuman do normal human things in a flawless manner. Derek had always put Cyndi on a pedestal. But here she was doing things that Derek did. Cyndi was here with him, and it was exhilarating for him to watch her do normal human things, like grocery shop. She was graceful and eloquent, composed, methodical, and as his eyes gleaned her up and down, he was stunned by her physical attractiveness. *Ridiculous*

attraction and fanatical admiration, Derek told himself, gifting her with a smile as he placed the garlic into the top basket of the cart.

Derek followed Cyndi towards East Taylor Township. Derek's thoughts were that this Wednesday was turning into the best Wednesday of his life. They pulled into a driveway off of a street called Stonewall Avenue—aptly named—for the entire length of the street was lined with a perfectly maintained stone wall next to the sidewalk. The neighborhood had a nice feel to it. Houses from the early to mid-twentieth century lined both sides of the street. Cyndi's apartment was on the second floor of a white, two-story colonial with wide clapboard siding. It was asking for new paint and was begging for window upgrades. But despite needing a few fundamentals, Derek could see why Cyndi was here—the landscaping—even for early spring, it was full of detail. An ornamental tree and tasteful flower gardens were already being attended to and they married up nicely with the stone wall that ran in parallel with the sidewalk in the front. All of this attention elevated the house's curbside appeal. The first few seconds are really all it takes for you to make up your mind on any sort of living arrangement decision, albeit an apartment or purchasing a home. Your subconscious asks you one simple question —*does it feel like home?* A few glances inside, a few on the outside and either it feels like it could be home, or it doesn't. Cyndi's choice for an apartment looked warm and homey.

"What do you think, kinda cute. It needs a bit of love, but the owner spends more time and money in her gardens than on the house itself," Cyndi spoke loudly, projecting towards Derek as they exited their vehicles.

"It is super cute," Derek responded, "great place for

a walk after dinner, or a jog. I like a place where you can take a walk just out your front door."

They gathered the groceries and entered through the front. Cyndi explained that the owner was a retired college professor. Thus far, all she knew is that her landlady was kind and respectful. They hadn't had many conversations yet, just those around the lease signing. "She just feels like a good person. My gut said, yes, this will work." As they entered, to the right was another door. Cyndi handed Derek a bag of groceries while she rummaged to find her key. "Up we go," Cyndi warmly smiled. Derek willingly took the warmth from her smile and returned one.

Salad and lasagna. Derek hadn't had comfort food like this in a while, especially with his personal aversion to cook for himself. Derek helped some in the kitchen while Cyndi prepared dinner. His main duty was to chop up the garlic. "Garlic," Derek started, "no vampires tonight." Cyndi looked as if she was searching for the right wit back.

"I'm not worried about vampires, but you're lucky there's no full moon tonight."

Conversation flowed easily between them, and most topics were in play, from silly things of present day to the reminiscing of their childhood. Derek's nervous energetic butterflies were now gone and were replaced with a surreal yet welcomed feeling of joy. After dinner, they cleaned up the table and kitchen together. The way they orchestrated their synchronized kitchen performance was as if they had done it before. Neither of them got in each other's way, nor asked for a particular job—they just did all the doing in a harmonious manner, like a river flowing in the only way it knows how.

Cyndi finished by wiping down the table. "Go sit down," she told Derek. "I'll be right there." Derek headed for the couch and sat at the end taking in the new surroundings; candles, decorative pillows, placid paintings of nature hung on the walls as well as a framed photograph of two distinguished golden retrievers. She had made it home already. Cyndi reappeared from the kitchen holding a bottle of red wine and two stemless glasses. "Not to get heavy, but I realize you've not been talking about your mom," Cyndi said, setting the wine and glasses down upon the coffee table. "In Vino Veritas." She began to uncork the wine.

20

"Sorry to eat and run," Derek responded in jest. "I have cows to milk, and on top of that I'm pretty sure I left the stove on." With a slow and graceful ease, Cyndi, while smiling, poured two glasses of wine and placed the cork back upon the bottle.

"I'm loving Malbec lately. Robust, yet smooth, it feels like it's been pampered." Cyndi held up her glass awaiting Derek's response. "A toast to our friendship and to new beginnings." Their glasses touched and they honored the significance of Cyndi's words with a large sip of the four-year-old Argentinian red.

"If you're wondering, Ken got the dog," Cyndi said after a moment. "As part of the engagement divorce. But I got the fine Corelle china." They laughed.

"Plans to have another one?" Derek asked. "A dog I mean, not another fiancé." They both took another sip of wine.

"When the time is right, absolutely. I get free doggy day care *and* they come with me to work; it would be a travesty not to have a dog. And besides, diamonds aren't a woman's best friend; like you guys—dogs are ours, too." Derek decided that it was not only a plug for the bond of canine friendship, but also a zing against her previous engagement. More importantly, it was her opening up to him, so that he could feel comfortable in opening up to her about his mother.

Derek knew he could stall no further. It was his turn. When there was a sufficient enough pause, he began, "Mom has been acting, well, *out of sorts* recently," the tone of the conversation shifted to the serious. "Fidgety, out of character, not in the moment, distracted," Derek was pleased enough with his description—these adjectives pegged his mother's current state of mind—at least from his vantage point. Cyndi patiently waited for Derek to continue. "Things were great at first when she retired, at least I thought. At first, I could tell she honestly enjoyed the time away from the grind. Then, almost imperceptibly, she started on this slow journey towards, well, distraction. She's been less her. More and more, it looks like she has things on her mind that take her three states away. I'll take some accountability, too. I've been living my own life, trapped in my own humdrum. You know, I get up, go to work, go to bed, repeat. I should be paying more attention to her, getting closer to her—emotionally."

Derek stopped and felt slightly embarrassed. Cyndi didn't need to know all of this; these were his deep feelings. He just showed Cyndi that he regretted not being or becoming closer to his mother. "I feel like I should be lying down on a couch, and you should be speaking with a thick German accent with a clipboard in your hand."

Then something happened that Derek did not expect. Cyndi's hand moved atop of his. Time stopped and a wave of peace broke upon him like the moment after water crests and falls against rock. He felt light, as if he were part of the air rather than fighting against earth's gravity. It was then that the floodgates of held back emotions, hidden feelings, and all the other things he never shared with anyone—not even Leena—were brought forward to Cyndi's ears. Cyndi continued to listen and from time to time, she gently squeezed his hand with hers; its meaning was clear—*everything will be OK*. In reality, Derek wanted to be much closer to his mother than he was and had no idea how to get there. It was as if he was still her son, and they loved each other, but as adults, they were not connected on the level he desired. On top of this, now she was holding things back from him, as evidence of her current state of mind. April Densmore, in her present condition, could not begin to let him in either. He felt helpless that he couldn't accurately diagnose what was going on. Yet, something was going on. All he knew was that his mom seemed like she was in some sort of trouble. The distance between them—an unconscious distance—seemed to amplify the pain of him wanting to be closer to his mother.

Derek hadn't realized, but he had consumed his glass of wine in quick fashion. Cyndi poured him another glass. "In Vino Veritas," Derek said as he looked up and into her eyes. He was hopeful that she didn't notice a growing excess of moisture in his.

"In Vino Veritas," Cyndi responded with a barely audible whisper.

He continued on, briefing her on all facets of his relationship with his mother and the subtle growing emotional distance between them that developed year after year. And of more recent events, he let her know about the gas grill, car key, and the vehicle storage invoice he had stumbled upon. "Leena doesn't seem overly concerned at the moment," Derek began again, "she knows something is up, in fact, she's the one that clued me in on her dramatic mood shift."

Switching from active listener, Cyndi began to participate in the conversation. "What do we do?" she asked. Derek was stunned. *What do **we** do?* He processed her words and was astounded to hear them from her; that she would invite herself into this thing, this mystery, of which Derek had no idea where to begin.

"I'm dying to know what this car key is," for that was the thing that was bothering him the most. "Do you suppose there's a connection between the key and the car storage facility? You know, not to state the obvious, but a car for this key." Derek reached into his pocket and pulled out the VW key showing it to Cyndi.

"Tomorrow I have a dentist appointment later in the morning," Cyndi responded, "then, what do you say about a drive to Galeton and a visit to, what is the place, *Twigg's*? We can investigate and see if we can find a car that fits that key? You and me. Your key is a glass slipper, let's see if we can find a match."

The thought of spending more time with Cyndi *and* taking a step closer of potentially unraveling what was going on with his mother, Derek's response was quick, "Do April showers bring May flowers?"

Their conversation shifted back away from Derek's mother-son relationship, and back to their own memories. They laughed for hours that drifted by like minutes. At 9:30PM, after Derek was certain all of the wine was out of his system, he decided it was time for a graceful exit. "Thank you for today. Pretty amazing to have you back," Derek gazed at Cyndi.

"It's so good to hear you say that. Oh, and thanks for letting me *keep* you today."

"I consider myself lucky to have been kept," Derek responded. As Derek readied himself to leave, they made plans for the next day after Cyndi's dental appointment.

Derek drove into his driveway—not remembering a thing about his drive home—his mind was still with Cynthia Vaughn, back at her apartment. The smell of her hair still danced upon his olfactory sensors. This day would forever be preserved, and no one could take it away from him. He sat back in his driver's seat and savored the day again—start to finish—and he filed it away in his brain's permanent storage facility. Lasagna. Derek's new most favorite meal, lasagna would always mean Cyndi, and smiles, tea, and wine, and grocery shopping, and tidying up the kitchen together in harmony. It was getting late. This incredible Wednesday was going to be yesterday in just a few short hours.

21

It was Thursday morning and he wondered how yesterday had evaporated into bliss. It was hard to grasp how fast the day went with Cyndi. Because of this new rotational speed of the earth, Derek had completely forgotten about connecting with Leena. Derek was staring at the text he received from Eileen about his mother's sweater. He didn't want to arouse suspicion with Eileen and thought it best to wait to respond. Still, it was now Thursday, and he had received that text almost twenty-four hours ago.

Derek made another cup of coffee and plunged deep into the couch to think. He needed to contemplate things, even more than needing caffeine. With his coffee in his left hand, his right hand took out his phone and proceeded to open his last text message with his sister. He then sent Leena a new text, *Mom get home last night? Oh, and good morning.*

His mother should now be home if she followed the same rulebook that she had for as long as he had known her, and that was all his life. Eileen indicated that she left a sweater, and that was on Wednesday morning. All of that meant that with a two-hour drive ahead of her, she should have arrived home at Clover Drive Wednesday afternoon. Three bubbles started to appear on his phone and with that mesmerizing effect that only those three bubbles can impart upon a human, conditioned to an impending response, Derek's gaze remained on the screen until the message returned from Leena. *Top of the morning to you. Mom said she would be home sometime Sunday. You good?*

Perhaps it was the assumption that he had made yesterday morning. Or maybe it was that he had one of the best days of his life yesterday. Whatever the reason, the text from his aunt led him to believe that his mother had left for home yesterday. Now, he sifted through the two pieces of information. Presumably, his mother left her sister's yesterday as evident by his aunt's text. And secondly, Leena now indicated that their mother would now be home on Sunday—some four plus days later. *Where is she from Wednesday to Sunday?* Derek thought.

He responded to Leena. *Doing well. Took a few days off from work to get my head clear. Feels good.* Derek's next message completely avoided their mother. He didn't want to alarm either his aunt, or his sister about these two disjointed tidbits of information—not yet. *Come visit, Everly would love to see you. I probably wouldn't mind it either,* Leena responded. Derek shut down the conversation for now. *Today is busy, I'll let you know tomorrow. Sounds good.* It was vague enough with no commitment. Derek, being unattached, flashed the definite maybe card more times than he should. But at this moment, he didn't know what to do. Should he call his aunt and simply ask what his mother's travel plans were? Should he go over to Leena's and advise her that they might have a missing mother on their hands? Should he even be going to *Twigg's Auto Storage* in Galeton with Cyndi—several hours away—with no plan, just reckless curiosity spurring them on. Doubt and uncertainty can rain on the emotional landscape, quickly ushering away joy as hastily as it had once appeared. And while Derek was no longer on the emotional high that he was just a few hours ago, he was glad for one thing. Cyndi would be here in just over an hour and they would spend the day together. Given that he had spued everything from his childhood-to-present-day feelings about his mother to her yesterday, he felt like he could bring her into the trust circle, or square, or triangle, of whatever was going on now. He took comfort in that. And he was excited to have her alone for a few hours, even if it was just driving in a car; the thought of that was both uplifting and soothing. On the other end of the phone, Leena let go of his last text, allowing Derek to be ambiguous, at least for the moment.

She arrived at 12:45PM, Derek couldn't hold back his excitement and started to peek out of his living room window starting at 12:30PM and kept checking about once every thirty seconds until she arrived. His butterflies were back. And there were more of them, all sorts of colorful varieties. There were probably some aesthetically pleasing moths down there, too. He was excited, the kind of excitement that doesn't come often in life, like seeing all of the numbers that you play on your lottery ticket equal the numbers on the screen. As she got out of her Prius, he noticed she grabbed a bag and what appeared to be two bottles of water. The same spell that was cast upon him yesterday at the café, the grocery store, and at her apartment, materialized yet again. Derek took in Cyndi's appearance as if savoring a painting at a gallery. She wore a tan wool sweater, black yoga pants, and upon her feet were light green sneakers which spot on matched the solid baseball cap upon her head. How this ensemble worked, he didn't care. She bent over and reached in to retrieve the last article—what looked to be her phone—before shutting the door behind her. "Ohh, Emm, Gee," Derek quietly said out loud to the window while biting his lip as he took in this angle of Cyndi.

After a soft but extra-long knock, Derek opened the door. "We don't want any, whatever you're selling," Derek blurted out, not being able to help himself.

"Fine," Cyndi responded, "I'll bring this delicious deli made sandwich elsewhere. I thought we could have lunch before heading out." Derek's breakfast was long ago now, and he admired her pro-active thinking. Good thing she was comprehending and acting on mealtimes; his mind had been elsewhere for the last few hours—attempting to piece things together—but failing miserably.

"How did the dentist go?" Derek asked as he opened the front door.

"Just a cleaning today," Cyndi said while pulling off her heavy sweater.

"Any cavities?" asked Derek.

"Zero. This brushing and flossing thing is paying off. You should try it," Cyndi's wit was as quick as ever. The two sat and had lunch around Derek's square, four-person table in what was less of a dining room and more of a dining space that was positioned to the left of his kitchen. Both he and Cyndi talked about yesterday. The fact that Cyndi had mentioned several of the things they did yesterday brought him satisfaction. It wasn't just him, she enjoyed yesterday, too.

They discussed what she liked and didn't like about

her new dentist and the same about her new surroundings. While she previously lived in the vicinity when she was younger, it had been a long time since driving around with her parents and high school friends. In many ways, Cyndi was new to the area, especially getting around and doing the things adults do, including of course, going to the dentist. The topic then went to today's adventure—each of them trying to envision how the day might unfold.

22

Derek made a travel mug of coffee for each of them. "Caffeine always helps at the beginning of an adventure."

"Ever been?" Cyndi asked as they both got into his silver BMW.

"To Galeton? Or on an adventure? I can't say that I have been to Galeton. You?"

"Not that I can recall," Cyndi responded.

They had done a few searches on the town of Galeton, trying to get some bearings on what to expect. They knew it was small, quite small, and its only claim to fame was having a state park. Other than that, they could find very little information. "We know it's 159 kilometers away," Derek said. "I've been trying to use the metric system as much as I can," stating the second part of his thought after receiving a strange glare from Cyndi.

"I think it's cute. We all should be using it anyway. If we took my car, we would use fewer *liters* of gas you know." Derek smiled; it was a nice double zinger in one jest.

"I don't think you need that cup of coffee, you're sharp enough already."

As they drove, their conversation mostly focused on how the surrounding towns grew and what changed the most since Cyndi moved away. "I miss it, and I can't explain it," Cyndi said. "It's completely average in almost every way. Very few tourists find their way here; there's no major attraction. Generic strip malls, commonplace developments, and regular-old schools. No one extremely famous has hailed from here, at least in current times."

After a pause, Derek responded. "I suppose that's the beauty of it. People living their lives with contentment—raising families, having holidays together, mowing lawns, watching television, working hard, maybe even reading a book to their kids before bed." Cyndi looked at Derek, she was afforded the ability to gaze at him, as he drove.

"You're saying I missed it because people around here live in the moment? Interesting interpretation, my Zen sensei." And with that term of endearment, albeit a mostly sarcastic one, Derek's face adopted a large smile, ear to ear.

Derek's car needed gas. The route they were taking was mostly state highways and at the sight of the first convenience store, Derek pulled up to the gas pumps. "Don't worry, my next vehicle will be a hybrid, or electric—providing I know that most of the electricity I use to charge it comes from renewable sources," Derek said before getting out to pump his gas.

"Good man," Cyndi responded, "can you pop the hood?" Cyndi proceeded, without hesitation, to check his oil level, then upon shutting the hood, grabbed the squeegee and set off to clean every window and then the headlights. Derek just took the entire scene in. She could have easily just stayed in the car, taking a passive role. Not with Cyndi. Derek fully admired this attribute. Even as children playing together with Leena, she was fully engaged with them—from playing tag to Monopoly. *And what a mediator*, Derek thought. Leena and Derek didn't fight all that much, growing up, but they were brother and sister. Cyndi would keep the peace when all three of them were together. As Derek finished pumping gas, his thoughts turned to the time when Cyndi lived next to him. He could not recall one contentious moment the three of them had while playing together all those countless times. Conflict seemed to resolve itself when Cyndi was present. Derek concluded that it was due to her ability to quickly ascertain personalities in a given situation and read them, fully inserting herself in the other person's shoes. She knew how much to push or concede in a particular situation, and how to factor in all the variables, put them together and then diffuse things. Many times, this talent afforded her the ability to sense things well before they started to near a boiling point.

Derek got back into the car—proud of himself for realizing all of this about Cyndi while pumping gas. "How's it look?" asked Derek, "my dipstick?"

"Derek G. Densmore, if you're referring to the current oil levels within your automobile, they are sufficient at this time." Then after a pause, while buckling his seat belt and starting the car, Derek, with a huge grin, began again.

"You didn't have to do that, but thank you," Derek looked at Cyndi while putting the car in gear.

"It was my pleasure. Habit, more than anything, you can blame my father for that." The next statement Cyndi relayed in a deep mocking voice—as close to her father's as she could. "Nothing can cause more damage to a vehicle than not having enough oil."

"Wise words in my mind," Derek said.

The sun went in and out that afternoon and the drive was full of active visor-up and visor-down participation for both driver and passenger. Their conversation continued to flow with ease. There was enough pause between subjects where Derek felt the need to discuss the latest about his mother. "I think Mom left my aunt's yesterday morning," Derek got it out of his system.

"She's home, that's good news." Cyndi asked, "Right?"

"I don't really know," Derek responded. "She could be, or most likely not."

Cyndi let a few moments pass. "Go on. I need help demystifying this," Cyndi said.

Derek brought up the texts he received from his aunt and also his follow-up texts with his sister from this morning, indicating that his mom would be home on Sunday. "Weird, but maybe not," Cyndi started. "Maybe your mom has things to do before she comes home. Errands to run, another friend to see, it could be that simple, right?"

"Yes, in theory it could be, I suppose," Derek responded. "But adding up her agitated state, and all the mysterious things—what could she be doing? I'd feel better knowing where she was. Mom has never been a mysterious person, at least the mom I know."

"You said just last night that you would like to know your mom on a deeper level—perhaps there are things that you don't know about her, or maybe don't want to know?"

"Maybe," Derek responded. "It's all so frustrating."

"I know you didn't want to get Leena alarmed at this,

but don't you think it's time?" Cyndi asked. "If I was your sister, I'd want to know that your aunt is under the impression that she went home *and* at the same time Leena is led to believe that your mom is still at your aunt's place—supposedly coming home on Sunday."

Derek couldn't argue with such a sound argument. "You're absolutely right, Cyndi," Derek said, his eyes on the road but on autopilot in terms of active vehicle operation.

"Hey, I like when you say that," Cyndi replied.

"What, that you're absolutely right?" Derek spoke louder.

"Both, but more when you say my name." At that time, the clouds blocked any sunlight, and he was grateful, fearing that she would see him blushing.

"After today's odyssey, promise me you'll contact Leena; bring her in?" Cyndi asked. Presently, Derek was incapable of telling Cyndi no—no matter her ask.

"Yes, I will. Promise."

"I know that I can trust you," Cyndi replied. He couldn't help but think there was a deeper meaning at play.

More time went by on their drive. It was approaching 3:30PM, and by Derek's GPS calculations, they would arrive at *Twigg's Auto Storage* just after 4PM. Derek was thinking about what they would do when they got there, having both the invoice as well as the VW key in the pocket of his jeans. Cyndi then changed the subject entirely.

"Do you want to have a family, Derek?" Cyndi asked, as bold and as calm as could be. "You know, someday. Do you want to raise a little Derek or Derek-ess? I know that Leena does, as evidence from her getting married to Eli and them having Everly. What about you?"

Derek shifted in his seat feeling slightly uncomfortable for the first time that day. "I think so, yes, if the right person came around and it felt right—everything about it. I never had a father, as you know. But I just might make a decent dad, at least I think so."

"Simply curious, that's all," Cyndi said. "You would make a great dad. I would also like a family someday. If everything felt right. Ken and I were just going through the motions of what we both thought we should be doing. I can't explain it other than that. Together, we were a painting of just gray; some darker gray, some lighter gray—but just gray. A relationship should be a canvass full of many bright colors, dimensional, vivid. At least, that's my perspective, my two cents," Cyndi finished.

"I like your two cents; those are some shiny pennies you just gave me," Derek replied.

A road sign appeared indicating that Galeton was ten miles away. "*Twigg's* is open until 5PM. Here's my plan. I'll present the invoice and ask to see the vehicle, as I'm April's son and she sent me to pick up something she accidently left in the car. What do you think?" Derek asked.

"Simply genius. Two potential pitfalls that I can think of though," Cyndi replied. "We're assuming the key fits a car in storage. And, what if they don't let you, because you're not the car's owner?"

"True, we are assuming this mysterious key fits this mysterious car. I'll play stupid if it doesn't, like I accidently took the wrong key. As to the second point, I'll keep appealing to them. I'm not above begging. They'll let us in." The GPS turned them onto Gilson Road, then after a two-minute ride, they took another right onto a dirt road called Twigg's Lane. "You think we're getting close?" Derek tried a bit of nervous humor.

The road banked slightly to the left and around the corner, it was there that they saw three buildings. Straight ahead was a small building, a construction job-site gray metallic trailer, presumably the office. To the right was a large four bay garage—all of the doors were open and in each bay a car or truck was being worked on by a mechanic. As Derek and Cyndi stepped out of the car, they could hear the clinks and clanks of tools and the unmistakable sound of an air compressor recharging. To their left stood a long, white, and rusting storage facility, capable of housing close to a hundred vehicles Derek guessed. Above the office door, a sign hung letting visitors know that this was *Twigg's Enterprises*.

"Here we go," Derek said to Cyndi, "care to join me?"

"This is exciting," Cyndi replied with a smile. As they walked to the office, Derek looked over at the garage, it was evident that each mechanic took a few seconds' pause to gawk at them. Derek knew it wasn't him they were gawking at. Cyndi rocked out her baseball cap and yoga pants, and they all stared without subtlety.

Derek opened the door for Cyndi, a small brass bell rang as the door opened. A heavy-set woman, with dark, square framed glasses, somewhere in her late fifties or early sixties approached them. "Hello, hello," she said, "here to pick up your car—it's been a busy day— everybody needs their brakes done it seems." After her run on sentence, Derek spoke.

"Wondering if you can help me. My mom forgot something in her car that's stored here, and she sent me to retrieve it."

"Hmmm, Hector usually does all of the storage arrangements. Does he know you're coming?"

"No, I didn't call in advance, we would only need a few minutes."

"Hmmm," is all she returned. She picked up a two-way radio and after a beep she began, "Hector, you there?"

They must have bantered to each other quite often on this device. "Yah, whatcha need?" a gruff and hurried voice replied.

"A couple is here to get something from a car in storage," the woman answered back.

"Be there in two shakes," the deep scratchy voice responded.

"Hector will be here shortly; he can help you."

After what must have been two shakes, a side door opened. They had already formulated what Hector Twigg looked like, using the woman who greeted them as perspective—presumably, Mrs. Twigg—and the rough voice that blurted back at them through the radio.

In walked a man similar in age to the woman behind the desk, but instead of being a large build with extra pounds and a beard, Derek's fabricated image was shattered. If he were 5'6" tall it would be a stretch, and he was lean, very lean. He was shorter than the woman in the dark glasses, ultra-thin and had a youthful face. Above his lip sat a salt and pepper, well-oiled handlebar mustache right out of 1904—or whatever year they were popular. Cyndi was also taken aback.

"What's your name?" Mr. Twigg threw his commanding voice at them without any cordial formalities.

"My name is Derek Densmore. My mother stores a

car here, and I'm here to pick up something she forgot in it," Derek responded confidently.

Hector turned to Cyndi, asking the same with his glance but with no words. "You his wife?" Hector asked.

"Oh, no, just a friend," Cyndi replied with a red face that Derek noticed.

"Hmmm, hmmm," is all Hector apparently had. And with no words spoken, the meaning was clear; *sure, you're just a friend.* Hector, still standing, went to the desk and typed in a few things into what looked to be a computer as old as Derek. "What's your mother's name?"

"April, April Densmore," Derek responded confidently.

"So, here's the thing," the rough voiced baby-faced man began, "a couple of years ago I got burned, badly." His moustache bounced up and down as he spoke; Derek found it difficult to look into his eyes because of the small piece of manicured facial hair that dominated everything else. "Few years back a lady came in and said she was the girlfriend of a customer that stores his Camaro here in the winter." Hector took a seat. He leaned back into the creaky metal desk chair; he had obviously delivered this soliloquy before and looked forward to pitching it once again. "Well, she *was* the girlfriend, as in the past tense. Turns out the two had a major falling out—must have been a doozy—if you know what I mean." Derek and Cyndi exchanged glances, knowing this wasn't going well. "Yup, she's the reason I now have a policy. Some of my employees sure did get a chuckle out of it, the end product that is. This lady, she must have been some filled with rage, I'm telling you. After she convinced me to let her in, *to retrieve some makeup from the car*—so she told me, she set to work with her nail polish writing some thought-provoking poetry on the doors of the Camaro." It became clear that he spent considerable time rehearsing this story as it came out too showy, too smooth. "Let's just say that some of the things she spelled out in pink nail polish would make a sailor feel uncomfortable." He paused for dramatic effect and to gauge his audience's approval.

Derek felt the need to make another plea. "We're not those type of people, Hector," he tried a personal play— either it would appeal to him, or it could be off-putting, calling him by his first name.

"I'm sure you're not, Derek," he mentally retrieved his name in time from the conversation just minutes ago. "But, because of that, I don't let anyone in unless it's the owner of the vehicle. The only other case is if the owner has passed away or is incapacitated and I have proof of Power of Attorney. Unless you fit that bill, I'm sorry and I know you probably drove a fair distance for a dead end." He watched their faces, both visibly showing disappointment. Cyndi, whether her face simply displayed sadness by the news, or she embellished the dejection with dramatic flair, it caught Hector's eye. "Tell you what. I have a number in my system for April, your mom," he paused and looked up to them. "I can call her now and if she says, yes, she knows you're here and are running an errand for her, I'll let you in to get her stuff. That's a big exception I'm making." Derek's stomach dropped, they just entered the space in-between a rock and a hard place.

Cyndi, never complacent in a passive role, spoke up, "A rule's a rule." Cyndi was aware of the dilemma they now found themselves in. More than likely April Densmore wouldn't pick up the phone, but if she did, it would become awkward quickly for all parties. "We had a nice ride up here today; it wasn't a wasted trip. There's a gift shop we stopped at not too far away, too, so this was a two for one." Cyndi was laying it on, impressively so. "We'll all come together next time and we can stop at that gift shop again, Derek, your mother would love some of that hand blown glass we saw." Derek stood halfway between awe, observing her cunning ability to think on her feet, and bewilderment, in shock of how deceptive she instantly became.

"That's a good point," it was all Derek could muster. The situation was diffused, Cyndi's forte. They could walk away, without embarrassment, but without accomplishing their goal.

"Could I use the restroom before we head back out on the road?" Cyndi finished, now with all routes closed on the prior subject.

Hector rose from his chair. "Sure thing, it's the door to the left," he pointed behind him to a two-tone door. It was bright red and below the chipping paint—probably a third of the door revealed its previous color, at one time the door was white. Even partially red and white, it was not unappealing for an old garage bathroom door. Hector moved towards Derek for some parting conversation. At the same time Hector asked Derek where he was from, Derek's eyes spotted Cyndi unveiling some more acting, this time silently, pointing excessively in a body language whisper, to a wall of keys, just to the left of the red and white bathroom door she was about to enter.

"I live just outside of Wilkes-Barre," Derek said, but he could not believe his eyes. Just before she entered the bathroom, Cyndi gingerly withdrew the key labeled *Storage Barn* from the top hook. The door closed behind her. Derek started to sweat and could barely focus on anything else Hector said. All Derek got out was, "Thank you for your time, I hope we didn't trouble you."

A moment later the toilet flushed loudly, and then the sink's water ran. It was not a highly desirable place to have a nature calls moment as Derek and Hector were just a few meters from the flimsy door and every sound could be heard.

"Thank you both for understanding. And sounds like we'll be seeing you soon." Hector departed this time out the front door. The heavy-set woman re-entered from what appeared to be a room full of old filing cabinets and a small kitchenette with a table. She had taken a small break while the three of them had their conversation. It was also obvious that she had been intentionally listening.

"I have a picture of the Camaro if you want to see it?"

23

Dusk was upon them. *Twigg's* was surrounded by forest, a mixture of tall white pines and hemlocks could be seen in almost every direction. The sun was starting to go below the tree line making it appear darker than it really was. They both entered the car and put on their seat belts.

"Cyndi, what the Hell are you thinking?" Derek wasn't angry, his emotion came from being stunned by her action.

"Sly, huh?" Cyndi was proud of herself. "Drive to the convenience store we saw a few miles away. We can discuss the plan there over a bottled water and some salt and vinegar potato chips."

A plan? Could it be that Cyndi already contrived a plan in the few minutes that she was inside the bathroom? Derek, for the moment, was glad to begin to drive away from *Twigg's*. The two were silent for the first few minutes of the ride. Derek was quiet, still in shock about Cyndi's key larceny and the disappointment of not getting in to see how this car may or may not fit into his mother's life and her current emotional well-being. Cyndi was also quiet, deep in thought, she was obviously scheming, and in the process of hatching a devious plan.

Derek, as instructed, pulled into a nearby convenience store. "I'll be back," Cyndi unbuckled her seat belt and headed into the store, apparently going in to purchase their unorthodox dinner.

The drive calmed him some and allowed him to process everything that just happened. Derek convinced himself that Cyndi's kleptomania was a sort of giving the bird to Hector for not allowing them to go into the storage facility. He continued to compose himself while Cyndi was in the store. His thoughts turned to how amazing her performance was at *Twigg's*. "Sharp as a tack, that one," Derek said out loud to himself in the car.

As promised, Cyndi bounded back into the car with two bottled waters, a bag of salt and vinegar Kettle potato chips and a Snicker's bar. She held up the Snicker's bar. "Devil made me do it."

Derek instantly came back, "Ah, um, so Satan had nothing to do with the Snicker's bar and everything to do with the key you just absconded with."

"Have a chip, it will make you feel better," Cyndi broke open the bag. "Everybody's doing it." She started to munch on a large chip.

"Stealing keys or eating chips?" Derek fired back.

"Are you ready?" Cyndi asked Derek.

"Ready for what?" Derek responded.

"Ready to hear my plan. I did the best I could to get a look at the layout of things, I didn't see security cameras—anywhere. And they close at 5PM. They look like a business that shuts down at closing time. Today's Thursday, tomorrow's Friday—the week is almost over. The storage facility abuts the woods, so we can approach from that side and park the car on the road after Twigg's Lane, what was it called, Gleeson?"

Derek interrupted, "Gilson. Wait, you're proposing that we actually sneak in, and actually use the key you took and actually break and enter a business that already told us they don't want us being there?"

"Actually, yes. You make it sound foul. It's just entering, there will be no breaking. I have merely borrowed a key, not taken it for good. If you think about it, it's all on the up and up."

"Ms. Vaughn, there's nothing up and up about any of this." His voice was louder than he anticipated it. Cyndi crunched on another crispy chip.

"I love salt and vinegar, they are my favorite," Cyndi replied. "Derek, do you want to find out if that key in your pocket fits a car in that storage facility?"

"Yes, I like salt and vinegar chips, too, and I also want to find out if this key fits the car that's in there. But this is dangerous. What we're doing is risky and my sense of adventure isn't; I have, shall we say, a *common* sense of adventure."

Cyndi paused and took two giant gulps of her water. "We'll be careful. Once we get beyond the woods and approach the door, if there is anyone there, or things look awry, we can abort the mission." Derek instantly went back in time when the three of them would spy on the neighbors. Of the three of them, Cyndi had the most spirit and sense of risk in approaching their neighbor's house—the house to the right of Derek and Leena's—as Cyndi lived in the neighboring house to the left. "My phone's battery is low; do you have a flashlight? You were a scout, always prepared, and so on?"

Derek reached into his glove box, "Excuse the reach —I'm not being fresh," Derek opened the glove box, just above Cyndi's knees. There, he pulled out a royal blue tactical flashlight, one that allowed you to concentrate the light's beam.

"It is settled, we have the tools, we have the means. Operation *Fishbowl* commences." Cyndi grabbed another chip and proceeded to chomp loudly.

Derek sighed and put his head back upon the headrest. "You're serious? You're absolutely, stone cold sober serious?"

"Stone cold, and there's no liquor involved in this mission," Cyndi replied. "We got this. We wait here another forty-five minutes or so. We find a place on Gilson and park, traverse up through the woods until we're parallel with the storage facility, then quickly enter, locate, and leave. I will leave the key inside the door and will wipe any fingerprints off of it. It will all be chalked up to oversight, by Hector. You know, someone forgot to take the key out of the door. All will be good." Derek took a chip, began to chew, and wished it turned into lasagna and last night's danger free good time.

As crazy as her plan sounded, she also sounded confident. It was almost thrilling in a way Derek could not describe. For a man with routines within routines, this was so far away from being typical. The plan involved risk, something he usually avoided. In addition to the element of risk, the element of excitement was amplified simply by being with Cyndi. Deep down, he didn't want to disappoint her. After mentally assessing all of the variables once again, Derek made the decision. "I'm in. But only if we never call it Operation *Fishbowl* again."

Cyndi opened the Snicker's bar and broke it in half and handed the equal portion to Derek. "I can compromise." She held out her hand to shake Derek's.

"We have ourselves a deal, mister. Let's find out what we came here to find out. Do you like my choice of dessert?"

They spent the next forty-five minutes talking about all they observed at *Twigg's* just an hour ago. "Are you certain there are no cameras?" Derek asked again.

"I didn't see any old bubble looking ones or newer ones, like you put on your front door. If there are none, it should be a piece of cake," Cyndi replied.

"I don't know, a piece of cake sounds pretty easy and a lot safer." Derek's stomach started to knot.

After another twenty minutes, the sky continued to darken. "They have been closed for almost two hours," Cyndi whispered.

"Why are you whispering?" Derek asked back.

"Practicing," she said again in a hush-hush tone. Derek gently shook his head trying to look appalled but couldn't help but be amused. He laughed. Cyndi's personality carried this sort of delightful charm she brought with her wherever she went. She had always had it, even with difficult topics, long ago when they were children. Wit, he supposed, but a special kind of wit. Her wit was ultra-keen and one that that made him feel specially connected to her. It had been many years of being away and here she was with the same wit, in his car, developing a scheme to find out more about his mother's mysterious vehicle. They each had a second life since they saw each other; Derek moved to the next town and had settled into a job he enjoyed and bought a house of his own. Cyndi had moved to a different state, found the love of her life—or so she thought—and was now starting over; back where she once came from. Derek couldn't help but think how strange it was to have her sitting in his passenger seat, taking in the last bite of a

Snicker's bar, her wavy hair smelling like some sort of intoxicating honey and orange blossom fragrance. Cynthia Vaughn, his crush of crushes, as clever as ever, right here, sitting next to him. And she was apparently equally as devious, too.

They each took one last gulp of water and flashed each other a glance that said it was time. No traffic appeared on Gilson Road for the few minutes they were on it. The lack of cars wasn't surprising, it was a dirt road and before the right hand turn onto Twigg's Lane they could only see two houses. They continued to slowly ascend the country road. Derek wanted to park out of sight of Twigg's Lane. Less than a quarter mile away, a corner bearing right took them out of the line of sight from the entrance to *Twigg's*. While there was not much of a pull off available, there was also no real shoulder and the road blended in with what would soon be tall grass in the summer months. Derek pulled his two right tires off the road while keeping the driver's side still on Gilson. *It would have to do*, Derek thought.

"Flashlight?" Derek asked.

"Check," Cyndi acquired it from the glove compartment, "and my phone for backup."

"Stolen key?"

"Double check," Cyndi made it appear in her hand.

"Balls to break the law?"

"I forgot those, but I did bring my titanium ovaries," Cyndi flashed a large, nervous grin. "Let's do this. I'm feeling pretty alive right now." In finance, you don't take chances. Derek was quickly learning that in marketing, you might have much more tendency to do so.

They got out of the car and looked around, instantly feeling like the police were about to surround simply for the thoughts they had circling around in their heads. "The forest, see, through there—if we go straight up that, the storage facility should be on our right, oh, less than ten minutes away if we walk quickly," Derek said, "I guess it's now or never."

Cyndi was in stealth mode already and had bolted ahead of him, quickly and quietly finding her way into the woods. Derek picked up his pace. The two were completely silent, not daring to make a sound other than their feet breaking an occasional small branch given up by trees during the previous winter. They could see their breath and being dressed for only a causal walk during the day, both of them felt the chill of dampness from the spring woods. It was definitely still April.

Just under nine minutes into their walking journey, Cyndi thought she saw the structure on her right and used the flashlight for a quick glean to confirm her target. They both knew the next move; assess the area for activity. If there was someone around—anyone—they had already discussed that they would abort the mission. Stillness. As their eyes acclimated, they could see that all four bays of the garage were closed, a florescent light emanated from inside. Floodlights at the trailer-office, pointed towards the *Twigg's Enterprises* sign, one light was out and needed to be replaced. A light right above the entrance of the giant storage building was also on. No other lights anywhere could be seen. An absolute silence identified itself. The two breathed for a minute, taking the scene in, listening for anything that could be human, assessing for movement, for anything that was making noise beyond their steady breathing. Only their pounding hearts kept them company, and the smell of their breath —peanuts and chocolate with a hint of vinegar.

After a few more minutes of taking things in, Cyndi flashed Derek a thumbs up. Derek responded with the same. This time Derek led the way, he wanted to show Cyndi that his anatomy also contained titanium. Cyndi followed right behind. Staying out of the light emanating from the entrance to the storage facility, they paused again to ascertain their surroundings. Things remained calm. Derek held out his hand, requesting the key. And with one more large intake of oxygen, Derek turned the corner, approached the entrance, and proceeded to unlock the banged-up metal and glass door. After a few turns and jiggles, the lock relinquished its purpose, and the door could be opened. Slowly pushing the door inward while keeping the knob turned—and leaving the key in the knob, he snuck inside. Cyndi was his shadow. Darkness.

This Thursday night, no moon was there to assist them. Poor lunar planning for a night raid, Derek thought to himself. The facility had many large windows at the top of the walls, there for natural light. But being night-time, and no moon of any kind to help, they had two choices. Use the flashlight only, or risk turning on some lights. The latter seemed far too risky to two normally law-abiding citizens. Cyndi brought her arm up, holding the flashlight, and projected it back and forth. All around them were boats, cars, and trucks in every direction. A Model-A Ford stood just to their right, more than likely used once a year for an Independence Day parade. A large army transport truck was to their immediate left. Hector Twigg, in addition to vehicles, allowed for all sorts of storage, including marine storage. Sailboats, motorboats, even a small yacht were scattered throughout. The winner: convertibles, they were too numerous to count. After some stumbling and stepping on each other's feet, they found a walkway in what they believed to be the middle path of the facility. Here they could walk in an almost straight line and observe each stored form of transportation. Not too far in, they discovered a grand piano almost touching a Mazda Miata on one side and a Harley Davidson on the other. Derek reached into his jeans and began to feel for the key he found in the fishbowl of his mother's bookcase, now days ago. He pointed to the VW on the key as Cyndi flashed the light upon it. Many vehicles either had specially fitted covers or makeshift tarps covering them— something that they had not anticipated; unwrapping cars in order to reveal their make and model.

They continued down the aisle, hoping a Volkswagen would jump out at them. After another two minutes of exploration, on the left, just after a lifted navy-blue Jeep CJ7, they came to an older style, extremely dusty, champagne colored Volkswagen Jetta. How long this vehicle had sat in this location without being driven or washed for that matter, Derek couldn't fathom a guess. "This car looks familiar somehow," Derek whispered, "yes, very familiar." Cyndi used the flashlight to peer into the vehicle, first in the front and then in the back seat. Nothing peered back. At this point, given their heightened state of borderline paranoia, not seeing a skeleton in the car was a disappointment. Taking a chance that the car was unlocked, he tried the driver's side door. It did not yield to his attempt. Cyndi nodded to Derek and touched his hand with the key. It was time to see if Leena's old goldfish's secret key was connected to this vehicle. Between the stress of entering the building without permission and the uncertainty of this bizarre mystery, Derek's forehead started to sweat despite being chilled by their brisk April walk, minutes before.

After a quick turn, the key successfully unlocked the car. "Oh my God," Cyndi whispered. It was at that moment, as Derek was opening the driver's side door that something fell out of the vehicle and made a loud noise on the concrete floor. Cyndi's light quickly found the culprit, a VW wheel's center cap, presumably to this car, bounced several times on the concrete floor before rolling and then stopping close to the Jeep. Derek could not believe how loud a piece of plastic could be on a concrete floor. But then again, when you don't belong somewhere, every noise is deafening. A few moments went by before Derek and Cyndi dared to do anything. He motioned for the flashlight and Cyndi offered it to him. Derek crawled into the Jetta's driver's seat and motioned the light all around him, trying to take it all in. *It's just an old car*, he thought. Nothing visibly could be seen other than normal car components—a steering wheel, a dashboard, seat belts, an AM/FM radio. He then approached the glove compartment. Upon opening, he found it busting with papers and documents. Derek grabbed the entire contents, just barely fitting them all into one hand. It was at that time that his entire thinking became engulfed by the gravity of things. He continued to sweat, and then there was the loud noise the center cap made, and the whole breaking and entering thing invaded his mind. His thoughts were many but now were reduced to one thing. He needed to get out of there, now.

Derek, still in the driver's seat, forced the glove box shut with his right arm and as he did so, his left arm fell upon the steering wheel and for a brief moment, a piercing horn blast launched from a late 20th century Volkswagen Jetta, and made itself known, announcing to everyone that it didn't matter the last time it was started; it still had enough battery juice for the horn to proudly sound. "Crap," Derek said, only not in a whisper. The *I-*

need-to-leave-now feeling he had just seconds ago blended now with a *I'm-here-come-and-get-me* sentiment. This blend of emotions created something in Derek he had never felt before, at least to this degree—genuine panic. Cyndi's eyes were larger than Derek had ever seen anyone's. They both took in a large breath and then exhaled. "Everything will be fine," Cyndi whispered. After Derek popped back out of the car, he closed the door and they stared at each other.

Their hearts were pounding, mouths excessively dry, and their pupils were the size of their irises. Just after another large breath, they both heard a switch being thrown, and above them, bright florescent lights flooded down on them. Their eyes, just a moment ago, adequately adjusted to the darkness, were now entirely useless against the ceiling's aggressive fluorescence. Unlike *Twigg's* office, all of the lights in the storage facility burned with authority. They were not alone.

24

April Densmore walked unstably back towards her car. Her shoes gently clicking on the sidewalk, away from the two-story gambrel house. It was evening and the entrance light showed her the way back to her car, parked on the side street that ran parallel with the house. There was no moonlight to guide her way—only the streetlights that reflected on the damp sidewalk revealed her path. She had done what she had come to do.

She glanced over her shoulder, finding the strength to take one final look at the house. Her hands were trembling. In the darkness, her eyes adjusted and were assisted by a nearby streetlight. She could still make out the color of the house. The second story was a dark forest green; the lower story was white with the same green paint as above used for the shutters. The street was quiet and more than likely she was the only one around at this time of night. She turned around to take in the scene. There she looked at the front door and its surroundings one final time. On the front left of the door, a black wrought iron number adorned the clapboard siding: number 114. Below the street number, centered perfectly, was a surname in the same black iron material. It spelled out the family name in a cursive font: Morello. Tears started to form in her eyes.

This evening, the air was still. Neither northerly nor southernly winds applied pressure on the changing season. To April, the night felt as if the air had less oxygen. It was stale. There was no smell that she could identify outside. Moments before, she was in the Morello house. It had a slight musty odor, like a basement of an old farmhouse and it mingled with several other fragrant candles that burned. That smell, while not necessarily putrid to April, already churned her stomach. All houses have smells; a mixture of the people and pets and soil on which the house was built. On top of that, add the cleaning fluids, perfumes, laundry detergents, and where you store the garbage before it's hauled away—they all add up to be the true aroma of a house. It wasn't a hideous smell. But there was a dampness to it, like the vernal equinox they were in. Still, each house has its own scent, and the smell of the Morello house began to make her sick. She wished for a breeze in the air to vanish the odor. Now that she knew this smell, if she ever caught anything close to it again, it would make her physically ill. After all she had done in there, if ever she encountered the smell again, it would connect the memory of tonight.

April, with robotic movement, opened her car door and sunk down into the driver's seat. Her hand found the ignition and she yanked on her seat belt. Driving away, April Densmore's windshield did not need the wipers turned on, however, her eyes went from misting to rain and then from rain to a downpour. She did what she had come to do. Her sobbing, the cause-and-effect relationship of what just transpired in the Morello household; she began to question herself already. Would what she just did make things better?

While the street was barren, if there had been someone walking on the lonely sidewalk, they would have heard the deep painful sob of a woman in tremendous emotional pain. The engine was now on. With her eyes leaking and hands shaking, April sped away from 114 West Avenue, with one of her three promises now accomplished.

erek and Cyndi's eyes blinked rapidly. Derek thought of three options. Capitulate immediately was easily first. But the getting arrested part of that seemed quite distasteful. The second option was to hide, but they had already announced themselves, loudly. Hiding in a finite place like this, under a car cover could only delay the unpleasant experience that was part of option number one. Escape was the third option and afforded the only chance of getting out of this without a record.

"I know you're in here," boomed a deep and angry voice. Cyndi's eyes, despite attempting to acclimate to the brightness, were bulging and wide—they reminded Derek of a cartoon character and at any other time he would have let loose an enormous laugh. They both looked around at their surroundings, this time with light enough to see everything. "We can do this one of two ways," the voice beckoned, "you come out now and wait for the police with me, or the police can come in and find you. I assure you, the last thing the sheriff wants is to play hide and seek. Course, that means breaking and entering *and* resisting arrest. Your call."

What kind of a building had only one egress? A homemade metal storage facility in Galeton, Pennsylvania built by the Twigg family a generation ago had only one human sized exit. The male voice boomed yet again, "I'm not playing games—what's it going to be? Answer *me*." The last word, *me*, was heavily emphasized; if you were this person's child you would be headed for a permanent grounding. Cyndi and Derek continued to survey their surroundings. Their eyes acclimated more with each passing second. It was true that the anxious shouting man was at the only human sized door, but it was not the only exit. Along the side of the facility, evenly spread out, were four massive, oversized garage doors, capable of allowing even the largest RVs to enter and exit with ease. From what they could gauge in their crouched position, they were close to one of them— more than likely the third one down from the door where the man with the hostile voice stood. They looked at each other, both pointing to the garage door. With that, they started to move towards it hunched over as if approaching a helicopter. Advancing towards the garage door, to the left was the back end of a monster sized speedboat. At any other time, Derek would have liked to have looked at it more closely and wondered at the price tag of such a thing. The speedboat was the last bit of protection before the larger-than-life size garage door. To the right of the door, they saw what they were hoping for —the up/down switch—green for up, black for down, and in the middle was a red stop button.

"What's it going to be?" The man's voice bellowed yet again. They looked down to the left towards the door and the man, peeking out from behind the speedboat's stern. They could make out only one leg, clad in faded blue jeans. Slowly they rose from the crouched position, a multicolored customized van, some ways down helped hide them from his gaze. With what courage he found, Derek mouthed the word "now" to Cyndi as he quietly tiptoed to the door and hit the open button—Derek did so with the VW key as not to leave any fingerprints. The door groaned loudly but slowly began to open. Without thinking, both he and Cyndi fell flat upon the cold concrete, as if approaching an obstacle course with barbed wire. As soon as the door was open enough for their bodies to fit, they wiggled out upon the cold concrete floor and found the night's darkness waiting for them on the other side. They bolted for the woods. Behind them, the man shouted in their direction. Derek was confident the first part was "Son of," but couldn't hear the rest, but he had a theory on the remainder of the man's expression.

In the forest, risking spraining an ankle, they ran as fast as they could in the dark, retracing their original approach. They said nothing, they only concentrated on breathing deeply and running, there was no room for any other thought or action. If this is what it felt like to run for your life, Derek had no desire for seconds, ever.

Breaking out of the wooded surroundings, Derek's car appeared. In the darkness, while running at full steam, Derek fished out his keys and found the remote to open the doors. The BMW's lights flashed. They flung themselves into the car. Derek became grateful for a push button start. He cranked the steering wheel to the left, turning the car around at the same time stepping down hard on the gas. They headed back towards the village of Galeton, accelerating down Gilson Road. All that could be heard inside the car were two people gasping for breath. Derek realized he had been carrying the contents of the Jetta's glove compartment with him and still had it in his left hand—even while steering the car. He handed the wad of papers to Cyndi. "Could you hold this?"

"Yes, of course," Cyndi replied. For the next fifteen minutes, nothing was spoken. There was one thing in their minds, and that was hope. The hope of not seeing a police car between now and finding their way back home. The silence was broken when Cyndi cleared her throat. "We just did that," she remarked, trying to convince herself as much as making conversation with Derek.

More time and towns went by on their return drive. Derek began to come out of the state of shock he had just visited; yet another new place—visited just today. "Do you think that will come back to haunt us?" Derek finally asked with about fifteen minutes remaining in their journey.

"I've been thinking the same thing," Cyndi replied, "and I don't think so." Cyndi's wheels were spinning, "Here's why. I don't think the man, had to be Hector, had a cell phone on him. I also think that, again, if it were Hector, he would want to check out things, to see if there was any damage before calling the police. My guess is he examined the whole place up and down. Most likely he would have been looking for some time, checking for break-ins, paint scratches, slashed tires. He would probably be expecting the second installment of the Camaro incident. Of course, he would find nothing out of sorts. You don't know this, but I placed the center cap that fell out back into the car just before you decided to honk the horn." Cyndi went on, "Well after closing time, on a Thursday night and finding nothing out of place, do you think that type of individual would want to call the police and bring attention to his business? I'm thinking he's the kind of person that wouldn't want any publicity; last thing he wants is someone catching wind of a break-in and them thinking their speedboat isn't safe."

"Or Steinway piano," Derek interrupted.

"My thought is, we did him a favor." Derek wasn't following her logic, at least her last comment.

"Say again?"

"We did him a favor, I would say; this will probably make him invest in security camaras, or even a full-on security system where entry after hours trips the alarm and the police come—post haste."

"And how did you know that there wasn't a security system when we did that, that thing that we just did," Derek asked.

"I didn't, but I also noticed there were no signs or stickers on the doors or windows announcing it. You know, you're spending a bunch of money on a security system, you want the full effect. Announce the security system so that it's one additional deterrent for would-be bad guys."

"Like us?" Derek asked, finally shaking things off, attempting to cut the heaviness with some humor.

"Like us," Cyndi replied smiling.

"I'm buying what you're selling on your logic about him not calling the police. But let's say he did, and they got our fingerprints, what then?" Derek asked, looking to Cyndi to assuage his fears about not wanting to be hauled off to the big house.

"Small town, really small town, no damage anywhere, and it was his key that was in the lock. How does that look? One further, my guess is he knows the sheriff—and probably well—small town and all. How does it look if your law enforcement arrives, and the office key is in the doorknob? No Bueno—he would have some explaining to do—and he would probably be given a hard time about not locking up his keys. Mr. Twigg didn't seem the sort that wanted to be told what to do. And while he enjoyed the storytelling of the disgruntled girlfriend and her artistic graffiti, I sense that he would like to keep drama out of the picture when it comes to his livelihood. It's on him to keep that place secure—when it got out that his own key was used for entry, well, double no Bueno." Derek could not believe how fast Cyndi was calculating all of this and piecing together the variables and assumptions. It made a lot of sense.

"OK, so he doesn't call the police, but he probably will put two and two together about you sneaking off with the key just before closing, and us being in the proximity of the door we opened, very close to the Jetta."

"Elementary, my dear Derek," Cyndi was beginning to have fun now that her adrenaline was back to somewhat normal levels, "he would have to admit to Mrs. Twigg that the key was stolen when he was in the office talking with us—he would have to tell Mrs. Twigg, if that was indeed Mrs. Twigg, and admit that he was conned. If I've got it pegged that they were a couple, I don't think he would want her to know he got scammed in his own office. I just don't think he is motivated to do so, you know, call the cops that is. And, as already produced in the evidence, nothing was out of place, nothing broken. More than likely, if he did put it all together, he'll think it was you and I, and we went in for what we came for. He will tell himself that your mom did send you, and you got what you were sent to get. He won't be happy with it, any of it, but it beats telling his wife or the sheriff. Ergo, he avoids excessive drama and prevents spoiling a perfectly good Thursday evening."

Derek was feeling better as they approached his house. Cyndi made great points with her logic. He was still amazed at how fast she could compile and break it all down. More than likely, they would feel no repercussions out of this, which to Derek, seemed miraculous. "Let's not do that again," he said turning off the car.

"I don't plan on it," Cyndi replied.

"What's the weirdest thing—is that I had the most incredible sensation of déjà vu when we got caught—or almost caught. I've had a few of those feelings, but never one this intense," Derek confessed to Cyndi right before they exited his car. "Come in for a beer before you head out?" Derek asked, hoping to continue to feel better by Cyndi's arguments, and wanting her company even if only for a few more minutes.

"*One* beer it is," Cyndi replied, "while I am now a professional burglar, I will not drink and drive. Thank you very much."

Derek returned with two green glass bottles of beer. "Fancy glasses," Derek said as he handed one to Cyndi.

"Very," she replied, "and I have a confession to make."

"Well, this evening can't get any more eventful—can it?" Derek said, gulping down some of his cold beer.

"While you were in the kitchen, I went through the stack of papers you handed me."

"Let me guess, registration and insurance, maybe a receipt or two from a mechanic?" Derek was relieved it wasn't a heavier admittance from Cyndi.

"Yes, exactly," she started, "and the original bill of

sale, it appears, and this." Cyndi handed Derek a piece of aging wide ruled paper with edges that were wrinkled and worn. It had seen some sun and was faded. The paper had a light-yellow hue and had creases as if being folded and unfolded many times. There on the paper were three names. Cyndi couldn't wait, "Did you know the car was purchased by your mom and someone named Lyle? At least that's what I think." Derek pulled on his beer again. "I can guess at the first name. Someone did a good job scratching out the last name. Look, it is scratched out with black ink, so much so that it went through the paper."

He closely examined the purchase and sales agreement. There in front of his mother's name, someone had intentionally tried to bury the co-owner's name. You could just make out the L and maybe a y, then nothing else. And it was a short first name. He then saw how Cyndi deduced the co-owner's name. His eyes went to the beat and battered paper. Out loud, he read three names, "Annie Morello. Gordon McKnight. Lyle."

The two spent the next ten minutes scouring over all of the paperwork, looking for anything interesting or out of the ordinary beyond that one piece of paper. Between sips, they kept coming back to the article that Cyndi had already identified. "I feel like I'm playing a game of *Clue*, but none of the clues mean anything," Derek said.

"We did find out that the key matched the car, right?" Cyndi replied.

"Yes, and it almost got us arrested. What were we thinking?" He paused and then changed his stance and tone, "Sorry, what was I thinking? Mom will be home on Sunday. I've become a snooper and I've involved myself in things I don't need to be. Quite frankly, I'm feeling bad about myself." Cyndi finished her beer and her mood changed. She looked Derek intently in the eyes.

"Knock it off, Derek G. Densmore. You told me your mother is out of sorts, distraught by the sounds of it. You tell me that she's basically missing in action. Her own sister thinks that she's back home. That's right, and her own daughter thinks she's still at her sister's house and will be back on Sunday. You find some interesting things and want to see if it is at all connected. Cut yourself some slack. And besides, outside of the dangerous parts tonight, I had an exciting time with you, and today will be, how does one say," she paused for impact, "unforgettable."

"That's two nice days in a row. Albeit, making lasagna isn't as dangerous as a break-in," Derek responded. Again, she made him feel better. "I guess who cares if none of these so-called clues add up," Derek continued. "However, I bet they do, I'm almost certain of it."

26

Cyndi left for the night and Derek was alone to process his thoughts. While he didn't want Cyndi to leave, he was glad to have a few minutes alone to think through all that had happened. Breaking and entering was one thing, almost getting caught for it, was something else. It was a lot to take in all at once.

Derek shifted from beer to water. The house was warm without the heat needing to kick on and because of that it was extremely quiet. The neighborhood children were now in their beds, only an occasional dog barking could be heard. Before she left, Cyndi confronted him again on making sure Leena knew the whole story, maybe without all of the details of today's adventure. He knew she was right. They needed to track down their mom, and he needed her help to do so. In the end, what his mother was doing, being so out of character, didn't feel right. She was in some sort of trouble—most likely. He wasn't quite willing to admit yet that they had a genuine situation on their hands with an

AWOL mother. He promised Cyndi that he would call Leena and let her know that he wasn't certain where their mother was. Earlier in the day, Derek had felt the intensity of panic; peak adrenaline created from being the most frightened he had ever been, and it mixed with the feeling of not knowing what to do next. He relived the day's harrowing events several times. It was too soon for him to laugh at it, but he was certain he would later on—much later on; providing mugshots weren't ever part of the story. But now his mind replaced panic, with worry. He never worried about his mother—ever. She was always so organized, consistent, and steady with her thoughts and actions. There had never been any diversion to this that he remembered. And it was starting to scare him. The fact was, she was not home, and she was not at his aunt's. *Where is she? What on earth could she be doing?* Derek shivered.

He picked up his phone. He had a powerful urge to reach out to his mother. He wanted to write a text asking her where she was and why she was being mysterious; it was too much for him. And then he thought that it was too heavy a conversation to bring up in a text. Some things should be reserved for an in person, tete-a-tete. But he did need to at least reach out to her. The feelings from dinner yesterday evening at Cyndi's surfaced and he focused on his confessions to Cyndi. He desperately wanted to be closer to his mother, at a much deeper level than he was now. He felt distant from her, not a coldness, but rather a wedge of limbo existed between them, preventing them from connecting and loving as a son and mother should—at least from his vantage point. His hand wrapped around the phone and started to text. *Hi Mom, just saying hi, I hope you're doing well. Let me know how you're doing.* The day's events had now caught up with him; the terror he had felt earlier in his escape, the knot in his stomach about his mother, the warm feelings that embraced him when spending time with Cyndi. He was about to head to the bathroom to brush his teeth, he was tired, but his phone lit up and vibrated three times. His mother texted back. *Hi Derek. Having a nice time with Eileen, be back on Sunday.* As Derek tucked himself into his bed his last waking thoughts were, *she's lying to me.*

27

After two hours of attempting to fall asleep, Derek decided to try something different. He got out of bed and made some herbal tea. He was a sleep fighter by trade; not fighting sleep but rather forcing himself to stay in bed until sleep came to take him. During his failed attempt to slumber, his thoughts were a pendulum, going from Cyndi to the trouble they were in a few hours ago. Then his thoughts went and stayed on his mother and whatever thing was going on with her. His mom was a lot of things but lying to her offspring—this meant something was wildly wrong.

Sleep would be very hard to find tonight he admitted to himself. These days, sleep usually didn't find him instantly, more times than not because of a work issue. Recently store number nine's manager refused to comply with his new monthly financial rollup process. He not only refused to submit his monthly sales and expenditures by the required dates, but he also only sent in partial information back to Derek. What complicated matters more is that this store manager was well liked by employees and customers. To further complicate things, he managed one of the top three performing stores. This seemed like a major problem not long ago, and one that robbed his sleep. But now, the only parent that Derek ever knew, was somewhere out there until Sunday. *Or maybe that's a lie, too*, Derek thought. He squirted what was more or less a teaspoon of raw honey into his mug, stirred it excessively, with more zeal than a chamomile-peppermint tisane required. Well after midnight, no noises could be heard and yet the spoon's clinking against the inside of the mug sounded like an alarm. He stopped his hand.

The silence returned; the hum of his refrigerator commenced to fill the void. If only this puzzle was as easy as how he solved his work plight. Derek was determined not to escalate the store manager to the regional director. He needed to find a way to persuade the manager to do what he needed. Derek did find a way and thus far, it was the best decision he made in his career. Two things happened. One, his determination for figuring out this complicated matter, built confidence. Secondly, the manager, by refusing to submit his monthly figures on a timely basis became an incredible blessing. Several months ago, on a morning after a poor night's sleep, he informed his supervisor that he was going to start visiting stores from time to time, in order to build better rapports with the store managers. His supervisor didn't balk; Derek was one to always get his work done, in time, and without error. It fit within her family-style, human-first mode of operation and was more impressed than taken aback. That day, Derek rolled into store number nine to meet with the disobedient yet well liked manager. His first thoughts were to go in with authority and to demand that he fulfill his monthly financial reporting obligations. Then, even before Cyndi was back in the picture, he remembered Cyndi's innate ability to diffuse and to solve; and he channeled it. And so that day, Derek visited with the store manager for an hour asking about his family, thanking him for his service, praising him for being one of the best at retaining employees. What is more, he meant it. Managing a store is a difficult thing. Managing a store well, is much more difficult. And Derek listened to every word the manager said and filed it away. The next week, now armed with information from their conversation, he called store number nine's manager and left a voicemail on his work phone. "This is Derek Densmore, I just wanted to thank you for your time last week. It was a pleasure catching up with you, and my plan is to come visit from time to time. Next time I come, I'll bring lunch. Oh, and I hope your daughter's leg is healing well." The next month, he stopped in again and brought lunch and they chatted for an hour and a half. Derek learned that his daughter's leg was healing nicely, and she would likely be playing soccer in the fall—obviously quite important to her and to her father. The next month, without a word, the manager submitted his reports on time and with precision. From that point on, every month, he was the first manager to submit reports. One further, he had no idea if the relationship they developed had anything to do with it, but the store was performing even better than it had been. Suffice to say, Derek visited with a different store manager each month. Something that at first caused him to lose sleep, turned into one of the best things in his career. It was after this when he was approached by his manager on a promotion. But now looking back at it, he was trying to draw parallels. For him it was a rocky time —something bad was happening. And that bad time transformed into something incredible; it made him a better employee, a better problem solver, and a better human being. This thing with his mother also felt bad, if not dire. He sipped the last of his tea, what was initially piping hot, now the last few sips at the bottom of his mug were lukewarm. This situation was different, he thought. How could something good come out of his mother lying to him? *It couldn't*—that was his last thought before finally succumbing to an unrestful dream of being in a car chase, running from the police.

28

Colder spring made way for warmer spring that Friday. A warm front moved in during the night-time hours, allowing one to forgo a jacket. Although long sleeves or a light sweater still seemed a wise choice, the weather was beginning to turn warmer. His sleep was less than restful. Derek's dreams were tormented by the surreal events from yesterday and the uncertainty of the future.

Coffee. Two cups. He consumed both cups with more speed than he had finished his one cup of tea late last night. He needed caffeine before making any attempt to call Leena. Cyndi was right, it was time to bring her in. Last night's text from his mother made this whole thing packed with uncomfortable eeriness and besides, it was Leena that had first brought up the point that their mother was acting out of character. Perhaps it was better to go see her, Derek thought. Not only did he feel obligated to go see his sister and niece because he was asked, but he also genuinely wanted to. Everly was still a ball of energy, and it took some time to get mentally prepared for this kind of uncle-niece interaction. He was certain that the calmest interaction with her would be a tea party with her and two stuffed animals she called Minks and Presto, her favorites. Minks was a not-to-scale grayish weasel-like creature with unsymmetrical eyes, so ugly it was cute. Presto, a gift from Derek, was a black and white rabbit—the coloring like a tuxedo cat—with the softest fur imaginable. It was the stuffed animal's soft fur that converted the sale at the toy store. Derek went in shopping for a birthday gift for Everly and the rabbit came out of the store with him. He would have to make sure he found time to get ahold of Presto if he got over there today. Those two stuffed animals made for the most bizarre combination of friends to have tea with. But it all worked. Everly was as kind and as accepting as anyone, being both tolerant and open-minded. Before picking up his phone he said out loud, "We need more Everlys in the world."

Can you make any time for your brother today? Derek sent the text. He craved a walk before heading to the shower. Like yesterday, today felt warmer than it had been. Turning right, he walked around the cul-de-sac and then headed back up the street—across from his house. He didn't know any of the neighbors despite living in the neighborhood for several years. He would wave and put on a smile whenever meeting anyone while out on a walk. It was a good neighborhood, and it was quiet and family oriented. Almost all the other homes in his vicinity were family residences. Some children in college, some families with kids in high school. Other families were just starting out and the toddlers could be seen out holding hands with mothers and fathers as the little ones splashed in the remnant springtime puddles. But Derek was the outsider in this realm. As Derek picked up his pace, he had a thought that he must look like a loner to them. Here he was, the only one coming and going from his house. He had no wife, no life-partner, no roommate. His last girlfriend came over now and then, but it wasn't with regularity, and that was now years ago. Several of his friends would come over to watch a game and have a beer periodically. The only other people that came over to his house was his immediate family. Leena, Eli, and Everly would pop in now and then. And even more seldom, his mother. Usually, it was Derek that went to see his mother. It was thinking on these thoughts when Derek became aware of a feeling that could only be described as loneliness. A hollowness inside of him surfaced after passing a woman who was outside looking at her yellow daffodils. He wondered how many true connections each one of us have in life. It's not very many, he thought. Even the most extroverted people he believed only had a finite number of real friends they connected with, the ones you can fully let down your guard with. The same people had an amazing number of acquaintances, and they knew how to converse with them at a level far beyond his introverted self. But still, how many people do we have in our lives that are truly close; the kind of closeness where a part of you falls away forever when they die.

Whether it was the emotional rollercoaster of the last few days or the dampness and lack of sleep, Derek felt alone. He threw himself into work, into sports, into hanging out with his friends. Up until recently he felt no void. Today, his soul walked straight up to the chasm of emptiness. In his thoughts, he asked himself a direct question, *Derek, what's really going on?* His answer came in three parts. *I'm getting older. I want to be closer to my mother. Cyndi.* It is an amazing thing when life hands you the things you need to see, to unlock the next steps, to enable you to move forward, to find the next new and different place. Whatever label you place on it, the Universe guides you when the time is right. Looking at himself in the mirror the other day was eye opening. The mirror could not hide his current face, the lines here and there, the diminishing chisel in his chin. And as for his mother, he had never been worried in his life about her—never once. Now all he could do is be concerned.

Lastly, there was Cyndi. From nowhere, out of left field, she walked back into his life. His life had to be some sort of strange cosmic screenwriting. The script calling for the emotional low of his mother's situation balanced by Cyndi's positive aura. His shoes picked up the pace and he headed back towards his house. His desires were becoming clearer with each step; get his mom home and to find a way back to her. And with Cyndi, he would be open to whatever happened. She always seemed too good for him. But why not him? Their bond was an adhesive, rooted in growing up together, and cemented in trust. Back inside the house, he hit the shower. As he lathered up, his last thought echoed again. To Derek, trust was love, love was trust, and Cyndi brought it by the truckloads.

Leena tried her best to be a dedicated mom and not be consumed with her mobile phone when Everly was nearby. She had seen too many of her parenting cohorts be obsessed by their phones. Leena found that one of the saddest things in the world was to watch a parent's face in the phone while their child was talking to her or him. What did it say to the child? You are not as important as this phone, what I am doing is more important than you. And the saddest thing she realized was in twenty years, that child, as an adult, would be doing the same thing to his or her son or daughter who desperately wanted to connect with them. She described it to Derek as a sort of deeply sad "Cat's in the Cradle", a la twenty-first century style. For Leena, it was beyond tragic, and she did what she could to put Everly first. Her biggest phone cheats were to peek at her phone during mealtime preparation, while the cooking needed her attention and Everly was involved in some sort of playtime or was allowed to watch a show. Other than that, she only went to her phone during nap time, which was slowly winding down being that Everly was already five. Her other phone time came at bedtime, or early in the morning if Everly wasn't already jumping on her bed.

Derek felt quite a bit better after feeling clean and freshly shaven. Despite having slept poorly and having some epic realizations during his walk, he was propped up by two things. He couldn't get his mind off of Cyndi, still in a state of shock about how fulfilling it was having her back in his life—in any capacity. The other, was that the sun was shining and the chill in the air was leaving. He loved the optimism of spring days that hinted at summer, they even had a sort of smell. The April sun was burning up the mist that covered the grass that was just starting its journey of growth. He needed another excuse to go out and fill his lungs with spring air. Derek put on his hiking boots and headed to his mailbox, again he thought how refreshing and stimulating this fragrance was. It was that special place between spring and summer and if a candle manufacturer could master it, they could double their profits. In his mailbox were a few advertisements and several grocery flyers. He brought them back into the house and sat them down on his dining table, next to his phone. He checked for texts, there were two. The first was from Cyndi, *Did you call*

Leena? The second was from Leena, *Come on over, brother of mine. What time shall we expect you? It's just me and Everly. Eli is at work.* That's right, he thought, it was a workday.

He wanted to text Cyndi first but found the discipline to text Leena. *I'll be over around 1PM, after Everly's lunch, so she's already loaded up with mac and cheese.* He realized it was going to be difficult to talk to Leena in the manner he wanted to, in the way he needed to. You don't just drop a bomb like our mom's a liar and has gone missing in front of her five-year-old. He would have to find a way.

Then, with excitement, he texted Cyndi back. *Did the police come for you yet? Need a good lawyer?* Immediately, bubbles. *They did. But I convinced them you kidnapped me in your gas guzzling BMW, and it was all your doing. I gave them your address.* A pause, then more bubbles. *I'll be your one phone call, if you want.* With a smile, Derek continued. *I'll take you up on that,* and then switched subjects. *I'm visiting Leena and Everly this afternoon at 1PM.* Another quick reply came. *Very good, proud of you.* Then came a thumbs up emoji. A few moments passed; *I have an idea.* Derek liked ideas that Cyndi had, although he could pass on the law-breaking ones. *I'll invite myself over, too. Internet technician will be here between 10:30-11:30, then I can probably be there at 1PM. Leena will be cool with it.*

Indeed, she would be, Derek thought. Most days it was just she and Everly. Today's Godsend: two adults to converse with and moreover, a dear old friend and her only brother. *I like your style, and I'm glad you're coming over.* Bubbles appeared once more. All that appeared was a smiley face emoji and then a, *see you this afternoon, I'll text Leena now.*

Derek savored the weather as much as he could given all the other thoughts that were occupying his mental space. Spring in the northeast was a reason to rejoice.

Upon heading to his sister's, he decided to spoil his niece with a treat. A few minutes later he pulled into a pharmacy to check out their minimalistic toy section. Puzzles, dolls, army men, card games, even small hand-held video games stared back at him. Nothing became appealing until he spotted something he had cherished as a child. The perfect toy, so simple and so satisfying; he picked up a purple-colored magnetic rail twirler. *Purple is a majestic color, whatever your age or gender*, he thought. Before purchasing it, he stopped and picked out a white and purple gift bag and some white tissue paper—in an instant, he had a spur of the moment gift for his niece. He reflected upon how some toys were timeless, this one fit into that category. He had one as a child and it was a go to. It wasn't flashy, but it was soothing, and he had many memories of sitting and watching the wheel wrap around the metal bars and come back again. It was also one of those toys that was satisfying on many levels. It was hypnotic, mesmerizing, and fulfilling in a tactile way. The toy was also quiet, something he was sure his sister and brother-in-law would appreciate.

He arrived just after 1PM. Leena lived in a newer development in Edwardsville, the same town they had grown up in and where their mom still resided. Eli and his sister had done well for themselves. He admired both of them. Eli was a worker. If he weren't working at his job as a manager of a local manufacturing plant, he was thinking about work and how he could improve the levers of people, process, and tools to drive efficiencies. Derek was sure that Eli would rise to become an executive in the not-so-distant future. He had the drive that others simply didn't have, and a passion for the dairy products his company made. Derek knew how to hold a lasting conversation with Eli, simply by raising the topic of yogurt or cheese and hours would pass by, much faster for Eli, much more slowly for Derek.

Eli was a good husband and father despite his strong work ethic. Work was still a means to an end, and the end was a family. Likewise, Leena also possessed a strong work ethic, but how could you not, being the offspring of April Densmore. She had taken time off from her lab technician position to raise Everly until the first grade, and that time was approaching rapidly. Everly was going to enter kindergarten in the fall. Leena had only one summer left after the one approaching before returning to work full-time. Leena was ready to return to work four years ago. It wasn't that she didn't enjoy being a stay-at-home mom—it was just that Leena had the need to be productive outside of the home as well. Despite that, she was always in the moment with Everly and whenever Derek watched their interaction, he could tell Leena's heart was always home. He couldn't pick up on her desire to be back at work, even if that's what she yearned for. Because there was always medical lab work, she could reenter her old position at any time. And like Eli, Derek was positive that Leena would rise to great heights within her field. She kept abreast of her industry and stayed in close contact with her co-workers. Securing employment is always difficult, even if you're experienced and have multiple degrees. But it helped Leena not to worry about reentering the workforce; her job was there for her, and she knew what to expect when she returned. Everly was clearly benefiting from their decision. She was bright by nature, and the nurturing love and education that Leena provided on a daily basis made Everly sparkle with enthusiasm and curiosity. She was joy on two legs, and despite the messes she made and loudness that echoed during her waking hours, it pulled at a desire within Derek.

Leena and Eli's home was a large two-story dark slate gray sided colonial with bright white trim and black windows. It was sharp and classic. The home reminded Derek of an older colonial with all the updates of a modern built home—made tight to keep the warmth or coolness in—depending upon the season.

Derek began asking himself how Leena might react to their mother's lie. Before Derek reached out to his mother, it was a selective omission. Now, her last text was a clear fabrication... *Having a nice time with Eileen, be back on Sunday.* She wanted them to believe she was still at their aunt's.

He entered through the garage; Leena had opened the door anticipating Derek. Already he could hear the chirps and expressive vocal ranges of his spirited niece. The first one to the screen door was as he suspected, a little person with bright brown eyes and she flung the screen door open almost immediately after he knocked. "Uncle Derek, Uncle Derek!" It is a wonderful thing to see excitement in a young person. As adults we learn to cover up our excitement. We make attempts to cover our sorrows, our happiness, our exhilaration—suppressing them in order to fit the part of acting like an adult. In that moment, Derek couldn't help but think how wonderful it was to watch this elation, to be so full of joy that you say the person's name multiple times while jumping up and down when you see them. At the café, he felt the same way about seeing Cynthia Vaughn. He wondered how Cyndi would have reacted if he had arisen from his seat and jumped up and down and let forth her name several times in a row. "Uncle Derek, Uncle Derek! Mommy, Uncle Derek is here!"

"Everly, Everly!" Derek returned her style of greeting and dropped on his knee to give her a large squeeze. "How is my little sprite?" It was good to see her, and she *had* grown, noticeably so by Derek's reckoning. The emotional ups and downs of the last few days had made him cognizant of all that he did have. While in that bear hug of Everly, he vowed to see her and Leena and Eli more often. Much more often. Life was moving too fast as reinforced by his bathroom mirror just two days ago.

"Well, hello there, *stranger.*" Leena came up behind them. After Everly let go, they both hugged.

"Great to see you," Derek replied. "I was thinking just now, let's see each other more often."

"You are welcome here anytime," both Leena's tone and body language let Derek know that his comment was well received. At that moment, Derek handed Everly the gift bag he had brought. "Here you go, Everly!" With eyes that continued to be large, she took the package from Derek.

"Thank you, Uncle Derek!" she issued without prompting from her mother.

"Such manners," Derek said to both of them.

"Can I get you some iced tea or lemonade, glass of water? Come on in and sit. Beautiful spring day, doesn't it feel great?" Leena issued a litany of questions and commands in one run-on sentence. It was Leena's way, or certainly how she communicated now having much less adult conversation than she used to.

"I'd love an iced tea if it's unsweetened, if not, a glass of water. And yes, today's spring weather makes my optimism feel optimistic." And just after his statement, he realized the true, undeniable dichotomy of his feelings. The sunny spring day, of seeing hyacinths and daffodils earlier that morning, taking in the smells of the vernal equinox filled him with joy. And then there was Cyndi—returning after all these years and them seeing each other two days in a row, and soon to be three. On the other side, he was too in touch with his anxious feelings. Their mother's change from an always grounded, predictable matriarch, to now being aloof, out of sorts, distracted, and missing; all compounded by a lie. This feeling of being high and low at the same time —it was too much drama and he did not have the tools to navigate this new territory.

"What do you think of that?" Derek asked Everly who was looking at the toy upon opening the gift bag. "Do you want me to show you how to use it?" Everly had opened all of the toy packaging and looked at it perplexingly.

"Yes, what do you do with it?" she asked inquisitively.

"You make the wheel go back and forth—it has magnets on it." He showed Everly how to use it. "Just like riding a bike," Derek spoke out loud, and for a minute, he was Everly's age, lost in the hypnotic, time freezing moment of the spinning wheel finding its way up and over the parallel metal bars and then back down again.

"Wow, can I try?" Everly's voice was full of excitement. Derek handed it back to her.

"You know, I used to have one of these." Leena came into the living room carrying a tall glass of iced tea. "Thank you," Derek said gratefully. At that moment, Leena was looking outside towards the street.

"Well, look who's here. One Cynthia Vaughn." Instant butterflies fluttered about in Derek's stomach.

Derek wanted to greet her in the same manner his niece greeted him, but he chose to tone it down. He intentionally stayed in the living room playing with

Everly while Leena went out to the garage entranceway to meet her. Wanting to stay in the moment with Everly, he could not help but also want to listen. Two childhood friends reuniting is something powerful to behold, even semi-eavesdropping from the next room. Hugs and "It's *really* you," and more hugs came from each of them— and animated speech.

Cyndi entered the living room. Leena went to the kitchen, apparently after a refreshment for Cyndi. "Good afternoon," Derek said sitting on the couch while playing with Everly. He knew his facial expression spewed *I'm-so-happy-you're-here.*

"Good afternoon," she responded in kind, "trust you had no run-ins with the law on your way over?"

"I'm playing things on the down-low," Derek responded. "It's not easy being on the lam. This is Everly. Everly, this is Cyndi." And it was at that moment that Derek noticed two things. The first was how fluidly Cyndi's engagement with Everly, a child she never met, took shape. Within seconds, they began talking about children's movies, several of them very recent of which Derek felt bad not knowing. You know it when you see it, Derek thought. Cyndi wasn't putting on an act, she was really good with children. The second thing Derek observed was just as Leena came into the living room, also carrying a glass of iced tea; Cyndi sat right beside him. Not right beside, as in next to. Right beside, touching, hip to hip, leg to leg, knee to knee. He felt an overpowering feeling of bliss and embarrassment as Leena faced them as she handed Cyndi her beverage. Then a look flashed from Leena to Derek. Perhaps it was because they were sister and brother, perhaps it was because they had known each other all of their life. But in that moment of facial expressive body language, it was crystal clear what Leena had signaled directly into Derek's eyes. *I've always wondered about the both of you.*

Shaking off the look, Derek thought that this was probably the best time he could to steal his sister's attention as Everly had a fantastic playmate and would occupy Cyndi as long as Cyndi had energy. "Got a second in the kitchen?" he asked Leena. Cyndi, as always, somehow understood the things that weren't being spoken and gently nodded to them both as if to say, go have your conversation, I'll be happy to stay here and entertain. Derek didn't want to get up, breaking up the close physical contact he had with Cyndi. But this was a must.

In the kitchen, Leena took hold of Derek's arm. "I'm so happy for you," Leena expressed with a gigantic smile.

"I'm not sure what you mean," Derek replied, he wanted to have a chat with Leena, but certainly not about this topic. In fact, because they had such little time, he forced the conversation away quickly to the perplexing and disturbing subject of their mom. He pivoted without any softness in transition to force their discussion.

"Mom lied," Derek said with a somber face. Derek went on to describe the mystery of their aunt's sweater text, and the straight up false statement indicating she was still at Eileen's.

"What if she's still at Eileen's, I mean we don't know for certain; she could have gone back, right?"

"That's unlikely," Derek responded, "you don't take off after spending a week and a half with your family member, then pack up your suitcase say good-bye and then return after a ride around the block." Leena couldn't argue. She had been pushing her mom's disposition off for some time after bringing Derek in on what she had noticed as agitation and un-mom like behavior. Leena had thought she would rebalance after a long visit with her sister, or at least that is what she hoped for. And that feeling of hope was what led her to pause any feelings about her mother and her current state. Now, with this news, Leena came back into the present, back to the reality that there was something more than just a little off in their mother's life. "Leena," he used her first name to express the severity, "I think Mom is involved in something and I don't know what it is. Something potentially dangerous." He stopped himself there, not wanting to bring up anything about the key, the car, the adventure Cyndi and he just had, nor the head-scratching list of names they discovered in the glove compartment.

"I'm calling her," Leena said, "we've got to make sure she's OK."

"I don't think she'll answer, but let's do it together, can you put it on speaker?" Derek replied.

29

April Densmore spent the night in a roadside motel. Well-kept and clean, although the motor inn looked as it must have thirty years ago, preserved in time. The walls, the carpet, down to the brass bathroom fixtures weren't quite vintage, more, simply outdated and stale. To her surprise, she found sleep despite yesterday's visit to the Morello household. She had paid for two nights so that she could sleep in and not be held accountable to the 10AM check out policy, although she didn't plan to stay another night. Already well after 1PM, in the half comfortable, half lumpy bed, she reexamined her notebook, flipping the pages intently. She found the last page again. With a ballpoint pen, furnished by the motel, April crossed off the name Morello.

Her phone went off; it was Leena. Texts she could avoid and respond to on her time. Phone calls from this point on had to be ignored—it would be too awkward. After all, she had her bases covered. In a call with Leena and a text with Derek, she informed them that she would be home on Sunday. She would deal with any consequences later, but not until Sunday.

It was Friday afternoon. The plan still hung together. Derek and Leena for all they knew, believed she was still at Eileen's. There was no sense complicating things and answering the call. April told herself that she would text Leena back later in the day to let her know that she was on a walk with Eileen and left her phone at the house. The plan still was intact. More importantly, one thing on her list was accomplished and she had underestimated the emotional toll of what she did. She touched her eyes, assuredly puffy and tender from the exodus of tears the night before.

April found a way out of bed. She had taken a shower the night before, and now needed another. After doing what she did, she craved another shower, another way to get clean. With one of the three names on her list crossed off, she was now committed to finishing her task. To some extent, the next would be easier. This time, the person she was going to see was already dead. April, focusing on her breathing to attempt to find some calmness, turned on the water and let the steam of the shower enshroud her anguish.

30

Leena and Derek stared at each other as their mother's phone went to voicemail. "I've got it, we call Aunt Eileen, maybe Mom had another place to go, to visit before she came home. Did your text from her, the one about the sweater, say anything about when she would be home?" Derek withdrew his phone from his pocket and reexamined the text from their aunt.

"No, it just says if I see or talk to her, tell her about the sweater she left behind," Derek relayed.

"We've got to eliminate the possibility that she didn't go somewhere else. You know, to see a friend perhaps. She's an adult, and she's retired, little to no responsibilities."

"But her agitated state and why lie about it?" Derek replied.

"We can ask Aunt Eileen about that, too. Ask her if Mom seemed normal to her," Leena fired back. From the living room they could hear Everly ask Cyndi if she wanted to see her room, Cyndi kindly obliged. Up the stairs they bounded, Derek thought that it was almost comical how a light as a feather five-year-old could sound like an elephant running up the stairs while an adult's ascent was barely perceptible.

"It sounds like we have time, now," Derek said.

Derek used his phone as it was in his hand having just looked at the text from Eileen. "She's going to freak; I never call her."

"I do occasionally, but mostly on her birthday," Leena responded.

"Hi Aunt Eileen," Derek started.

"Hi Derek," an unsure female voice answered.

"I hope you're well. Listen, I have Leena here with me—you're on speaker." Derek decided not to pause to allow Eileen to insert a comment. "Hey, we're puzzled by something. Do you know when Mom is coming home?" There was a large pause.

"Really? She left Wednesday. Well, she alluded to taking the scenic route, so I expected her back there Wednesday late afternoon, maybe early evening." Derek and Leena again glanced into each other's eyes, the overwhelming feeling of dread and uncertainty was now confirmed. Leena and Derek began to downplay things with their aunt rather than worry her.

"Just confirming more than anything, she's told us that she would be home Sunday, so we're not worried," Leena lied. But the lie did the trick and allowed them to assuage any apprehension that crept into Eileen's mind.

"Strange that she didn't tell me. Maybe her saying that she would take the scenic route meant that she was going to make a few stops, perhaps see some friends." Eileen went on. "Well, if she told you that she would be back on Sunday, she'll be back on Sunday," Eileen finished.

"I'll call you soon, it will be good to catch up. I've got

guests over so I can't right now—Derek and I were simply curious about Mom."

"OK, sounds good. Oh, one more thing, I hope your mom becomes less tense," she paused, "less distracted. She just wasn't herself this trip."

This time Derek jumped in, "We'll be sure to keep an eye out for that."

Another pause, "Love you lots, Eileen," Leena closed the conversation.

"Love you both, too. Please keep me posted and Leena, yes, I would love to chat and hear all about Everly." As if on cue, Everly's excited voice echoed from upstairs, overjoyed to be showing Cyndi around her natural habitat.

"Of course, talk soon," Derek chimed in with a soft good-bye.

"Well, there you have it. Mom is officially MIA," Derek said to Leena after terminating the call with Eileen.

"I go back and forth on this one, Derek," Leena started. "I know Mom is, well, *off* right now. But she is also a grown woman and has told us she'll be back on Sunday."

"You're forgetting a big part of what we know," Derek began, "she wants us to *believe* that she's still at Eileen's. And, she was nebulous with Eileen about her return home. Since when does Mom lie *and* be illusive? It's just not her. I'm worried about her, Leena," a few seconds passed, "something is going on with her and I'm starting to become afraid." Hearing the words worried and afraid come from her brother's lips flipped a switch in Leena's stance. He was right, she thought, something was off, *way* off with a mother whose actions were always consistent, always predictable. She knew something wasn't right from the last time she visited her mom, now it was an unavoidable glaring neon sign.

"What do we do?" Leena asked Derek, "where do we start?"

Derek took a deep breath in. "I think Cyndi and I already started, yesterday."

31

"**A** lot has happened in the last two days," Derek informed Leena.

"Apparently," the response was somewhere in-between shock and sarcasm. Time to come clean, Derek thought to himself.

Leena and Derek stood in the kitchen while Derek unfolded his story of all of the recent events in as a condensed fashion as he could, aware of the limited time they had with Everly upstairs with her new best friend. Leena was expressionless. She stood with her arms folded taking in every word and didn't interrupt until he was completely finished. Afterall, how do you interrupt a story about your mother that seems entirely fictional? The words coming out of her brother's mouth were foreign. On top of adding another bizarre layer onto their mystery, her brother was now a fugitive from the law—at least by his confession.

"I think I need a drink," Leena said. "A big one, or two big ones," she followed up.

Her arms were still crossed when she had the courage to respond to what felt was a jargon of jumbled words that spewed from her brother; none of it made any sense. "It's Friday. She's not at Eileen's, and she's not home. Do we assume that she'll be home Sunday?" Derek paused a moment before responding. He imagined waiting all of today, all of Saturday, and who knows how long into Sunday—all the while not knowing.

"I don't know. But for one, I don't think I can sit still while Mom is off her rocker. And, as I said, I think she's in trouble." For the first time, he removed the words 'could be' in front of the word trouble.

"But what do we do? What can we do?" Leena's question was more rhetorical. She decided to answer her question with another question. "Do we call the police? I mean, do I call the police?" After last night, she was thinking that Derek and Cyndi should keep a low profile from the long arm until things blew over.

"The police wouldn't attempt to do anything but file it. We have it in writing that Mom will be back on Sunday. I don't see what good any of that will do. If Sunday comes and she's not here…" The unthinkable cast its shadow on Derek and Leena. To think for the first time that she might not come back was overwhelming; overwhelming and motivating.

Everly and Cyndi, by the loud giggles and thumping noises, were now engaged in some sort of game made up on the fly. To Derek's surprise, Cyndi's giggles were as contagious as Everly's. The sounds emanating from upstairs were enough to break the darkness of their thoughts. "We have some clues," Derek began. "We have three names. Annie Morello, Gordon McKnight, and a person with the first name of Lyle. And we can conclude that she owned a car with this Lyle person—at least it would seem."

"Who's to say those names have any correlation with anything to do with Mom, at least in her present *condition*?" Leena emphasized her last word.

"We don't," Derek replied, "but when I last saw Mom, the way she peered over at the fishbowl. It was as if she was trying to hide something but doing a horrible job. The fishbowl had the key. The key fit the Jetta. The Jetta held the names of these three people. One of the people look like they owned the car with Mom. I admit there is a leap of logic in all of this, nonetheless, it's still logical. I'm telling you, when we saw each other last, the glances over to the fishbowl sitting on the bookcase, it seemed to make her more antsy. It's a hunch, Leena." Leena knew Derek wasn't one to use the word *hunch*. Derek was a straightforward guy. He liked the habitual rhythm of his life. He chose the right occupation; numbers meant the same thing each time you looked at them—the only difference was how large or small, or how positive or negative they became and how that impacted whatever lens you were examining them through. For a cut and dry personality like Derek's, using the expression, I have a hunch, was enough for Leena to believe there was a connection with the names to whatever was going on in their mother's life.

"We can't keep them upstairs forever," Leena said, "although they are having a blast." Today held something positive. Their friend had come back to them after so many years. They both had a feeling that Cyndi was here to stay. The bond they had formed as children wouldn't go anywhere. With Cyndi Vaughn back home, Derek had a new feeling sweep over him. With Cyndi, he felt closer to his sister. The sensation was indescribable.

"Do you think this has anything to do with," Leena

paused thinking about how to phrase her next thoughts. "With our father," the words finally coming from her lips. With an equal amount of pause, Derek took a moment to collect his thoughts.

"Perhaps. But why three names on the list? Why two males and one female? Why does one of the names only have a first name?"

"I don't know," Leena responded. "Have you done any internet searches yet? For the two with full names?" Derek now realized that his thoughts had been scattered over the last two days. The enormity of illegally entering *Twigg's Auto Storage* coupled with his feelings for Cyndi was compromising his normal train of thought.

"No, I haven't gotten around to that, I guess," he said timidly.

"I don't want to disturb Everly, about this. Whatever is going on." Leena had another idea. "I'll make us all a snack," Leena was already at the refrigerator, "and you can play with Everly for a few hours, I'm sure Cyndi would like the back-up." Leena had brought out some cheese and was reaching for some crackers in the cupboard. "When Everly has a nap, I'll start to research the two with last names. You and Cyndi, if she wants, should go to Mom's house and try and find anything that makes sense given what we know." Derek watched as Leena started to fan out the crackers for a cheese plate.

"You mean snoop?" Derek asked.

"I mean investigate," Leena began, "Mom lied to us. She's not at Eileen's and she's stressed out—per her own sister. If we're going to act, we need to take action." Leena was now fully engaged in whatever was going on. She continued, "Tonight, we can regroup over the phone. See what we were able to uncover. Formulate a plan for tomorrow." It seemed reasonable, Derek thought.

Everly was leading Cyndi downstairs. "My mommy works in a lab. She tests people's blood," Everly was offering up free edification to Cyndi.

"I actually knew that," Cyndi responded, "your mom is a smart cookie," she finished.

"That's silly," Everly giggled, "my mommy is not a cookie." All four of them converged in the living room at the same time. Leena was bringing in the cheese plate. Derek brought forth the apple slices and four small plates with napkins.

"How about a snack, everyone?" Leena asked.

"I'll get beverages," Derek said. He looked at Cyndi and nodded his head in the direction of the kitchen. She picked up his body language and proceeded to the kitchen. As they topped off their iced teas, Derek recapped the conversation he had with Leena moments ago. "I'm not sure what you have planned for today," Derek started. Internally, he had committed to go over to his mother's house—with or without Cyndi. However, the prospects of being alone, looking for clues in places he shouldn't, sounded dreadful.

"I'm ahead of schedule in terms of my move. Everything is in place at my apartment, I now have internet, I have clean teeth and some random guy and I went grocery shopping the other day, so I've seeded my kitchen. All of my laundry is done, too."

"Some random guy, huh?" Derek raised his eyebrows. Cyndi fired back a smile.

"If you're asking me to poke around with you at your mother's house—I'm in."

Derek responded with, "Are you sure?"

"You forget, Derek, I spent so much time at your house growing up, it's like I had two mothers. And you and Leena are my friends. You would do the same for me." Derek was in awe of her willingness.

"Where have you been all these years?" The question fell out of his mouth, his filter obviously broken. He regretted it instantly. Cyndi took it and ran.

"I took a detour. One that I needed to take in order to know what I really wanted. Luckily for me, the road, although a long one, brought me back here."

Lucky for me, Derek thought, holding it inside, this time his filter working.

After some cheese and apple munchies, they played Jenga, then moved on to Chutes and Ladders. For almost two hours Leena, Derek, and Cyndi pushed aside the string of uncertainties of April's current whereabouts. More than ever, the moment cemented his commitment to see Everly—and Leena and Eli—more often. Life was moving too fast. The command of language that Everly now had was shocking to him; it felt like a few weeks ago when she was in diapers.

As excited as she was to see him, Everly was equally as disappointed to see Derek and his cool new friend leave. Derek knelt down at eye level with Everly and made his commitment known to her. "I will see you shortly, I promise. Soon it will be warm enough to go outside and we can toss a baseball." Everly, a year ago, would have thrown a tantrum at him leaving. She was growing up and knew that people had to leave after a visit.

"I'll call you if I find out anything on my web research," Leena informed Derek. "Cyndi, I'm so glad you're back. After this, whatever it is, blows over, let's go out for some wine and dinner. I can't help but feel slightly distracted right now."

"Deal," Cyndi said, with empathy. With several embraces, Cyndi and Derek walked towards their respective cars. Everly's face pouted as she and Leena waved goodbye.

32

At least they had a plan, of sorts. Derek was alone in his car. Behind him he could see the Prius keeping pace with him. Derek's eyes repeatedly went to his rearview mirror, to glimpse at the sunglasses donning woman driving the Prius. His thoughts went to earlier this morning when she sat next to him on the couch, their legs and knees touching. Every sign pointed to her liking him. Not liking him as in the friends that they were and had always been. Liking him as in interested in him. Perhaps even interested in him as in relationship material. Derek smiled and wondered if this was really happening. Cynthia Vaughn, his girlfriend? He had countless fantasies of this ever since high school. And well past high school. But the fact was that Derek gave up on even the remote possibility of he and Cyndi once she moved away. That is when he and Leena started to grow apart ever so slowly. After college, Derek threw himself into his work life and his friends. Leena after college, did the same, and then Eli came into the picture. And now the two of them had Everly. Cyndi had been an ingredient that complemented he and his sister. She was a part of the family that ceased to be when she and her family moved, some fifteen plus years ago. Could it have been that long? Almost as much time had passed since Cyndi moved away than he and Leena had known her for, growing up together in neighboring houses on Clover Drive.

He glanced up again as they came to a stoplight. Derek's eyes only focused on his rearview mirror. Her wavy hair with that hint of strawberry flattered the black framed sunglasses she was wearing. Intelligent, optimistic, and funny, Cyndi was now driving behind him and they were about to spend their third day in a row together. "I could get used to this," he said out loud with a smile. His eyes went from the traffic light to his rearview mirror once again. She must have been looking at him, too. For in answer to his smile, the woman in the sporty shades smiled back.

Derek's attention focused on what they were about to do. How would they tackle his mother's house? What they were about to do felt like an invasion of privacy. In fact, it was a violation. It also felt like a breach of trust. *Desperate times called for desperate measures or was that simply a justification. What the Hell, Mom*, he thought to himself, alone in his car. Why was his mom acting so weird, why was she doing this? What could she be going through? What was the tangled web of trouble she was in?

Leena's question about their father surfaced. Several times as young children, then as older children, as teens, and then as adults, Leena and Derek approached their mother on the subject of their father. The last time they did so was probably a half a decade ago. It was then that Leena and he pressured their mother together. Their mother stood firm to the same answer she had always given them throughout their life. "It's not worth speaking about," is usually all they got. And that last time they chose to press her on the subject, they pushed her as hard as they ever had. They thought that if they came together, united, in an intervention style dialogue, their mother would finally spill the story, or at least shed some light. She became angry and the last thing April ever said to her children about the subject was, "If you care for me, you'll stop now." And it was after this moment that Leena and Derek resigned themselves to the fact that they would never know anything about her relationship with their father, let alone anything about the man who put them on this planet.

rriving at Clover Drive, Derek parked on the
street in front of number 23. Cyndi followed
suit. Derek visited the mailbox. He found only
one article, an advertisement for a credit card. Cyndi
shut her car door and walked up behind him. "Some
random guy was checking me out in the car ahead of me
on my drive over here." Having no control, Derek knew
his face was as red as the apple they had for a snack just
a few hours ago.

"I'm sure he was handsome," he decided to roll
with it.

"If he asked me out for coffee, I'd go. Oh wait, he
already did." Derek was instantly sent on another high.
Could this really be happening? Something crossed his
mind; what if he had stayed with his last girlfriend,
forcing it to work. She was a good person, and she was a
good companion. If he had stepped forward with her on
the natural continuum of a relationship, he could even
be married to her. But something stopped him from

taking the next step in the relationship journey. Or was it someone?

"What do we do first? I'm used to bigger, more seedy jobs," Cyndi said cheekily as they entered the house. Inside, it was as cool as the outside air. Derek had kept the heat down. There was no sense heating a house with no one in it.

"I was thinking on the way over," Derek started.

"I could tell the way you were looking at me in your mirror," Cyndi replied with a sly smile.

"I was simply ensuring my mirrors were positioned in the best vantage points for optimal driving," Derek answered, "And, I was thinking how nice it is to have you back—back with Leena and me."

"Nothing else?" she asked. Again, Derek blushed.

"Maybe… In Vino Veritas," he responded, "after today, I'll need a beer." Cyndi let it go; they had a house to rummage through.

"It seems to me that somewhere in this house, my mother *must* have some sort of documents connected with my father. My suspicion is that they were married. Maybe some sort of court paperwork, marriage certificate, divorce paperwork." His statement was more of a question. He wasn't adamant, but it seemed logical.

"I'll buy that. If there were such paperwork, I'd have it in one of two places," Cyndi replied.

"Where?" Derek—always fascinated by her quick thinking—was eager with curiosity.

"I'd keep an important document that I had to retain, one that you don't want anyone to see, deeply hidden in my house. Or I would put it in a safe deposit box in a bank."

"OK, I'll buy that," Derek chewed on the potential of this. "If it's a safe deposit box, we're screwed. No bank will let us in if it's under my mom's name. Even if we found paperwork alluding to her having one or found another key." After more thinking, he added, "Mom has always been frugal with money. I was shocked she had a car in storage. My thoughts are that if there is such paperwork, it is somewhere in the house. It's not in the car, all we found were papers in the glove compartment."

"Divide and conquer? You have an attic I remember," Cyndi asked.

"It's more of a crawlspace where we kept some camping supplies and some board games, holiday decorations, that kind of stuff," Derek replied.

"One attic, one basement?" Cyndi asked.

"Wait," Derek said. He paused for several long seconds. "The basement and the attic. Those were not off limits to us growing up. Leena and I had the freedom to go anywhere. If your line of thinking is right, it would be hidden. But it would be somewhere that we wouldn't stumble upon as kids or even as adults for that matter. I come over and am always retrieving things or storing things—still to this day. It has to be in a hidden nook, an ideal hiding place."

"I agree," Cyndi said. "Freezer, medicine cabinet, back of the toilet in a waterproof container?"

"Perhaps," Derek replied, "using the same logic, none of those were technically off limits to us growing up. Especially the freezer. Recall, Mom was big into popsicles for us in the summer."

"Oh, I remember hours of using the slip and slide, having your famous PB&Js, and your mom bringing out popsicles for dessert. A Densmore lunchtime staple in the summer. Not just any popsicles, always the red, white, and blue ones."

"I propose we walk through the house together, room

by room. Maybe with four eyes we can see more than with two."

"I'm game," Cyndi replied, "you sure you want me that close to you?"

"There are few things I am sure about these days; I am sure on this one," Derek replied and flashed a smile.

Calling the basement and attic out of bounds, for an initial search, they started upstairs. They both aligned on the theory that unless there was a tremendous hiding place, it wouldn't be in Derek or Leena's bedrooms. Although Derek's room was now a catch-all of books, magazines, and a myriad of neatly stored tchotchkes accumulated through the years. His former bedroom took in any excess accumulation from the house so that other parts of the house weren't cluttered; the room as always kept shut. April Densmore had the ability to make a junk drawer look organized, so it was the case with Derek's old room. Leena's room became the immaculately clean guest room—ready for a visitation from Eileen at any time.

They started with his mother's bedroom. This made him the most uneasy as it felt like he was encroaching upon the sanctity of her privacy. To Cyndi and to his mother's room, he said aloud, "Forgive me, Mom, I'm just trying to help." At that moment he opened her top drawer and began to forage. Cyndi began in the closet. For the next fifteen minutes, no words were spoken. Only the sounds of two silent bandits rummaging through clothing could be heard, in search of some unknown quarry. Derek found several British pound notes, which was an interesting find, but nothing connecting anything to the VW, or to the list of names.

Cyndi found a box of old photos in April's closet and got lost in perusing through the loose photos. She couldn't believe how many of the photos had her in it. Almost half of the pictures she examined were all three of them, right up until around high school. What a powerful thing to live your life and get to examine it again through the camera lens of your best friends' mother. The pictures became fewer and fewer the older they got. When the conversion to digital happened, the hardcopies of photos almost dried up completely. "Who was *she*?" Cyndi asked, breaking the silence. She handed a photo to Derek. There in a classic black and white tuxedo stood a younger, more awkward looking Derek, going to his one and only prom. Beside him, stood what could only be his prom date. "I don't recognize her?"

"Is that what you've been doing over there for the last ten minutes? If you must know, I think her name was Loren."

"You think her name was Loren? C'mon it's your prom, you remember who you went with," Cyndi teased. Derek let out a sigh.

"Her name was Loren. It was a friend date. You know quite well I didn't have a girlfriend in high school."

"I always wondered that, too," Cyndi said. "I didn't either, you know—have a boyfriend in high school."

Derek looked under his mother's dresser. The eight drawers had yielded no contents other than clothing and the foreign currency which looked to be a souvenir. Nothing stood out underneath the solid wooden structure. He took out his phone and with the flashlight, examined under and in the back of the dresser. He stood up and glanced over to Cyndi. In any article of clothing that had a pocket, she put her hand in and explored with her fingers hoping something would reveal a secret. Like the dresser, the closet relinquished no clues.

"What do you have in your hand?" Derek asked Cyndi.

"Two photos. One of all of us. One of just you and me." Derek reached out his hand. The first photo from left to right was Derek, Leena, and Cyndi—the first day of school—in some year. Derek guessed he was in eighth grade—it wasn't flattering. The second was an action photo. On more than one occasion, Leena would sneak in and grab the camera off the bookcase. "I think we were playing tag," Cyndi spoke up. Even as an action shot, the picture was crystal clear; a smiling girl with long wavy strawberry blonde hair was chasing a taller boy in a blue hoodie with joy stamped all over his face, in the back yard of 23 Clover Drive. And like a song where you have a favorite part, and your ears are compelled to hear it before moving on to the next thing, Derek's eyes could not turn away from the depth of the smiles upon their faces.

"We were so happy in this photo," Derek said after a long pause.

"We were," Cyndi replied. "I was playing with my best friend," she paused, realizing what she had said, "while my other best friend took the photo."

"Memories," Derek said, his heart starting to pound.

"Suppose your mom would mind if I permanently borrowed these? I'd like to have them," Cyndi said looking hopefully up at Derek.

"She'll never miss them," Derek said, for it was obvious that the photos had been stashed away for well over a decade.

Their attention turned to under the bed and then below the mattress and finally they checked the slats of the bedframe. Still, nothing of interest surfaced. "Your mom doesn't have many pairs of shoes. That's my vice. I like shoes." Cyndi then went on, "I *love* shoes."

"Let's revisit that subject later," Derek responded, his head spinning from side to side, searching for places where one would hide important paperwork. Still nothing spoke to them.

"We ruled out the basement, the attic, my old room, Leena's old room. And we've searched her bedroom. What's that leave?" Derek asked, knowing the answer. "The bathrooms, the kitchen, and the living room."

"I'll tackle the bathrooms, you raid the kitchen, we can meet in the living room after that."

Derek's search found only the most typical bathroom accoutrements; a toilet brush, a plunger under the sink, and the medicine cabinet of each bathroom revealed nothing but what should normally reside in medicine cabinets. Though in different quantities, both the upstairs and downstairs medicine cabinets were over half full of what you would expect, bandages, medical tape, eye drops, nasal spray, allergy meds, over-the-counter painkillers, ear swabs, tweezers, and fingernail clippers. Certain it would be a dead end, he peered in the rear tanks of each toilet. Nothing. Finishing up, in the downstairs bathroom, he listened to kitchen cupboards, continuing to open and close.

"Anything yet?" Derek asked as he stepped into the kitchen. Cyndi was up on a chair with her head in the cupboards closest to the ceiling.

"I just couldn't see. I'm not short."

"I didn't say you were," Derek replied. "I just asked if you found anything yet." She finished up while sweeping her phone's light deep into the back of the cupboard.

"A few cookbooks here, muffin tins there. Silverware

where you anticipate silverware being. Pots and pans, it looks like any other kitchen on Clover Drive. Did you know your mom still has a bread maker? I haven't seen one of those in years."

Cyndi tucked the chair she was using back under the dining table and followed Derek into the living room. They searched under chairs, under the couch, in the couch. "A dollar and fifteen cents in silver—no pennies," Derek said while putting the change into his pocket. Noting that sofa cushions are always good for that.

"Anything else in those cushions?" Cyndi asked while visiting the bookcase.

"Popcorn kernels."

They scoured the bookcase together. Derek was hopeful that this could be *the place* after finding the key there earlier. The bookcase was the focal point of the living room, it was wall to wall on the west side of the house. Several books resided on one shelf, several on another. But the bookshelves were there for more than just books. Derek and Cyndi stepped back for additional examination. On the top shelf were a grouping of books, a ship in a bottle, a trophy Leena had earned for a science project. What was most obvious was that it wasn't cluttery. Although everything on the shelf was eclectic, nothing appeared out of place, nor was there too much of any one thing. They opened each book to see if papers could be found inside. On the bottom shelf, Derek picked up the *Count of Monte Cristo*—the last book, but it revealed nothing other than the printed words that belonged inside.

"Alexander Dumas, Classic," Cyndi said to Derek.

"It sure is. There are a couple of good movie versions of this, too."

"I'd like to watch one with you," Cyndi responded instantly.

"I'm sure I can make that happen," Derek smiled back at her.

His eyes performed a final vetting of the bookcase and ended looking again at the fishbowl with pink stones at the bottom, that no longer contained a key. "This is where I found the key to the Jetta." They spent the next minute trying to digest everything they just did in their search that proved unsuccessful.

"Strange thought," Cyndi finally broke the silence.

"What?" Derek asked.

"What if our hunch was right about a safe deposit box?"

"We didn't find a key, or bank statements alluding to her having one," Derek replied.

"But you *did* find a key," Cyndi took a moment to collect her thoughts on what she was going to say next. "What if, the car *is* her safe deposit box?"

"Huh? We were just there, nothing, other than normal paperwork and the list of names."

"A car is bigger than a glove box. We didn't look under the seats, under the hood, or inside the trunk." Derek let that sink in for a moment.

"It's a long shot."

"But," she paused again for dramatic effect, "but, you did find a list of names, and a purchase and sales agreement with your mom's name and another person's." Derek couldn't refute her logic.

"Wait a second. You're not suggesting that—" Cyndi interrupted him.

"We need to get a better look inside that car."

"Nope, no way," Derek responded, "there is no way we can go back there after what we just did."

34

Naps, Leena knew, were almost over for Everly. She would be entering kindergarten this fall and then by the next summer, scheduled naps would no longer be a thing. But Leena was grateful for this moment. Instead of her normal routine of tidying the house, Leena Pielski went directly to the living room and began her reconnaissance due diligence.

Leena encountered several difficulties in her internet search. She started backwards on the list. She learned quickly that just having the first name of a person was useless. Unless you were famous, whose moniker was one name, it was impossible to gather anything useful in terms of background. If they were going to solve this mystery, the other two names would have to yield results.

Another trouble with searching for people on the web Leena noticed, was that you really should know where the person lived in the past—or at least have some idea. And yet another problem; for both Annie Morello and Gordon McKnight, she found multiple people with the same name—or some sort of derivative. For Gordon

McKnight, she encountered six in Pennsylvania alone. Carving out the northeastern US, she found seventeen. If she made it a national search, she found forty-eight matches, although a few appeared to be duplicates. The more she looked, the more she wondered how much of the data was real. She started to become frustrated.

Then there was Annie Morello. Annie was some variant of Ann, she thought. And then her national searches started to yield Annettes and Annas, and Anas and Anikas and Hannahs. For some of the geographically close matches, it became apparent that the person married and took the name Morello. Leena hadn't thought of that when she began her search; maiden names threw a wrench in being able to find someone. Again, she narrowed her search to Pennsylvania. There were at least four people that could possibly fit; and no exact match on the first name.

Leena needed more time than just a ninety-minute nap window. With roughly twenty minutes remaining before Everly awoke, Leena wrote down every close hit she could find; it was more of an art than a science. Her score so far: zero for Lyle, four potentials for Gordon McKnight, and four for Annie Morello. Tonight, after Everly was tucked in, she would re-examine her work and dig deeper into the searches to eliminate some of the contenders and hopefully, to uncover connections to her mom. She could hear Everly stirring; naps were getting shorter. Phone still in hand, she texted Derek, *This searching for people thing is harder than I thought. I'll do more tonight. Stay tuned.*

35

Wolves, a large insidious pack. She was in fight or flight, and she was fleeing. Voracious wolves hunted her relentlessly and the direction she was running offered no safe harbor. The only place away from the hungry pack was towards a menacing gray industrial looking building with chain link fencing that fully surrounded it. Her feet were numb, and the cold stale air reeked of decay. She could make out people in the windows of the building cheering on the wolves as she picked up her pace towards the structure. The closer she got, the more she could make out the heinous faces of the window people, their arms flailing outside, gesticulating unpleasantries as they hurled out insults towards her.

These were bad people, people that wanted to hurt her, not just physically, but emotionally. They knew that real pain doesn't come from hitting your thumb with a hammer, or of breaking a bone; real pain came in the form of permanent emotional wounds, deep wounds— leaving forever scars. There had to be at least a dozen of the window people, casting out stones of tormenting language—they knew things—things that picked her apart. Their verbal assaults knifed into her lifelong insecurities, tore into things that they knew would injure her heart and soul. Despite the hateful cries of the windowed mass, she finally reached the sterile and cold building. She began to pound upon its massive wooden door, adorned with black iron, crisscrossing vertically and horizontally with an artistic flair, it now looked more like the entrance of a medieval castle than that of a factory. Again, she rapidly beat upon the door. Both of her hands in fists, she flailed upon the wooden door with all of the force she had. She twisted her head to gauge how long she had before the wolves were upon her. The gray alpha was snarling, and he began to communicate the capture strategy to his comrades. With everything she had left, she screamed, "You will let me in!!" and reintroduced her fists to the door, this time, her fists started to make a loud pounding noise.

Startled, April awoke to a loud knock on the door. She shook off sleep and the wolf nightmare. She must have gone back to sleep—something she did not mean to do. Panicked, she shot out of bed. Who could it be at her door? No one knew where she was. She had deactivated the location services on her phone. She even paid cash for the two nights in the mediocre motel. Her mind flashed through all the scenarios her post nightmare mind could fathom. Police? Her hands shook, her mind went blank. She ran towards the door and shut her left eye. With her right eye she peered out from the motel door's classic brass peephole. There, in front of her stood a small woman, somewhere in her sixties. She had a bucket in one hand. The other hand was attached to a metal pull cart, on which fresh towels and bedding were neatly folded. "Room Service," a voice sounded. April let out a large sigh. A wave of relief broke from the top of her spine and flushed its way to her toes.

"No thank you," April said loudly attempting to be heard through the door.

"OK, just wanted to make sure, your door had no sign." Even from what little line of sight she had, April could tell the woman was happy to be turned down; one less room to clean today.

April sat at the edge of the bed. Her nerves were breaking. Between the traumatic dream and how she awoke, April decided to stay another night. It was only Friday. She still had Saturday and part of Sunday—and had two more visits on her list; two more, to make things right. She still had plenty of time to get home by Sunday evening. More importantly, April Densmore did not feel like visiting a desolate cemetery on a cloudy Friday after being chased by wolves, even if it was a dream.

36

They were already more prepared than they were the night before. Rummaging through Derek's house, they gathered headlamps, ski masks, a crowbar, and duct tape—although neither could articulate why they had to have duct tape—this wasn't an abduction or a murder.

Cyndi volunteered to drive to *Twigg's* this time. "I don't know," is all Derek said over and over in the passenger's seat. "This is a reach and a gamble." Cyndi had convinced Derek that they needed to eliminate any potential mystery the car still might possess.

Cyndi drove the car in silence with her hands on the steering wheel in a ten-two position. She was listening to the conversation Derek was having with himself. "Then again, if you never wanted your children to find a trace of paperwork about your past, about their father, you wouldn't have kept anything in the house." He knew his mom never liked to worry about things within her span of control. She would tell Leena and he often that we have things we can influence, and we have things that we can't. Whether it was an idiosyncrasy or a valuable lesson, she regularly taught them to control the things you can control. Not having any paperwork as evidence in the house that Leena and he could stumble upon, was span of control for April. While visiting the car once more seemed a stretch, Derek agreed with himself that it was a very mom like thing to do.

"Did you get yourself there?" Cyndi asked.

"Huh, what?" Derek asked, coming out of his trance.

"Did you come to the conclusion that there are decent odds that there are more things in the car?"

Derek sighed.

"In a way, I guess."

"Good, then we can proceed. What's for dinner?" Cyndi asked. It was Friday evening, and they would need some energy for what they had ahead of them.

"I'm not hungry," Derek discounted her question. He had no desire to eat and then break the law, for the second night in a row.

"I'm not either, but we have a drive ahead of us, and we'll want something in our stomachs before..." she dropped off.

"Before we go to jail?" Derek responded with nervous wit. "And who am I going to call now, you were my one call if I get put in the hoosegow." It was then that Cyndi's face lit up and her smile beamed with a sense of joy. She enjoyed his sense of humor, even under duress.

"I've missed you. I've missed you terribly—all these years. Don't worry, I've missed Leena, too. I don't want your head getting too big, Mr. Densmore. The fact is, I have. Ever since I left town, things were good, but something was always missing. The only way I can describe it is," Cyndi paused, finding the words, "not feeling hungry, but not feeling full. Or, watching a movie that's decent, but lacked depth, too." As if Cyndi was a radio frequency, and he was the receiver, Derek picked up on her exact meaning. And even more, he deeply felt the meaning of what Cyndi described.

"I know exactly what you mean. Today I felt something when you and I were at Leena's. With you at her house, with you playing with Everly—just knowing you were upstairs and the three of us were together again—I felt closer to my sister."

"Well, how about them apples?" Cyndi asked.

"Pink Ladies," Derek responded, "those are my favorite."

"Of course, they are, Derek, of course they are."

They stopped at a deli and split a large vegetarian sandwich along with some salt and vinegar potato chips, a weakness of Cyndi's, Derek was starting to realize. They ate inside the Prius, discussing how much Everly looked like Leena but acted like Eli. Their conversation drifted to guessing their favorite sandwiches, favorite colors, and favorite numbers. "Mine is six," Derek said.

"That was your baseball number," Cyndi replied. "Remember, I used to come to your games. A pretty decent third baseman you were," she locked his eyes, "I wasn't there just to root for the home team." It was Derek's turn. Derek informed Cyndi of her favorite number.

"And yours is fourteen. If I recall it was your soccer number. I used to come to your games, remember? But I came solely to support the team, being the gentleman, I was. And still am." They talked longer than they should have, trapped in-between wanting to enjoy each other's company longer and the inevitable task ahead of them.

"So, what are we doing, Derek? Do we storm the

place with torches and pitchforks and take it by force? How are we going to do this?" Derek wished that like the previous night, Cyndi had the plan already formulated. But this time they didn't have a key to the facility.

"Tonight is Friday. Everyone wants their Friday nights off. Not to stereotype, but I can see a few of Hector's mechanics going out to the bar for a few beers to celebrate a long week. I have to think we'll have the place to ourselves." At their current pace, they would arrive at *Twigg's Enterprises* just after 8PM.

"Too soon for Hector Twigg to install cameras," Cyndi added. "The top part of the entrance door to the storage facility is glass—windowpanes if I recall. It could easily be broken. Still, I just don't want to cause any damage, you know? I feel horrible just doing this, as it is, for the second night in a row." A few miles went by, each searching their own thoughts.

"Do you have a rope?" Derek asked. "We could climb up on the roof and use the windows at the top of the building, use the ropes to shimmy down? Remember the windows where it would have been nice if there was moonlight to help us find our way last night?"

"Possible, very possible," Cyndi responded deep in thought. "You know, this whole thing is ridiculous. It is your mom's car and all we want to do is look inside it."

More time went by. The GPS told Cyndi to take her next left. "We're smart people, we'll figure this out," Derek said after Cyndi had completed her turn and was on the final paved highway portion of their journey.

"The garage door we escaped under—it had a decent gap at the bottom. What if we pried it open as far as it could go, and then you crawled underneath?" Cyndi flashed him a glaring look. "What? You're smaller than me and we have a crowbar."

"We're not very good at this," Cyndi said, "novices, that's what we are."

"Does this car have a tire iron?"

"Yes, when I bought the car, I checked out everything —spare tire, jack, and tire iron."

"We'll bring that, too. You never know. But first, let's try to find a way in through the entrance door. It's a pretty tired looking door. If someone wanted their way in, I can't think it would be too difficult," Derek said trying to be optimistic.

The rest of the drive they contemplated the known variables and attempted to make plans for the unknown ones. To save time, they weighed the option of driving up the main road and parking directly next to the storage facility. If no one were around, they could park the car near the buildings in such a way as to be ready for a quick exit. If someone were there, they could back out and would have to come back later in the evening. After more reflection, they decided to park in the same location as the previous night and traverse through the woods. It was better to be cautious.

"I'm nervous, Cyndi," Derek confessed as they crossed into Galeton. "I'm nervous about this, I'm nervous about my mother. I've never remembered a time I've felt more frazzled. And I can't think of a better adjective than frazzled, that's how frazzled I am."

"We will figure this out. Together. The three of us," Cyndi reassured him. "Speaking of—any news from Leena?" Cyndi asked.

"She said her initial search was harder than she anticipated and would try again tonight."

37

W hile she normally stayed completely present with Everly, tonight, Leena was distracted. Bedtime was rushed and she leaned on Eli to read to Everly before turning out the light. Leena had work to do, to sort things out from her earlier web surfing. She had just enough information thus far to make her confused and anxious. *When you're anxious, you're not in the moment*, Leena thought to herself. It was an expression her mother always used. Eli was understanding. "Your mother is the top priority," he kissed her on the head as he commenced with Everly's bedtime ritual.

This time she decided not to spend another second on Lyle. Without a last name, she would not be able to identify any concrete leads. Forgoing her phone, she found her laptop, better to use for her continued research. Armed with the pad of paper she had earlier, plus a cup of tea, Leena focused her attention on the two remaining names... Annie Morello and Gordon McKnight.

She was hopeful that a break would give her some clarity on her search. This time, like earlier, each search she did ended about the same way as her prior investigation. It wasn't that the searches didn't lead anywhere because they did. If you don't know what you're looking for, that is when things can become frustrating. Leena was trying to give herself some forbearance but became discouraged after she drained the final few sips of her herbal tea. Powering through the frustration, she decided to concentrate on birthdates as the primary focus of her search. Assuming the people she was searching for were close to her mother in age, it was probably the best gauge to measure a potential connection. Proximity and age. Their mother never lived outside of Pennsylvania, and as far as Leena knew, she lived only in two counties; the one she lived in now and the one she lived in growing up.

Her new strategy eliminated two options for Annie Morello. Leena's mood soon turned from frustrated to being fascinated by what she was seeing. The first of the two most probable was of an Ann Yvonne Morello. She was four years younger than her mother. And she had moved around considerably, in several states. One of them in Pennsylvania. From the internet's point of view, right or wrong, she currently resided somewhere in Virginia. The other was Anika T. Morello, around eight years older than her mom. But Anika never moved out of Pennsylvania, and the addresses revealed that she was always in the proximity of her mother. She even lived in the same town as her mother while her mother was still a child. This one seemed the most promising. Leena's search only yielded one other solid connection to Anika Morello. Roughly twelve years ago, she and her neighbor became entangled in a legal dispute about property lines in the town of North Wales. The only thing this exposed was that she probably still lived at the last address listed, for it was in the same town as the lawsuit—North Wales. She was close to a decade older than her mother. Leena wondered if there was any digital footprint for her. It was quite possible that this person didn't have one, and who knew if she even had an email address.

Only one Gordon McKnight fit the bill. In terms of proximity, he lived in the same area. In terms of birthdate, he was her mother's age. And that's when Leena's search for Gordon McKnight turned much stranger. Two pages down after keying in "Gordon McKnight Edwardsville"—the search engine revealed an interesting hit; a cutout picture of a newspaper article from many years ago. Not just an article, it was an obituary.

38

It was darker than the night before. Again, there would be no assistance from the moon to illuminate their way as they retraced the same path through the bordering woods of *Twigg's*. Cyndi drove to the identical spot where Derek had parked his BMW. The only difference was that she turned the car around, pointing her vehicle towards their exit route. Leaving the car, they could make out many of their own tracks from yesterday evening. With their headlamps turned on, it was easier to identify the long strides and heavy imprints in the matted wet grass from their escape back to Derek's car.

"Some good news. Lightning doesn't strike twice," Derek told Cyndi, more to internally motivate himself. He gathered the duct tape, crowbar, and tire iron from the back seat of the Prius. "I can't imagine tonight being more," he hesitated, "any more *disturbing* than last night."

"You just completely jinxed us," Cyndi fired back.

"Lucky for you I'm not superstitious, but I'm hella nervous."

"That's two of us," Cyndi replied, "my stomach is a mess. I wonder if I could use their bathroom again." Derek had no idea how he could laugh under the circumstances, but with Cyndi, he was relearning that it was possible.

They donned their black ski masks, and headlamps—only their eyes shown. Fully dressed in dark clothing, their lawless ensemble was complete. Derek wore a pair of dark gray gardening gloves; Cyndi wore black leather driving gloves. "I've got to get a picture of this," Cyndi pulled out her phone.

"Like we need proof of this," Derek said above whispering level.

"Come here," Cyndi closed in, "duck down just a bit." She pressed her cheek next to his and with her flash on, Cyndi proceeded to capture the gangster selfie, forever memorializing the Bonnie and Clyde moment.

Before she backed away, she kissed him on the cheek through his mask. "That's for good luck," she smiled and started to tuck her phone back into her black jeans. Derek surprised himself with his next action. Whether it was the culmination of all of the emotions running around in his head for the last several days or just raw pre-crime adrenaline mixed with how incredibly attractive and racy she appeared wearing form fitting black jeans, he didn't know. But her simple kiss on his cheek was all that was needed to create the catalyst. Derek ripped off his ski mask and tore away Cyndi's. He placed both hands around her head and brought her towards him and applied the most sensual kiss upon her lips that his skills in this arena permitted. And the two pressed up against each other silently on the side of a lonely road they had no idea existed a few days ago. It was quiet and cold, and for that one moment in time, there was no one else in the world but the two of them.

"That was for extra luck," Derek began, realizing that this moment that they created could not last.

"With that kind of luck, I'm ready for Vegas," Cyndi replied with a soft kiss on his cheek and a satisfying smile.

They set off, retracing their previous evening's steps. Cyndi was carrying a hefty amount of rope and the tire iron. Derek forced a half-used roll of duct tape into his jacket pocket and in his right hand he held up a large flashlight, in his left he carried a full-size crowbar. Just before starting on their quest, a realization washed over him. Most of life, through the daily hum of its activities, we are completely oblivious to the changes that steer us in a certain direction. We accept the subtle changes and course corrections without a conscious awareness. Conversely, there are times in one's life when you are fully aware of a change, a shift, a fundamental alteration in how things were, and a second later, how things must now be going forward. There was no way back to the Derek and Cyndi that *were*. The moment they just experienced together; their kiss, that long time in coming, pent up emotional release of need and passion said good-bye to strictly being childhood companions. Even if they wanted to find their way back to that place, he realized that it no longer existed. It was as if looking back in your rearview mirror and seeing the road behind you was now filled with rocks from a landslide. There was no way back, their relationship from this day forward would be different. No sadness existed from his realization, just the opposite. A feeling of abundance and a wave of relief cleared his mind—even in this insane moment of pre-misdemeanor drama—Derek felt something he had never felt. He deeply sensed an awareness he previously could not reach, that he was where he should be at this moment. He was supposed to be next to this person, with this woman, his long-time cherished friend. The feeling was overwhelming, rousing and all together highly invigorating. If Derek were to be called upon to lift a car with his own strength, tonight was the night to do so.

"We're close," Cyndi whispered just audibly.

"What do you see?" Derek asked. Both of them scanned the entire area of *Twigg's Enterprises*. So far, everything looked as it did the night before; the same lights were on, and the location was void of human presence. They stayed silent for several minutes, peering out from between two enormous white pine trees while searching for the moxie to take the next step. The only sound they could identify were peeper frogs, somewhere in a distant pond. It was Cyndi who turned to Derek and gave a thumbs up while shrugging her shoulders. "I think so," Derek replied in as quiet a whisper as he could find, almost mouthing the words, "Our eyes are adjusted, that's a good thing. Are you sure you see no cameras; they can look pretty inconspicuous these days?" Cyndi was mindful of that, too. Nothing seemed different than yesterday evening.

"Nothing that I can see anyway," Cyndi replied in the same low-level whisper.

"How about we both go to the door first; I'll see if I can find a way to open it—you be the look out?" Cyndi agreed to the plan.

And for the second consecutive night, they sprang out of the woods towards the rusty industrial storage building, tiptoeing as best as two inexperienced people could in the art of sneaking. Once they made it to the door, Derek dropped on his knees. His first reaction was to turn the handle. As expected, it was locked. He then examined the top window portion of the door, assessing how easy or difficult it would be to break it, and then to reach in and turn the knob from the inside. The door was indeed old and tired; however, it wasn't ready to forgive intrusion without some sort of fight. Derek's mind spun around. He brought forward the crowbar, and as he was just about to insert it between the door and the frame just at the lock mechanism, he felt a tap on his shoulder. A tingly cold chill went down his spine.

39

Leena continued her search for almost two more hours, hopeful to unearth more information on the names. Letting out a big sigh, she realized she was at diminished returns. Nothing more could be found other than the same few intriguing pieces. It was approaching 9PM.

A thought occurred to her; perhaps it was time to enlist additional help. While her mother had always been tightlipped about the past, she believed Aunt Eileen knew much more. And with Mom missing, her aunt would have to come clean. Leena went back and forth on this idea for some time. On one side, she didn't want to involve Eileen. Getting her entangled in this meant upsetting her immensely; after all, her sister was missing. On top of that, it meant that Eileen would have to spill some secrets that were only meant to be between sisters. She weighed the predicament in her head for some time. Tipping the scale was the deceit their mother brought to them. Her mind went to the text Derek received: *Having a nice time with Eileen, be back on Sunday.*

After discussing things with Eli, she decided it would be best to visit Eileen in person. Tomorrow, as early as possible. Not wanting to frighten her aunt, she hatched a white lie and placed a call. It was almost 9:30PM, hopefully not too late. "Hi Aunt Eileen, it's Leena—your favorite namesake," Leena started, attempting to keep it light, at least for tonight.

"Oh, hi! How are you?"

"I'm good, everybody's good," she lied. "Hey, listen, I'm actually down your way tomorrow and if you don't have any plans, I could stop by for a coffee, and we can get caught up." She paused to await the response.

"Will you be bringing that little spitfire of yours?"

"Not this time, Aunt Eileen, but we can make it happen next time. How does sometime after 9AM work?"

"That would be fine, I'll get up early enough to make us some coffee cake."

"Don't go to too much trouble," Leena told her aunt.

"Nonsense, coffee and coffee cake it is." And before Eileen could start asking any probing questions, especially about her mom, Leena shut down the conversation.

"Then expect me there then, sometime after 9AM and unfortunately I have to go right now. I'll see you tomorrow," Leena owned the entire conversation.

"OK, looking forward to it."

Leena hung up. *No*, Leena thought, *you wouldn't be looking forward to it if you knew why I'm visiting and the questions I will be asking.* Leena packed some extra clothing in a backpack, she just didn't know where this was going, or if she might need a change of clothes. It was around a two-hour drive if you didn't stop. She would have to get up around 6AM; she set her phone alarm. And now she needed to talk to Derek and Cyndi about her findings and inform them of her new plan. For a moment, her mind came off of her mother and she smiled a little. She thought about how nice the two names flowed together: Derek and Cyndi.

40

The searing adrenaline chill dissolved when Derek realized that nothing was wrong. Cyndi had tapped him on his shoulder, asking for a crack at the door before calling in the big guns of a prybar. "Switch places?" He nodded, now it was his turn to stand guard. "Had an idea," Cyndi whispered, or that's what Derek thought she said. "Got a credit card? This is an old lock."

Unzipping his jacket, Derek fumbled around his pocket, fishing out his wallet. "Do you take VISA?" Where the humor came from, he had no idea. Maybe they were good at this and could handle the stress and tension of a life of crime. Cyndi snickered, appreciating the jest.

She held up her hand. "I promise not to spend too much," Cyndi then went to work. Derek looked into the blackness of the night, nothing stirred. He started to fumble and play with the VW key, already out and ready.

As quiet as she tried to be, the sound of a hard plastic credit card against wood and metal rattled together and announced itself to the evening. More rattling and tinkering. And still more. "It's time for the crowbar," Derek whispered, "my money's no good here."

"Wanna bet?" Cyndi asked while rising from her kneeling position with an accomplished grin upon her face. She pushed open the door with flawless execution.

"Not bad, not bad at all," Derek nodded with an equally satisfied look. Cindy handed the credit card back to Derek. "My card is just about ruined, you didn't say you were going to destroy it," Derek whispered as he examined what used to be his go-to card.

"I guess I'm bad with credit," Cyndi replied, continuing with the pun. Now inside, their attention turned to finding the Jetta, this time to conduct a thorough search of it and then to get out of there as fast as they could. "Should one of us be a lookout?" Cyndi asked.

"I had a good luck kiss earlier; I think we're fine," Derek responded.

With renewed confidence and with headlamps on, they navigated their way over to the late eighties VW. It was much easier tonight having the knowledge of landmarks—the speedboat, piano, the CJ7. "I'll take the trunk, you take the front, check under every seat, nook and cranny," Derek issued the plan.

Cyndi began to look under every seat, starting with the driver's side. She found only candy wrappers, faded receipts, pennies, and chewing gum that bonded to the aging stained carpet from years of wear. Under each seat, nothing of importance stood out. While examining the interior, Derek was busy in the trunk. Some jumper cables were visible, otherwise, emptiness. Emptiness until he pulled up the lining of the trunk, exposing the cavity of where the donut sized spare tire should be. Instead of a tire, his headlamp's light shone upon an old, wrinkled plastic freezer bag, inside of that was a manilla folder. He could feel his heart pounding. Inside the manilla folder, a collection of paperwork revealed itself, about a half an inch thick. "Interesting," Derek whispered to himself.

It was then that several things started to happen, one right after the other. Cyndi finished up her search and came out to visit Derek, "Find any junk in the... you know." Then, their ears perked up. Something was getting louder. They picked up what could only be the sound of a vehicle's engine, approaching the building. They froze.

"Not again, not again," Derek's heart started to pound. The winter attire he had on to blend in with the night was too much for what was a warm spring's evening. The nervousness and the cold weather gear compounded, and he started to sweat profusely; more than he did on a run on a humid day at the peak of summer. The shock of hearing the engine dulled their senses, and it wasn't until they heard a car door open when they had the sense to turn off their headlamps.

They stared at each other with bulging eyes, with the same *we-are-going-to-prison-tonight* expression and in the same exact location as the night before. Now they could hear voices, one male and the other female, gruff voices, displeased voices, fight or flight voices. A loud human whistling noise is what came next, and the first discernable language could be understood. "Get 'em, Truman!" It was now evident that if the Twiggs came for a visit, they brought their dog along with them. Finally, as if wanting to reveal their location, Derek's ring tone announced that his sister was trying to get ahold of him; it was Leena's worst timing, ever.

Panic assailed them. There was a dog, and at least

two others, and by turning off their headlamps late and Derek's phone announcing their location inside the building, things looked grim. Grim was an understatement. It was bad enough he would be arrested, but the thought of involving Cyndi in this mess was too much to handle. Derek thought only one thing; *how could a situation go from easy and smooth to horrific so fast?*

Perhaps it was muscle memory, already sculpted from the night before, they both pointed to the oversized garage door and bolted to it, carrying everything they had brought with them, plus the newly acquired plastic bag full of papers. Cyndi pushed the green open button with her elbow. The door started to rise. As soon as the door was at the needed height, they crawled under and through. Cyndi was out first. Derek, needing just a little more space before fitting, felt something clamp down upon his leg, as if his calf were now in a vice. A warm, sharp vice. The vice growled. He had never been bit by a dog before this evening, and to his credit, he had never practiced breaking and entry until the previous night, and so on a certain cosmic level, it didn't faze him.

Now having ample room, he pulled his body through with all his strength, the canine, not small by any description let go as his head hit the garage door. "*Run, run!*" Derek yelled. His next thought was that going from whispering to yelling with nothing in-between is a strange thing for your ears to handle.

Warm liquid began to ooze out of Derek's left calf; pain would have to wait he thought. They bolted for the woods, exactly as they had the night previously. Perhaps this is why Derek's sensation of déjà vu last night was so intense. Just before entering the woods, Derek turned his head for a look. He never regretted turning around more than he did just then. His cheek, at that exact moment, encountered another feeling he had never experienced. Now in one night, he not only checked off dog bite on his list, but now he could proudly boast that he got shot in the face with a BB gun. Not just any BB gun, from the pain the center of his cheek was feeling, it was a high caliber BB gun. "*William Shatner!*" Derek screamed as loud as he could, not being able to help himself.

"Get back here, Truman! Come!" They ran, faster than yesterday. Get to the Prius, get to the Prius, it was the only thought on their minds.

When they got to the road and approached Cyndi's car, they were expecting the Twiggs to already be there. Derek was well behind Cyndi and was limping to the car. He was afraid they would already have their weapons ready again. But there was silence. Without a word, they entered the car. Cyndi's hands were shaking badly. Nervously she found the ignition and began to drive away—away from *Twigg's Enterprises*. In shock, the next ten minutes were reserved for their own thoughts, for processing what just happened.

Derek's pain shifted. The humiliating pain of the bite and his cheek's sting began to be overpowered by a throbbing ache in his ankle. They turned left off of Gilson Road and onto one of the state highways that would bring them back home. Several minutes of driving time elapsed, when a police car with flashing lights approaching in the opposite direction whizzed by them, heading to what could only be towards the direction of Gilson Road. "Let's get home," Derek said to Cyndi, as she did her best to keep her hands from trembling.

41

The first half of the ride home for Cyndi and Derek was pensive. Derek thought back to less than a week earlier, while he was sitting in a restaurant making faces at a two-year-old, without any cares. If someone told him at the restaurant that in less than two weeks, he would be sitting in the passenger's seat of Cynthia Vaughn's car, bleeding from a dog bite and reeling from a stinging cheek, plus a swelling ankle, carrying a stack of what appeared to be documents from his mother's past, he would have laughed at them.

Cyndi was lost in her own thoughts—spending considerable energy on simply driving the vehicle—something that usually came automatically. She asked Derek if he was OK several times already but couldn't stop asking. "Are you sure you're OK?"

"Yes, I need my leg cleaned and wrapped, my cheek is fine, it just still stings," Derek replied yet again. For the first few times, she probed his voice to try and hear if he really did need a trip to the hospital. Now after some time went by and their initial shock was wearing off, she picked up on the sincerity of his tone, the bite was more likely superficial, and he would be fine.

"I'll clean it thoroughly when we get back to your place," Cyndi advised him. "It's a good thing I kissed you for luck. If I hadn't, there's a good chance you would have got shot in the eye." Humor was good medicine. They began to realize that they were going to be OK, that they had avoided the police, yet again, and they may have been successful in retrieving some of his mother's secret documents. "How do we know Truman had his rabies shots? Should I put you down? When should I put you down, at the first sign of your mouth frothing?" Cyndi asked.

"Can you believe it?" Derek asked. "Shot and bit the same night. I didn't tell you, but my ankle on the non-bit leg is killing me; I fell in a hole and sprained it on our run back to your car."

Cyndi shook her head. "You're a mess, did we just do the same thing, because I'm feeling fine." Derek began to laugh, and then Cyndi mirrored his lead. The two laughed until their stomachs hurt, and it erupted again several minutes after it died down the first time, prompted by Derek's groan when he lifted his ankle.

Limping and bloodied, Derek stumbled up his front steps when they arrived home sometime close to midnight. His outside light snapped on, sensing the motion. Behind him, Cyndi asked for his keys to unlock the front door.

Derek immediately went to the bathroom sink to view his new face. Dead center in the middle of his left cheek, a dark red circle had formed with an expanding outer rim of pinkness; it was sore to touch. This particular BB gun wasn't the entry level variety. This one was designed to take down squirrels. As bad as it stung, he was glad he wasn't any closer to the shooter. Cyndi went to the kitchen to get some water and sat down the two glasses on the coffee table of the living room. She entered the bathroom as Derek continued to examine his face. "Galeton has *huge* mosquitoes," Derek said as he examined the diameter of the welt more closely.

"Your face is still pretty," Cyndi answered. "I think the real carnage is below. Put on some shorts and I can take care of your other battle scars." He hobbled to the bedroom and did what Cyndi instructed. Having never been bit by a dog, he had no idea what to expect. He peeled off his jeans and threw them in the corner telling himself that he would take care of them later. Dried blood prevented him from seeing the wound very well. Beyond the bite and his stinging cheek, his biggest concern was his ankle; it ached and felt stiff, and he could feel the swelling.

"I can get myself cleaned up," he told Cyndi while slowly walking down the hallway.

"Yes, I have no doubt, but I can do it easier because I can see it better," Cyndi said, already having lined up the rubbing alcohol, bandages, washcloth, and a container filled with warm water. "Let's do this."

Cyndi set about icing his right ankle while cleaning out the bite on his left calf in quick fashion. "The bite's not all that bad but wow your ankle is mighty swollen. That's quite a sprain."

Derek shrugged.

"I can move it, it's just tender," Derek showed off his range of motion to Cyndi. "Leena's going to my aunt's tomorrow morning," he had time to listen to Leena's voicemail as he changed his clothes. Derek caught Cyndi up on what Leena had found during her internet searches and what she planned to do tomorrow. "She's serious."

After cleaning up the first aid supplies, Cyndi returned to Derek with his legs up on the arm of the couch. She carried another glass of water and something in her right hand. "Take these, they'll help with the swelling and maybe a smidge with the pain," Cyndi dropped three painkillers into Derek's hand.

"Thank you for," he delayed his next thought, "for all of this."

"You would do the same for me, although it remains to be seen if I would have got into the mess you did tonight. You may want to keep your day job. Stealth and escape may not be your jam." Despite three distinct bodily areas sending pain impulses back to his brain, Cyndi found a way to make Derek's face break into a smile.

"Why didn't they come after us?" Derek asked. "I mean, they had a dog, they had a BB gun." It was obvious Cyndi had thought the same thing.

"Remember that our car was parked around the corner to the entrance of their road. If they came up the way we did, they would have had to drive past their own entrance to identify a car, in this case, our car. If they hadn't, they would have no idea if we even had a car. And, you never know, going on the attack versus defending your own place is quite a different thing. For all they knew, we had BB guns too," Cyndi gingerly kissed his cheek below his pebble sized bright red welt. "They called the police after all, something I'm sure they really didn't want—deep down," Cyndi finished.

Derek's mind drifted away from everything that had just happened at the moment Cyndi planted the small, loving kiss on his cheek. Whatever was developing between them, it came naturally, and he admired it. Earlier this evening, they had kissed for the first time, a loving peck and then a sensual kiss. He hoped he was able to articulate everything he felt in that kiss and at that moment upon the side of Gilson Road, clad in their nefarious garb. The kiss, to Derek, spoke at many different levels and meant so many things. It was a thank you for returning into his life. It was for feelings of joy, something he had not felt in years. It was also a display of the carnal hunger he had for Cyndi. But on top of the many faceted kiss, was the loneliness component. In that one moment with his lips upon hers, he had hoped to communicate that he didn't want to be alone anymore and that she was the cure for an emptiness that had been growing for years.

Despite the physical pain he was in, worrying about the police knocking on their door, and concern for his missing mother, Derek looked upon Cyndi and offered up a tender smile.

"What's that for?" Cyndi asked, already knowing.

"Many things. Happiness, joy, glee, contentment, the list goes on." As if understanding all of the meanings of what he conveyed, Cyndi seemed to be in the same place. She then kissed his good cheek and lay her head upon his chest. They had so much to discuss about what their next steps were, but they both savored this moment; Derek listened to her steady, calm inhalations. Cyndi felt Derek's chest move up and down while listening to the rhythm of his heart.

It was getting late, and sleep started to call for them. "I need to open the contents of that bag." Cyndi picked up their plunder from the coffee table and handed it to Derek. In pain, he sat up and opened the freezer storage bag, battered and wrinkled through time and weather. At the beginning of the stack of papers were years of copies of federal and state tax filings, paperclipped together by year. Some of these dated back to when Derek was in elementary school. It was strange to see so many together, each one represented a distinct year as a family —together. While the papers only represented income, deductions, and tax to be paid, to Derek they meant much more. He examined one from when he was in seventh grade. That was the year he was promoted from outfield to third base. He had never worked so hard fielding ground balls that summer. It was the year Leena got glasses and they went out to celebrate so that Leena wouldn't feel bad about getting them. It was the year they had to get a new furnace, and it wiped out much of the money his mom worked so hard to save. Each year's filing looked almost like the prior year with just a few numbers changing. What was changing in those years were Leena and he, growing up, entering puberty, being rebellious, finding independence, Cyndi moving away, going to college, leaving home, leaving Mom. All the time, Mom working endlessly to keep them clothed, warm, fed, and loved. Derek sifted through more returns, returns up until the last few years—long after he left his family home for good. The realization from earlier in the week returned; each year that went by he felt more distant from his family, especially his mother. Derek was overcome by sadness sparked by the memories they had together, the three of them taking on each day as a family unit—and many times the four of them, Cyndi included. It is a strange thing to reflect upon your past, seeing your hurry to grow up, to launch from the nest as soon as you can; sometimes so much in a hurry that you fail to enjoy the growing up part of growing up. It is a cold feeling, realizing the emotional distance with a loved one who you just want to feel close to, who you just want to love. Derek began to stare at nothing while taking in his thoughts.

There was another thing that Cyndi's presence stirred in him and that was the desire to find his way back, closer to his family, to feel connected to his mom. Continuing to flip through each piece of paper, Derek realized he was close to finding the end.

"It's all taxes, Cyndi," Derek lifted his head. She watched patiently as he flipped through the paperwork, and she could see he was reflecting upon many things as he sifted through the pile.

"You really went deep there, I could tell."

"Yes, sorry. I felt like Walter Mitty. It's just that time is going by so fast, you know. All these papers reflect years of time—time before I knew who Walter Mitty even was, times where we all played tag in the backyard —like that picture you found in Mom's closet."

"It does go by fast and that's why it's important to find happiness and do your very best each day."

"Without a doubt," Derek replied back. There were only a few papers remaining and at that point he was expecting the entire stack to be tax filings. The next paper had a different texture than the copier paper which made up the tax documents. It was a letter, an actual pre-email, pre-text, letter, written on a piece of stationery. Derek removed it from a stamped envelope. "Do you mind if I read it with you?" Cyndi asked, scooching herself next to Derek on the couch so they could both read the letter at the same time.

"Please," Derek motioned her to come close.

"It's a love letter," Cyndi said immediately and excitedly after seeing the introduction. The letter, like the bag that held it, had been ravished by time. More than likely, it had been unfolded and then folded back into its original mailing position many times. It was printed handwriting, and Derek imagined that the writer was trying his best to be as neat as possible with his penmanship. It was a male; this was evident from both the writing style itself and how the letter took shape. For the next few minutes, they read and reread the letter in a trance of curiosity and awe.

My Dearest April,

What more can I say? I have found the one in you. Your smile is sunshine, and your touch is a warm breeze. Your kindness is gentle rain, and your love is a harvest in autumn.

I pray you feel the same way as I do, for I do not have the words to express the feelings I have in a simple letter. I'm not certain if the words may exist, or perhaps I just am incapable of transcribing the magnitude and depth I feel for you in written language form.

I know we are young, but I also believe that I will not find what we have with anyone. I have found the one in you.

Life is about to separate us, my dearest April. The only thing that gets me through the sadness of our separation is knowing that we will be back together again. I know we'll find ourselves together after the next four years and then we never have to be apart.

I'm so proud of you for finding the job at the energy company. And thank you for your support as I join the Navy. The next four years will be hard in so many ways. The hardest will not be basic training or being tested by a senior officer. The hardest for me is all of the breath I will put in and out of my lungs without you near me. All that time away. Already I feel the ache of missing you.

By the time you read this, I will be on the road, a step closer to wearing my uniform. I will send you a photo of me in it as soon as I have one. I'll send you three; one for your nightstand, to say good night to and to see me in the morning. One for your office desk, so that you know I'm with you during the day. And one for your purse, so that you have me with you wherever you go.

I meant what I said last night. I don't have enough for a ring yet, but the next time I'm home I will. My April, I love you. I need you. I have found the one in you.

With a heart that now knows love,
Gordon

"Whoa," Derek said, not finding another word available.

"Whoa is right," Cyndi replied. "Oh my God they were in *love*," Cyndi's excitement continued. "With a heart that now knows love… Are you kidding me? This is amazing!"

"I'm stunned," Derek answered. His eyes were never meant to see this correspondence between his mother and this unknown person. He turned over the letter to examine the envelope, sure enough, the return address spelled out the author's name, Gordon McKnight. "Whoa," Derek repeated.

"*So* much love," Cyndi said again, "I have found the one in you. Do you see that? That's incredible. He and your mom—amazing."

"I'm having a hard time processing this." Derek was speechless. He was starting to see his mother through a completely different lens. Although the letter wasn't dated, he was certain that it had to be just after high school. As far as he knew, his mother worked for the same company all of her life, directly after graduating high school. And the timing would also make sense for this man to enter the Service, if they both had just graduated high school together. It was eye opening; his mother was loved, was in love, and had all the entanglements of genuine romantic love. One thing he had never thought about was that his mother could be just like him. The feelings he had bubbling up inside for Cyndi right now; could it be that his mom felt the same way at one time, for this man? Gordon McKnight, who could he be? He meant nothing to Derek other than being a name on a piece of paper, and now seeing a love letter from him to his mother. It was mind blowing. It wasn't just a simple love letter—it was a proposal and a *want-to-spend-the-rest-of-my-life-with-you*, letter. Both Derek and Cyndi could see from the depth of the prose that for this man, there was no other woman on the planet other than April.

"My mom, in love like that?" Derek asked the question, not to Cyndi, but for him to process it all.

"I just think this is the most amazing thing," Cyndi started, "and I'm going to look at your mom in a whole new way when I see her next."

Cyndi's last statement jarred Derek. When would they see her next? Derek picked up the remaining few papers—these were not photocopies of tax forms either, although they appeared to be from a copy machine by the tactile feel of the paper. Four or five papers with printing on each side; it was a divorce decree between his mother and Lyle Densmore.

42

"**I** think I've found my father," it was all he found for words.

While he had never seen a divorce decree before, he was positive this was as generic as one could be. It seemed like there was little customization in the boilerplate lawyer-ese, other than the names of his mother and Lyle Densmore. It only indicated that his mother had full parental rights for him and an unborn child. No assets were listed, no child support, no spousal maintenance. However they had reached an agreement, there was either nothing in terms of assets to split up, or they each chose to move on and let go.

"All I know now, is my father's name is Lyle and he and my mom divorced before Leena was born." The memory of the man in the khaki jacket walking out the door flashed into his head, finally sure it was his father.

Cyndi shifted on the couch. "We know two names," Cyndi replied. "Your dad, and what appears to be your mom's boyfriend, or even fiancé."

"He's not my dad, he's my biological father," Derek said instantly.

"I meant nothing by that—your father," Cyndi reissued her statement.

Derek didn't hesitate, he went directly to his phone and called his mother. "Pick up, Mom, pick up," Derek barked the command at his phone. "Tell us you're OK." After a few rings, the call went directly into voicemail. As he anticipated, his mom was not going to answer. In his head, he went back to her statement about returning Sunday. "Why would she say she would be back on Sunday? Was she buying time? Will she even be back? What's a lie and what's not?" Cyndi could see that he was getting deeply upset. Seeing his mom through the eyes of a lover's note, looking for the first time upon his father's true name, it was causing internal friction and a deep sense of confusion.

"It's late, Derek." Cyndi put a hand upon his back and slowly rubbed in-between his shoulder blades. "It's tomorrow in fact," her phone illuminated 12:16AM. "We can't do anything right now. We made progress. Leena's going to your aunt's tomorrow to give Eileen the Densmore inquisition. We're tired, you're hurting on many fronts. Your body needs rest."

Derek couldn't think about sleep even though he was exhausted on many levels. Above all he didn't want Cyndi to leave, and he expressed it. "I don't want you to go." Derek found her hand and grasped it while his eyes met hers.

"Who said anything about me leaving?" Cyndi responded reciprocating the gentle squeeze with her fingers. That was all he needed to hear, for just knowing he would not be alone this night was enough for his tension to let go.

They found their way to Derek's room. Derek removed everything but his T-shirt and boxers and found his way under the covers. Just to know Cyndi was with him in the same house was enough for Derek, he had no expectation of her sleeping near him. For the next several minutes, Derek listened to the only sounds in the house. The refrigerator's hum was on a break, kicked off by it reaching its set temperature. Derek heard the bathroom sink run and some gentle rustling behind the bathroom door. It was nice to hear other sounds in the house, he thought to himself. Not just other sounds, it was the sound of Cynthia Vaughn and that was a beautiful thing, better than a perfectly composed piano and string ensemble opus. The bathroom door opened.

"Oh, you're not asleep yet," Cyndi asked in a statement. She must have rummaged through Derek's dresser. Standing in front of the bed in a *Property of the Philadelphia Phillies* T-shirt, Cyndi crawled in next to Derek.

"The Phillies are pretty lucky to have drafted you." Despite being exhausted, Derek tried a stab at humor.

"I would say so, do you like it? I wasn't planning to spend the night. I even used your toothbrush."

"I just might have cooties," it was Derek's last words before slipping into a strange dream. He was being chased by large shadowy dogs that ran on two legs, each of the dogs carried BB gun pistols which never ran out of ammo.

43

Leena could not believe how evil the alarm sounded on her phone. "I'll have to change that sound," she told herself as she climbed out of bed, the early light of morning was starting to show. She had her clothing all laid out the night before. She walked over and kissed Eli. "Thank you, Love, I'll call you later. Kiss Everly for me." Eli did his best to acknowledge and flipped over on his side; he was already back into the sleep she had interrupted.

She gathered her things and hopped in the shower. Annie, Gordon, Lyle, the names, and search results were all she thought about. And as if on autopilot, her shower was done without her remembering anything about the act of washing her body or her hair. Her mind was on the names and then moved to the questions she would pose to her unknowing aunt. After getting dressed, coffee was the next item on the agenda. She found a banana to take with her. A piece of toast with peanut butter would work for now, the banana was a good road trip snack. She had a full tank of gas already and that meant that if her coffee filled bladder would allow it, there would be no stops on the horizon before reaching Lansdale, about a two-hour drive.

After the grogginess faded, she started to enjoy the drive. Very few people were out on the roads just after 6AM on a Saturday. She started to wonder about the people that were; most of them going to or coming from work most likely. But what about the others? What about the people like her that are driven out of bed for reasons that sound like fiction? Her mind returned to the Saturday when she visited her mom without Everly. Where was her mom? And it wasn't just the question about her physical whereabouts, it was the question of where she was mentally. *Where do one's thoughts take you when you're aloof and agitated?* Leena thought.

Her thoughts turned again to the purpose of this morning's journey. Aunt Eileen was going to have quite an interesting morning and she dreaded getting her aunt upset. Still, it was time for all of them to put their heads together.

Leena drove up the interstate ramp. An hour on the highway was what she needed to focus on the tact to take with her aunt as well as start to make a mental list of the questions she had for her related to the three names Derek and Cyndi had found. She would arrive in her aunt's hometown with plenty of time to spare. She wanted some extra time to give Derek and Cyndi a call, perhaps they had more information for her. The car continued on its way and just like her shower, the drive went into autopilot mode.

44

After many dreams where Derek was continually searching while running, the next dream switched genres. He was now in a restaurant, and more than likely because recently, he was sitting at *Unwind*, this time he was in the booth where the older couple ate their meal in peace. The sun was coming in from the window and was hitting the table, there was a glare off of the napkin holder on the booth's table. The smell of eggs, spices, and coffee filled the air. As if somewhere in the middle of waking and dreaming, his conscious informed his subconscious that it was time to awake.

Filling his lungs with air, his eyes opened. The sun was shining brightly. The smell of eggs and coffee stayed in the air. Cyndi was no longer in bed, and he had a fairly good idea who was in the kitchen making noises that can only be described as the sounds of breakfast.

Derek started to take inventory of his wounds, starting with his cheek. Sore and most likely black and blue, it would heal. His next thought went to his legs. Out loud he vocalized his next thought. "Oh yeah, I got bit by a dog last night." He touched the back of his calf; it was also tender. He was lucky the dog didn't get a stronger grip on his leg. As bad as it was getting bit by a dog, it could have been much worse. He was thankful for the way he was positioned on the ground attempting to get away—lurching under and through the abnormally large garage door. And then he moved his right ankle. Of the three conditions, this was the most concerning. His ankle ached, and while it tolerated bearing weight, it had no desire to do so. Up and out of bed, he found his way into the kitchen, limping and in pain. He wanted to see Cyndi. He couldn't remember the last time he woke up to anyone making him breakfast. It was exciting, not because he was being made breakfast, but because Cyndi was the one making it.

Derek found Cyndi in the same T-shirt as the night before, facing the stove. She was tending to the eggs, and it looked like she was adding some flavoring. Derek took in the sight and could hardly take his eyes off her legs, going all the way up to the T-shirt. She was humming and it was evident that she was enjoying herself. Finally unlocking his eyes from the contours of her legs, he finally got the nerve to speak. "Eggs and legs for breakfast?" She didn't turn around, still attending to what was either scrambled eggs or an omelet.

"Funny for a guy without coffee in his bloodstream," she replied holding up and waving good morning with the spatula—still with her back turned to him. Derek moved to the cupboard to retrieve a coffee mug.

"Another coffee?" Derek asked her as he grabbed a coffee pod out of his carousel.

"Yes please," Cyndi handed him her mug.

"First off, it smells amazing. Secondly how did you sleep?"

She removed the pan from the stove and turned off the burner.

"It should, I'm good with eggs," she migrated towards a cupboard and pointed her finger for Derek to see. Derek, knowing what she meant, pointed to the one with plates. "Thanks," Cyndi responded, "and I slept well, believe it or not. I usually don't sleep well in strangers' houses. Come to think about it, I rarely sleep in the houses of strangers."

"That's encouraging," Derek said as he handed her a fresh steaming cup of dark roast.

"But," Cyndi continued, "I am not in a stranger's house, I'm in your house." A warm vibration tingled and encircled Derek; dopamine helped against the pain.

"You would think that after being bit by a dog and shot in the face that they would be the real source of pain," Derek started after taking his first sip of coffee. "Nope, it's my own stupidity that hurts most. My ankle is a mess."

"I am hoping it isn't broken, it's really swollen," Cyndi replied scooping out a perfectly prepared omelet to pair with some cut up apple with a dollop of peanut butter. "Your refrigerator needs some stocking up."

"Thank you, this looks amazing, and my ankle's just really tender, I'd say it's just a bad sprain." They sat down to begin their meal.

"I have bad news," Derek said. Cyndi's eyebrows went up asking what he meant. "My ankle will prohibit me from being able to run away from *Twigg's Enterprises* this evening. You'll have to do Act Three without me," Derek said just before sinking into his first bite of omelet.

"I think I've had enough fun in Galeton. Although I

met a good kisser there once," Cyndi took a bite. They needed the high protein breakfast, and the sunlight and coffee cheered their spirits.

Derek's ringtone sounded. As best he could with a sprained ankle, Derek went to retrieve his phone from his nightstand. He was hopeful it was his mom. Instead, Leena was calling, and it was sometime after 8AM. Derek answered.

"Hey, are you up?" Leena asked while parked outside a coffee shop. They began to exchange everything they had found out the day before. Derek put Leena on speaker and the three of them conversed for over thirty minutes. Several times Leena asked, "You really got bit by a dog?" "Are you sure it was a BB gun?" What Derek was telling her was atypical for the brother she thought she knew.

"Leena, we found more about Gordon and Lyle," Cyndi jumped in, keeping the conversation going. They went into every detail of their findings and what made sense when they combined the information they both had. The only linkage thus far was Gordon McKnight. It appeared that Gordon was Mom's boyfriend, during and after high school, and that Gordon died in a car accident shortly after the writing of the love letter. Leena explained that the obituary indicated that he was on his way to basic training.

"Horrific," Cyndi said, "so sad." After another pause, Leena asked the question that they were so far unable to solve.

"But why him on a list, why the three names? OK, now I understand Lyle is our father, Derek, but what's the motivation of a list—for Mom?" Derek and Cyndi looked at each other, both shrugging their shoulders.

"No idea," Derek said. "And who is Anika Morello?"

"That is exactly what I plan on finding out," Leena responded. "Aunt Eileen has no idea how strange a morning she's going to have."

H unger woke April. Meals weren't on her agenda, yet even more than the hunger, she could feel an overpowering thirst. Though hunger and dehydration forced her up out of bed, she felt somewhat rested. She was glad to have spent another night in the roadside motel. Despite her stomach growling, she felt better than she did the day before. What's more, she couldn't remember any of her dreams. Last night provided some forbearance, a reprieve away from running from a pack of wolves towards a building filled with sinister faces. April shivered as she recalled their voices casting globs of malice down upon her.

Reluctantly, April went to the small bathroom and poured some tap water. She let the water run for a minute, but it stayed the same temperature. She gulped down the tepid water; not only was it lukewarm, but it stung with a sulphury quality. Thirst winning the argument, she poured another cup and gulped it down quickly in an attempt to taste as little of it as she could.

Her stomach, now full of water assuaged the cry for hunger, at least long enough for her to take a shower.

She packed her few things and put a five-dollar bill on her nightstand for the housekeeper she saw yesterday through the door's peephole. While rest helped, April was anxious again today. Being anxious, like every mental state, is a series of degrees of relevancy. And while April was anxious, she was less so than the prior day when she did what she had to do to Annie. It was done and it was over. She would never be haunted by the woman again.

Initially, she was unsure if there would be some satisfaction caused by her actions. Or perhaps she would even regret what she did. But there was satisfaction. And this gratification, she sensed, was the reason she wasn't feeling as apprehensive and as highly strung; this was an important realization for her. It was motivating, and she needed the inspiration. April had two remaining names on her list. Today, in a way would be easier due to the fact that the other person couldn't talk back, couldn't strike back, couldn't counterattack. This aside, April knew it was going to be a challenge to stand before a grave she had never once visited.

She was in no hurry. It was early on Saturday morning and Reading wasn't that far. Eggs sounded good to her. Maybe an omelet, if she could find a restaurant serving breakfast, perhaps a diner. She had fond memories of diners as a child, when her parents would treat her and Eileen to breakfast. She keyed in a search on her phone. As luck would have it, April was less than twenty minutes from what the reviews told her, was a perfect match. She pulled out into the sleepy traffic of a Saturday morning. An omelet it was, she thought to herself. And some nice strong coffee. She would need the energy to cross the two remaining names off her list.

46

It was now Leena's turn to have butterflies. She dreaded the borderline torture she would be performing on her aunt. "What I should be doing is bringing Everly here for a pleasant visit," Leena told her steering wheel, inside her car as she pulled into her Aunt Eileen's driveway.

Aunt Eileen and Uncle Bo lived in a typical suburban three-bedroom ranch on the outskirts of Lansdale. Uncle Bo kept both the house and grounds up meticulously. In retirement, he put in a forty-hour week into their house and vehicles. If he wasn't washing his car, he was waxing it. If he wasn't cleaning the gutters, he was painting the floor of the garage. Every day he had a list and did something related to the house or their vehicles. And that's how he kept himself busy and out of Eileen's line of sight. Uncle Bo's fascination for keeping everything in order probably saved their marriage more than once. As Leena straightened her hair in the rearview mirror, she thought it funny why they called him Uncle Bo. His name was Wesley. It didn't matter. To Derek and

Leena, he was Uncle Bo. And the good part about Uncle Bo having this borderline unhealthy fixation with home and vehicle maintenance was that she was sure to find some time alone with Eileen, while Uncle Bo did whatever he did, outside the house.

"Leena! How are you?" Aunt Eileen opened the door as Leena's feet scaled the front concrete stoop to greet her. After some additional greetings, Uncle Bo, as anticipated, grabbed a travel mug of coffee and headed outside.

"Time to rake, if you don't mind," he said already halfway into the garage.

"He can't sit still, never could," Eileen said, already offering Leena some coffee cake.

"Keeps him young," Leena said. She was as ready as she ever would be, ready to turn the conversation into what she came here for.

"Aunt Eileen, thank you for the coffee cake and thank you for seeing me," she paused, and swallowed a bite of the perfectly baked treat. "I'm down here because of Mom. I have *questions*. Derek and I are worried."

"It's because of how she was acting, isn't it?" Eileen asked somberly. Her mood shifted from the joy of a visit with her niece, to the grave reality of what was happening with her sister.

"We think so," Leena began her story which would set up the many questions she had—armed with the names, her search results, and the findings that Cyndi and Derek unearthed—albeit, avoiding parts of the story relative to the less than lawful means of acquiring some of the clues.

47

Derek insisted that they go for a walk after breakfast. "I need to loosen up this ankle, it's too stiff, and besides, I can't sit still." Cyndi was glad to get some air. Spring was here and there was a warm wind carrying flowery spring-like fragrances. They needed the pick-me-up.

"I'll take it easy on you," Cyndi told Derek, observing his slow, painful gait.

"I could get used to this," Derek informed Cyndi.

"Getting shot, or bitten, or a walk after breakfast?"

"I was thinking a walk after breakfast," Derek retorted, and paused for effect, "with you."

"Why Derek, are you enjoying my company, or are you just saying this because I make killer omelets?"

"Could there be a package deal scenario, a bundle perhaps—because I would be somewhat interested in that." Derek was limping, but the more he walked, the less stiff his ankle became; it was good to move.

Two children, what must have been a brother and sister, were playing in the front yard of a house down the street. They were playing in some remaining driveway puddles in front of their house. A parent was outside with them assessing a flowerbed. "What are you both doing?" Derek asked the children in as non-threatening a voice as possible.

"We're making lakes. Do you think we'll have fish in them later?"

"Quite possible if you keep at it. Good luck." They continued on their walk.

"You like kids, don't you?"

Derek's mind went back to *Unwind*, when he made faces at the young girl eating French fries.

"You know I'm kicking myself for not spending more time with Everly. That's going to change."

"Where is the change of heart coming from?" Cyndi asked.

"This, this thing with Mom—whatever it is—I'm just realizing that all I do is get up and go to work, sleep, watch a game, get in some exercise. I might change my oil, make myself an English muffin, but then it is more sleep, then get up and go to work, repeat. I'm on a hamster wheel. Granted a good one. I like my job, I like my house, but it's not a home. Does that make any sense?"

"You have no idea how much sense that makes, Derek. You could say, that's why I'm here with you now walking down this street. My life with Ken, it held some goodness, I'd be lying if I said there wasn't. But it didn't feel like home. I had a house with Ken, and a really cool dog. But it wasn't home, it never was. The last time I felt home, was when my parents and I were on Clover Drive." She allowed Derek a few moments to take in what she said. "I feel so much better already, like my apartment is home, being closer to where I grew up.

Leena, Everly, you. I haven't even started my job, but I'm going to go in there and hit a homerun. I'm going to drive success in something I care about—animals. And I'm going to grow something that is important and means something. I want to bring so much value to *Vet Med* that they'll always be able to take in strays, give free spaying and neutering, and place pets into their forever homes. I know it's not solving world peace. Nevertheless, I'm excited. So yes, already I feel much more at home."

Derek could relate. Despite the current crisis with his mother, Derek was already starting to feel more connected to his sister, a step closer to the feeling of home.

They walked quietly for several minutes. The silence was anything but awkward, in fact it was quite satisfying. They didn't need conversation to feel close. Derek was caught up in how wonderful a feeling it was just limping along with her in silence.

"Let me ask you this," Cyndi asked, "when you write a list, what do you do with it?"

"Well," Derek started, "I suppose if it was a shopping list and it's something I need to get, I cross it off after I put it in my shopping basket. If it's at work, it's usually a list of action items that I need to accomplish, and then I cross them off."

"What if your mother needs to cross those names off her list?" Cyndi asked Derek. The back of his neck started to tingle.

"That could mean many things," Derek responded. And inside, he thought that not all of the many things were good.

48

Are you there? a text came in from Leena after Derek and Cyndi returned from their walk. *Yes, what's up?* Derek replied quickly. *You better come down here, how soon before you can leave?*

Derek couldn't stand that kind of a teaser. He immediately called Leena and put her on speaker. "All I had to do is say Mom's in trouble and Eileen answered nearly every question I could think of. Not all, but nearly all. Are you ready for this? Annie Morello, she was their babysitter. Eileen doesn't remember too much because, well, she's five years younger than Mom. But," there was a hesitation, "she remembers Mom not liking her—*like at all*. Mom likes everyone. My sense is that when Eileen says Mom didn't like her, it means she abhorred her. It sounds like for a period of two to three years, Annie was the babysitter during the summer and after school—she was the go-to babysitter for anytime that their parents couldn't watch them. I've got more on Gordon, and more on our," another pause, "I've got more on Lyle.

Can you come down, Derek? Cyndi, I'm sure you must have things going on."

"Yes, I do, Leena, and that's to help both of you. I'm coming, too."

"I'm so glad you're back," Leena said. "I'm going to hang out with Aunt Eileen some more, I've got to calm her down. As expected, I worked her up, *a lot*. But I think I can get her in a good place after some downplay. There's a strip mall not too far from here; let's meet there in, say, two hours and fifteen minutes, which will put you here around 1:45PM." Leena gave the address. "From there I want to check out a cemetery near Reading—the three of us can go together. I'll fill you in when you arrive. See you soon."

"A cemetery? All I can say is I'm glad we're not going to *Twigg's* today," Derek said while processing the words from his sister.

"I'll drive," Cyndi informed Derek, "you know, because of your *condition*."

They grabbed some bottled water and Cyndi entered the location that Leena provided in her phone's GPS. "I didn't take a shower today," Derek told Cyndi as he buckled his seat belt.

"One better, I'm still in yesterday's clothes—*all* of yesterday's clothes. I wasn't expecting to spend the night at some random guy's house."

"I'm glad you did, although maybe some other time we'll get a do-over on how it all shakes out. What happened is not exactly how I visualized it happening— you know, spending the night together."

Cyndi waited a few seconds before replying in a coy fashion, "And how, pray tell, did you visualize it happening, Derek G. Densmore?"

"I have a good idea," he was red in the face again, "how about we move on to another subject."

"Fair enough for now, but I reserve the right to press you on this at a later time."

"If you must," Derek replied.

Well into the drive, Derek couldn't help but talk more about Everly and how he wasn't visiting as much as he should. "Next weekend I'm going over—depending upon how this thing with Mom materializes."

"You really are kicking yourself, aren't you?"

"No reason for it, I guess I just got trapped up in my own thing. I'm feeling guilty and more than a little depressed about it."

"Like we talked about, all you have is now. The Derek I know will visit more often. Forgive yourself."

In the car, Derek watched the scenery outside his window, they were passing through some countryside. A few more warm days like this and the entire state's deciduous tree population would be full of green leaves. "You asked me a few days ago if I wanted a family. I said some lame answer, like I thought so. I do, I want a family. I want a little boy or girl, or both and I want to make them waffles in the morning. And I want to come home from work and let them know how much I missed them. And if I'm lucky, they'll come running into my arms screaming, *Daddy's home*." Cyndi just listened.

"It's not all like that, as long as you're aware," Cyndi said finally. "Sometimes they fight, and make messes, and later on, when they're teens they might not give you the time of day, unless they want money."

"Yeah, the good and the bad," Derek replied. "I'm ready for it all, I haven't been, but I am now."

"Well, I'm glad you can bare your soul to me about such thoughts. Now we just need to find you the right woman," Cyndi said, her eyes roaming from side to side, navigating the traffic in front of them.

"Too bad you don't have a sister," Derek said, smirking.

"See if I clean up your next dog bite or make you an omelet again," Cyndi took a second to send Derek a glaring grin.

49

E ither she was much hungrier than anticipated, or it was the best omelet she had ever consumed. The mushrooms, sharp Vermont cheddar cheese, and scallions were perfectly united with fresh garlic, and they used real butter to top it. April was always aware of her calorie intake, but today, after not eating much the last few weeks, she indulged.

The diner reminded her very much of a place her parents took her to when she was a child. Her dad and mom always knew people there and it was as much a socializing event as it was breakfast. Today, she was one of the younger patrons. This was a dying part of Americana—the diner. Good food, easy on the wallet prices in a venue that held no pretenses. And often your plates were delivered from someone you knew, or at the very least, knew your name. She reminisced for almost an hour, savoring her food, and eating every morsel of her eggs and toast. She also enjoyed the water, it was cold and had ice, unlike her drink at the motel. The coffee was better than average, and the caffeine was a blessing to her spirits.

She was trying for low-profile; she didn't want to be seen. Despite what she had already done on her trip, she could not resist striking up a conversation with the waitress. She wanted to feel human and connect with another person.

"This omelet is amazing, it really is," April began.

After learning a few things about the waitress' children, April let her know that she had two children of her own, that they were fully grown and had moved out long ago. April tried not to brag, but she was happy they were successful. She agreed with the waitress, that the worst part about having children is that they grow up. The void it creates in your heart when they move away to live their own lives is irreplaceable. The conversation was moving for both of them, each of them identifying how much they missed their children, needing them, as they once did. They shifted the conversation to the positive, complimenting themselves on being good parents, or at least good enough parents, so that their children were living fulfilling independent lives. That was a good thing indeed, April told herself. "We have that—don't we?" the waitress asked April.

April left the waitress a large tip. After using the restroom, she proceeded back to her car. She had a drive to a cemetery ahead of her, one that she had never been to. The guilt of never going to see Gordon's grave loomed large in her mind. She calmed herself and whispered out loud, "It's OK, April, it's all part of making things right."

After today, there was just one thing remaining on her list and it would take more combined courage than

what she was about to do, and what she did two
nights ago.

50

As expected, Leena spent the next hour calming her aunt down. Eileen's immediate reaction was to call the police. Multiple times, Leena had to go over the fact that they had it in writing from her mom that she would be home Sunday and that involving the police at this point wasn't going to accomplish anything.

"While this isn't like Mom, we have to give her the benefit of the doubt and expect her back on Sunday." Leena added, "Everything will be OK," numerous times. While Leena was certain Eileen would be on edge, and more than likely not sleep tonight, she would wait until late Sunday before taking the next step—placing a call to the police.

Derek and Cyndi would be there soon and so Leena drove to the designated strip mall, in the shape of a giant U with the parking lot as its center. A small bakery caught her attention and she decided to find another coffee. Although her nerves were on overdrive, she had no idea how long a day it would be.

Sipping her coffee in her car, Leena let go a long and deep sigh. She intentionally parked away from the mall so that it would be easier for Derek and Cyndi to spot her. The coffee lacked depth, but it was hot and for that she was thankful. She picked up her notes and began rewriting and circling the important aspects of what she learned from her aunt. Leena had a few ideas on what they might be able to do next. Her thoughts turned to how fortunate they were to have Cyndi back. She wasn't just back for a visit, she was already fully invested in them, and in finding their mother. Away from Cyndi, her thoughts shifted back to Eileen. Leena told herself that she would visit her aunt shortly, for a real visit, and without bringing any drama. Eileen deserved a visit with Everly, too; a more typical kind of family visit where you talk about how fast children are growing up and how good it was to see each other.

51

"See that convenience store up ahead?" Derek asked.

"Yes, do you need a stop?"

"Please, I need to put some weight on my ankle and walk around a little—it's getting stiff." Cyndi pulled into the store's parking lot. Derek got out and limped around the car several times, then proceeded to go inside the store. After several minutes, Derek came out holding something, and he was doing his best to hide what it was. "Put your window down," Derek told Cyndi through the glass. She did as he asked. Derek handed Cyndi a bag of salt and vinegar potato chips, delivered with a big smile. "Thank you for being you," he said as he circled the car to get back into the passenger's seat.

"You're alright, Derek," Cyndi replied. "How did you know?"

"Just a crunch," Derek said, regretting the pun. "OK, let's get going, we'll make it there in time, just about perfectly," Derek informed her. "My ankle, it gets really stiff, but it's better if I move it. Although, I'm not too fast at getting out of your car."

They were back on the road and Cyndi couldn't stop smiling. The bag of chips, while probably one of the smallest gifts she ever received, was one of the best. As Derek was repositioning his legs, she glanced over to him. She was lucky, she told herself. She continued to smile, knowing that the real reason Derek asked to stop at the store wasn't to stretch his stiff ankle. The real reason was to buy her chips and her favorite flavor. The depth of Cyndi's smile came from how well she knew Derek, even after all this time; Derek asked to stop here for her—not him.

"I try to watch my intake of these things," Cyndi informed Derek just before popping two chips into her mouth. Derek nodded in agreement while reaching into the bag for a few chips.

"I have a question for you," Derek took a swig of water. "Did I snore last night?"

"No, I didn't hear you."

"Good, because it is something that I worry about. I've read articles about how some couples who are completely compatible and then *it* happens—the snoring. One person can't stand the nighttime noises from the other and the entire relationship goes south." Cyndi glanced over to Derek with a *why are you telling me this* glare. "I just don't want to snore. I can control the way I act when I'm awake, unfortunately I don't believe I'm capable of doing the same in my sleep." Cyndi reassured him that she didn't hear anything from him during the night. "Good, it happens," Derek said believing Cyndi.

"Are you saying that you would like for me to spend the night with you again to determine if you snore or not?"

"No, I just want to make sure my sleeping body doesn't ruin," he paused, "ruin anything." Cyndi let it go, it was a considerate thought.

"We're getting close. Time to change subjects. Back to your list theory," Derek began again. "If we assume that the names are a list and she's crossing the names off," he waited for the right words to come. "You don't think that she's actually," another long pause, "that she's doing anything bad? I mean she's my mother, she's not capable of causing harm."

"I believe that too, Derek. Deep down, I believe it. As I've said, April is like a mom to me, too. And while extremely unlikely, we should probably consider the fact that sometimes bad things happen to good people." Cyndi's speech stalled.

"What do you mean?" Derek asked, all the while he was looking for reassurance from Cyndi, yet now, she was headed down a different route.

"What I mean is, sometimes people can just break, they snap, their mental facilities crumble. More scientifically, brain neurons can fire differently, and they get rewired." Derek thought on this for a moment. "How much time have you been spending with your mother recently, you know, in the last year?" Cyndi asked.

"Not as much as I should. And that's another thing I'm going to cure—more mom time. More sister time, more niece time, and definitely more mom time."

"I understand. I'm not trying to make you feel guilty. My angle is that I'm wondering if you've noticed things happen, gradually. Could it be that over time, her mental state has been slowly changing, maybe so subtly that you couldn't even detect it?" Derek tried to recall events and times he was at his mother's; the visits were all too few. And why? And then Derek delivered the answer that was the truth, as painful as it was to articulate.

"I'm ashamed, Cyndi. I couldn't even tell you if I noticed a change in her behavior—even if it was a slow change—over time. I don't know my mother very well." He said it. Hearing the words out loud, coming from his own mouth, in front of his best childhood friend—it was crushing. Derek's head started to ache, and it was followed by a feeling of lightheadedness.

"I didn't mean to make you feel bad about any of this, Derek," Cyndi said, glancing over to watch his duress manifest as sweat on his forehead. Derek put down his window to let the air find his brow. After a moment, he put the window back up again.

"You're not making me feel bad, Cyndi," Derek responded after composing himself. "It's just a hard realization. You know, feeling so distant with my only parent. So, a theory is that my mom could have lost her," a long pause, "bearings? That is what you're saying."

"Yes, *could* is the important word here."

"And she is highly agitated. And she has a list of people. And people make lists to cross off whatever is on the list." Derek's lightheadedness turned into full on nausea.

It was Derek that spotted Leena's car first. "There she is, over to the left." Leena had already gotten out of the car and was waving to them. Derek grabbed a folder with several of the critical papers they had obtained.

"Thank you for coming," Leena said while giving them each a warm hug. "Derek, your cheek looks awful," she paused and noticed his limp. "Do you need crutches?"

Derek shrugged it off.

"I've been through the wars."

"There's a bakery-café over there, let's grab a table. It will be more comfortable than sitting in a car," Leena pointed to the bakeshop. As they headed into the bakery, Derek held hard onto his folder with his right hand. Then, something touched his left hand, and then felt the surrounding of fingers, clasping onto and around it. Leena, walking ahead of them opened the door. Behind her, Cyndi walked with a limping Derek, side by side, holding hands. Leena thought to herself that if they weren't there because of their mother's current predicament, that she would have embraced them right there in a giant hug. Seeing two of her favorite people on this earth, together, was immeasurably heartwarming.

52

The bakery was long and skinny with a handsomely tiled two-tone gray floor. As you walked in, to the left were five small round wooden tables, each with three bistro chairs. On the right, was the counter where you ordered along with several large display cases which ran almost the length of the locale. The glass display cases revealed every imaginable delicacy contrived by the pâtissier. Separating the counter and tables ran a narrow walkway. What the establishment lacked in size, it made up with fragrance and appetite aesthetics. On another day, Derek would have been likely to try the baklava that was seductively posing through the glass. His hunger, like Leena and Cyndi's, was missing; their minds were on their mother, and what to do about her.

Leena led them to the fifth and final table allowing for as much privacy as they could find in such a small location. They removed their jackets in silence and sat down. The counter worker started to stare. "We should order something," Cyndi suggested.

"I'll buy. Iced Tea?" Derek asked.

He returned from the counter with the iced teas and lemon wedges teetering on the rim of the frosted glasses. They all sipped at the same time. In sync, the glasses found their way back to the table. Derek and Cyndi waited for Leena, the meeting coordinator, to begin.

"Aunt Eileen and Uncle Bo say hi," it was an awkward place to start, but there was no easy transition with today's topic. "I guess I'll start with Anika, then Gordon, and then Lyle," she reflected before finishing, "Densmore. I know Eileen's not a gossip hound. She would never have told me anything if I didn't say Mom was in trouble."

"Is your aunt OK?" Cyndi asked concerningly.

"Well, yes and no. She's going to be wound up pretty tight until we find Mom, or Mom arrives back home. Annie, or Anika Morello," Leena started, "as I told you already, was Mom and Aunt Eileen's babysitter for years. She was about eight years older than Mom, and about thirteen years older than Eileen," she took a sip of iced tea. "Eileen doesn't have many stories about her. But then again, Mom was half a decade older than Eileen. Mom would have the stories, right? One story that Eileen did have is a time when, in the summer, it must have been when Eileen was nearing five; she awoke from a nap and tiptoed down the hallway and saw Mom standing on one leg in the living room, facing out the window. Annie was laying down on the couch watching TV." She took another sip. "And when Eileen confronted her about it later on, Mom said that Annie always made her do things she didn't want to do—but Mom never confided in Eileen on it. And, aside from that story, she remembers Mom *hating* her. Eileen went on to say that she used to beg her parents not to go anywhere so that they would never have to be babysat by Annie. Mom is never one to make fuss, right? She's always been one to never give up, to just take on what needs to be taken on." A ding sounded as a customer walked in and started to examine the plethora of delectable pastries.

"Mom always used to say, that we have to play the cards we're delt. Good or bad, they're the only cards you have," Derek chimed in.

"She sure did," Cyndi answered. "I'm sure you got that one a lot, but I remember hearing it from her, too." Cyndi continued, "So, do you think Anika Morello was an abusive babysitter? Is that what we're looking at here?"

"In my mind, yes. Certainly not a role model that's for sure. But nevertheless, someone you remember." Leena's iced tea was nearly gone. "A bully, and probably a really bad one. From what I can guess, is that she screwed with Mom's mind for a few years and what's a bully's most powerful weapon? Fear."

"Annie was about eight years older than Mom?" Derek asked.

"Yes, right around there," Leena replied.

"Well, then can you imagine the power dynamic of someone in their teens versus a ten-year-old? As a bully, you have serious power and control at that age. If I'm a bully, I'm going to tell you that if you say anything about the way I treat you, I will hurt you or hurt your sister, or parents—whatever poison that is the most hurtful." Derek finished and stared off into the distance, looking at but not paying attention to the customer now making a purchase.

"Right, your mom had to take that abuse for who knows how long; your aunt was buffered from it due to the age disparity and, well, your mom took the brunt of it."

It was quiet again in the shop after the bell chimed announcing that the customer had left. "That makes me sick inside," Derek finally said, disturbing the silence.

"Me too," Leena answered. Cyndi nodded her head in agreement.

"We close at 3PM, do you mind if I put on the radio?" The young employee behind the counter asked the group in a run-on sentence.

"Please do." They responded in unison.

"Thank you, I like the company as I do my closing chores." They began to hear pop music, loud enough to easily hear lyrics, but not loud enough to make their conversation difficult.

Cyndi began this time, "We've got a list with three people. One of them appears to be an abusive babysitter. A babysitter, where your mom could still be holding quite a grudge. The next name is a curveball then. Derek, you still have the letter?" Derek opened the folder he had brought in and passed the handwritten letter to Leena.

Derek and Cyndi looked at each other apprehensively while Leena read the letter. It was so foreign to her that she asked for more time to reread it. "Whoaaa," is all that Leena could find.

"We had a similar response," Derek replied.

Leena shifted about in her chair. "OK, so I'm halfway between being in shock of Mom having this sort of relationship and still trying to figure out what this, what he, has to do with a horrible babysitter."

"Or our biological father," Derek replied.

A catchy ear worm started on the radio. The employee's spirits were up; her shift was ending and with that, started to get into both the song and her closing duties. Leena started to twirl her pint glass, watching the remaining ice swirl about. "Aunt Eileen was loose lipped about everything, except that. All I know is Lyle Densmore is our father and she believes he lives in or near Reading. And Mom and he had a falling out."

"I'm not a detective, but that last statement is fairly obvious," Derek concluded.

"Do you suppose that some secrets are so buried that it would take more than what's happening now to uncover them?" Cyndi asked.

"I'm not following," Leena asked for more.

"Well, my sense is that your mom didn't ever want you finding anything about your father. As evidence by you asking as children *and* adults, and her always deflecting the topic. And equally as evidence by the divorce decree being tucked away in a stored vehicle, many miles away. Do you suppose that Eileen didn't want to expose anything to you either—about your father, even given the current circumstance?" Leena and Derek looked at each other; what Cyndi was saying was logical.

Derek shook his head. Another song came on, this one not as catchy, but fast paced. The DJ announced that after this song he would be back with weather and the news. "OK, let's get back to what we know. A list, three names. A potentially abusive babysitter that Mom hated, as one would. A boyfriend who was head over heels in love with her and died in a car accident. And we have a biological father that lives in or around Reading." They took a moment and gazed about, all of them thinking hard about commonalities, searching for linkages.

"If we're to take some action, what do we do?" Cyndi posed the question. "Do we go and try and find this Anika Morello? Do we go find the cemetery where Gordon McKnight is buried? Do we do try and find Lyle Densmore, I mean, your father?"

"Biological father," Leena responded.

"Leena, where's Gordon buried?" Derek asked.

"Eileen was fine telling me that. He's buried in Haven's Fields, on the outskirts of Reading. I'm thinking we start there."

"It's been a while since I've been to Reading," Cyndi said. "Anyone game? I mean, it's something."

The DJ came on and informed them that it was going to be significantly warmer next week, and that spring was certainly here. He also announced that a local business was closing its doors. The last thing before more music was a story of a woman's body that was found in North Wales but there were no other details at this time. Leena's eyes bulged and her face tightened. "Um, Anika Morello is from North Wales, it was in my search that I did," Leena said quietly.

"You don't suppose Mom is capable of..." Derek tried not to say it. He tried not to say it earlier in the conversation with Cyndi. But this time it came out. "Murder." The next song started; the young employee started to dance with the broom she was using.

"I'll drive to Reading, let's go. Leena, can you search the address of the cemetery?" Cyndi did her best to bring her friends out of their thoughts of darkness. They had things to do and worrying was the expenditure of useless energy.

53

I t was a solemn ride. At any other time, the three of them reunited, would be laughing at old times, and rejoicing about the things to come. "Coincidence, about the body being found," Cyndi said while looking at Leena in the rearview mirror.

"I don't know what to think," Leena responded. Derek was silent. His thoughts turned back to the week that had started and the week that was now. He was at work earlier this week and he fixed his mom's bathroom wall. He broke the law twice, got injured in some sort of twisted cosmic trifecta, and now was wondering if his mother was doing the unthinkable. He reflected upon what Cyndi had said earlier. Can someone just lose it one day after keeping it all together for years? It was not out of the realm of possibility.

Cyndi tried again. "Any luck finding anything about Lyle?" It was awkward for her to call him anything. Leena was buried in her phone while Derek was buried in his thoughts, peering out the passenger's side window.

"No, not really. There are quite a few Densmores in

Reading, but I'm not having much success with the name, Lyle."

"And your aunt gave you nothing on him?" Cyndi said, desperate to keep the conversation going.

"No, I couldn't believe how tight lipped she was, at least about him. Everything else, she opened up. In hindsight, I'm shocked that she admitted he was our biological father. Nothing else, well other than he lives somewhere near Reading."

Derek could stay quiet no longer. "We are going to Reading, why?" Doubt started to infiltrate his thinking.

"We are going to try and find your mom," Cyndi replied as she passed a large silver SUV. "We can't give up hope." For the next ten minutes, the inside of the Prius was completely silent. Normally, the three introvert-leaning individuals savored quiet. But during this window of time, their thoughts ran in all directions; the silence was painful as it allowed their minds to go to places they never imagined—dark places, seeing things unfold about their mother that were inconceivable.

"We're getting close," Cyndi finally said. They had been in the car for forty-nine uncomfortable minutes. "The cemetery's coming up on the right in about three minutes." Derek's only comfort was in Cyndi's voice. Through observing her strength, he clawed back from the darkness of his thoughts. He looked up at her, with her hands on the steering wheel, eyes on the road. It was then that he convinced himself that no matter what happened, she was here now, and it was a gift. She filled a chasm of the recently revealed seclusion in his life. He vowed to himself that he would not only find more closeness to his sister, brother-in-law, niece, and mom, he would stay connected to the woman beside him forever.

It didn't matter if they were simply friends, he couldn't bear to be without her in his life.

On the right, as Cyndi had foretold, a large black iron gate was open, inviting them into Haven's Fields. It was as typical of a cemetery as one could picture. To the left and right of the gate was a stone wall, cobbled together by rocks a century and a half ago. The entrance was paved, at one time. Weeds sprouted up everywhere amongst the remaining pieces of cracked blacktop. In certain places, potholes could swallow a tire. Each of them looked upon the cemetery with eyes that wondered how much investment is really given to the deceased. The dead have no voice to ask for new pavement.

"This place is enormous," Derek started, "it looks to be at least two or three levels." The first section was flat with vast rows of gravestones appearing on their left and right.

Soon, Cyndi's car started to climb up the narrow, ragged, one lane road. "I hope we don't meet anyone coming down," Leena said from the backseat. Just as Derek suggested, after they ascended, things leveled off again—it was multi-tiered. Just as the first level, the second level revealed seas of headstones in every direction. This section, somewhat newer, offered multiple turns in both directions. "I don't use this cliché often, but this is going to be a needle in a haystack," Derek said in a dejected tone.

"The place keeps going," Leena was conducting some backseat driving as she pointed ahead. Sure enough, the cemetery had a third level. Up another hill, they leveled off once more. While not as large as the second level, the final level also contained a considerable number of headstones.

"I've never seen such a large cemetery," Cyndi

exclaimed, "and no one to be seen—anywhere." She took one of the left-hand turns, it was more a dirt path than what could be classified as a road. She pulled over onto as much grass as she could, trying to respect the nearby burials. "Top to bottom search?"

They split up, attempting to cover more territory. No living soul was around other than the three of them. They began their search with nothing to go on other than to search for a stone that was somewhere close to forty years old and possessed the name of Gordon McKnight.

Derek entered his section of the search and began to walk steadily up a row and back down the next. So many different names, last and first, the many different nationalities, different religions, the different ages of a lifespan. The slight lift in spirits he had while near Cyndi a few moments ago was fully depleted. The heaviness of everything began crashing against the ocean of death that surrounded him. His thoughts turned to the ultimate sadness of each passing stone he encountered. They all had lives. They breathed the same air he was pulling into his lungs right now. They ate meals, went to school, had friends, families, hopes, diseases, had desires, had children, found love, lost love, were lonely, were happy, were crestfallen, had jobs, took out the trash, lost parents, some lost children, they walked in the rain, they came out of the cold, they cut grass, they sang songs, they got their hair done, they played tag as children. Now, all that remained was a small plot; a memorial on a grassy plain, on some acreage, grouped together in a row with other strangers. The weight of the emotional awareness, for Derek, was too much to bear. He picked up his pace and forced his mind away from the melancholy focus. All he wanted was to be with Cyndi. Better yet, to be sitting down for dinner with he and his mom, with Cyndi, with Leena, Eli, and little Everly. He fantasized about the dinner conversations they would have about Cyndi's return, about Everly's upcoming launch into kindergarten, about his job, Eli's job, about how excited Leena was about going back to the lab next year, and about how everyone was doing at the energy company where his mom worked for decades.

He was close to finishing his defined section. Leena was heading back to the car and Cyndi was also finishing up with her back row. Nothing. And really, Derek thought, even if they found what appeared to be his mother's boyfriend's grave from long ago, what good would it do?

They found their way back to the Prius. "Nothing, you?" Cyndi asked. Leena shook her head.

"The only thing I found over there was depression," Derek conveyed the mood of the party.

"Let's try the next section," Cyndi was the leader now, the two siblings continued to be exceedingly distracted.

They descended back onto the second level, it was the largest and most daunting. "Do we tackle the left section first?" Cyndi asked.

"Wait," Leena interrupted, "there's a car over there now. It wasn't there when we first got here—we had the place to ourselves." About a football field over to their right was a car parked on one of the offshoots. "Hold on. Does that look like Mom's car?" Leena asked Derek.

"I can't tell from here. Besides, all I can see is the back. But it could be a Ford Escape. It's the right color," Derek replied.

"I have an idea," Cyndi started to take the next right-hand turn, it was still a long way from the other vehicle.

"Your mom doesn't know what car I drive, and she would never expect to see me walk out of the blue in a random cemetery near Reading, Pennsylvania. You both stay in the car. I'll walk closer to whoever it is and see what I can see. I'll be discreet, pretending to be looking for a grave." She opened the glove compartment and pulled out the green cap she wore on the outing with Derek. She put on her sunglasses even though it was a mostly overcast day. "What do you think? Could April spot me?"

"Doubtful, you're too much out of context. And if that is Mom, she's focused on other things," Leena informed her.

"Stay in the car," Cyndi once again ordered.

"Are we dogs?" Leena and Derek asked at the same time. At any other time, in any other location, they would have all laughed together, but not today.

Cyndi began to leisurely walk along the same path as she parked, towards but not directly at the parked vehicle. She looked at the gravestones, only occasionally glancing over to her acquired target. "She's good at this," Leena said, filling the car's silence.

"You should see her escape from danger," Derek answered. "We've got some stories for you."

"I noticed—you look horrible. How are your—legs?"

"Both are sore in different ways. I'll live."

Cyndi was making progress and was almost at the furthest row, inching towards her goal. They guessed she was only ten or so car lengths away now. Then Cyndi ducked down and started to make her way to the vehicle, using it as a screen. "What in the *freakin' hell* is she doing?" Derek asked. It was a long way off and hard to make out. They wished for binoculars. As far as they could tell, Cyndi was very close, if not almost touching the passenger's side of the vehicle. A few seconds later, she did a 180-degree spin and started to bolt in the same crunched up fashion until she felt she was far enough away. Then, like nothing happened, she slowly walked over to a random headstone and knelt down. She spent the next several minutes, from how it appeared, talking directly to the large chunk of chiseled granite.

"She always excelled in drama class," Leena said, "look at her go." Cyndi was still a long distance from the Prius. In the distance, they heard a car door shut. Derek and Leena looked at each other as they started to watch a dark blue Ford Escape turn and start to head back towards their direction.

"It's *Mom!*" Derek shouted. "Duck!" He and Leena slouched as low as they could within the Prius, doing their best to fit their visible parts below the windows. The SUV slowly drove out of view and turned to the lower level, making its way to the exit. Because of how far down they had compacted themselves, Derek and Leena had no idea if their mother slowed down to look at them. After enough time went by, they recoiled and straightened to a more normal car sitting position. Cyndi was running towards them.

A minute later, but what felt like much longer, Cyndi arrived gasping for breath. "Your mom—that was April," it was the first thing that came from her lips.

"Yes, we could tell. She didn't see you, did she?" It would be a few more minutes before Cyndi had a sufficient enough compliment of oxygen.

"No," she started, "I think she was aware," they watched her chest call for more air, "of me, I mean of another person," her lungs took in more, "in the cemetery," and she breathed deeply once more, "visiting, mourning at a grave." She got into the car and took the time needed to fully catch her breath. "You will never believe what I saw through the passenger's side window of your mom's car." Leena and Derek waited as patiently as they could.

"What, what did you see?" they asked assertively. Cyndi was now breathing normally.

"I saw a knife, half hidden under a black notebook, more like a leather-bound journal. It was a good-sized knife, old, but big. I'm no expert, but I would say a hunting knife."

54

After the run back to the car and getting caught up on what Cyndi had discovered in her undercover reconnaissance, they concluded that too much time had gone by to try to catch up to their mother. "I'm not sure why we hid. I think we were in shock. In reality, Leena and I should have jumped out and tried to catch her," Derek said shaking his head.

"Yes, I panicked, I guess," Leena responded. Due to the multiple levels and the angle they were parked, they hadn't seen which direction April took as she exited Haven's Fields. What's more, going either direction could take you into Reading proper, if that were the direction she was even headed.

A knife in her car. A visit to her dead boyfriend's—perhaps fiancé's—grave. What could it all mean? And then there was Annie Morello back in North Wales. Was she the body that was found? What did make sense is that there were three names, and assuming she had already gone to find Anika Morello, she then came here to find Gordon McKnight. There was only one name remaining on the list. Derek's thoughts circled back once again to the conversation he and Cyndi had about lists and what people did with lists; when you're done with an item on the list, you cross it off and move to the next item. While they had no idea what was going on in the mind of their mother, nor her motives, they at least now had a good idea of her next step. And unless Cyndi was mistaken, there was a knife involved.

They continued to sit and contemplate things in the car with the windows cracked for air. The sky was threatening rain. Cyndi spoke next, "Your search for Lyle didn't yield much, Leena?"

"No, there are Densmores in Reading, but no Lyle, not even an L. Densmore." She pulled up her phone and listed the choices. "Alan Densmore, Charles Densmore, Vincente Densmore. I found a few female names, too. Janice Densmore and Roxy Densmore. And there are three with first initials. B. Densmore, D. Densmore, and Z. Densmore."

"We've got to find the right one, and we've got to get there soon. If Mom is mentally unstable, we've got to ensure she doesn't hurt anyone," Derek said, choosing not to think about what might have happened to Anika Morello. Derek turned to Leena, "Eileen's got to come clean about Lyle."

"Your turn, Derek, I can't torment Aunt Eileen anymore today," Leena answered. They circled the second cemetery level and found Gordon McKnight's headstone. Like many of the other stones that surrounded them, it was also made of granite. A small terra cotta planter with bright purple hyacinths stood upon the stone's bottom ledge. "Beautiful flowers. Mom?" Leena asked.

"Had to be, it looks new—like it was just placed

there," Derek replied, remembering them from his last visit with his mom. He recalled her strong reaction when he asked if she would like him to plant them. It felt long ago.

The stone stood waist high, and the engraving could still be read easily. Derek read it out loud.

Gordon E. McKnight
Born – February 16, 1965
Died – August 22, 1983
Loved by All, Missed by All

Leena took several photos of the gravestone and headed back to the car. "Let's go somewhere else, anywhere else. I'll call Aunt Eileen," Derek said, wanting to leave this place as soon as they could. While it wasn't dark, the sun was beginning to make its way down, more than likely hovering just above the horizon—the heavy gray clouds intensified the gravity of what they were all feeling.

Cyndi chose to go north after exiting the cemetery. After several minutes, they found a middle school with an empty parking lot. Derek checked his reception and limped out of the car. Leena and Cyndi started talking as Derek walked towards one of the school's outdoor basketball courts. It wanted to rain but was still holding back. He looked down on the court. It had recently been resurfaced. With a large heavy sigh, Derek retrieved his contacts and dialed his aunt.

"Hi Aunt Eileen, it's Derek." There was a long pause before the response came.

"Hi Derek, I guess I was expecting your sister. Is everything OK, did you find April? I mean, your mom?"

"We found her for a moment, I should say, we stumbled upon her, but we lost her. The good news is we found her."

"Thank goodness," it was evident that Eileen was quite relieved to hear this. She said it again, "Thank goodness."

"Aunt Eileen, we need a favor. We're still worried about Mom."

"What can I do, Derek? I don't know what she's doing."

"We don't either, but we are almost certain where she's headed next." Derek waited for a moment, thinking about the best approach; direct seemed the best. "Leena and I believe she's going to Lyle's; we need to know where he lives, his address."

"Derek, I swore to your mom I would never speak to you about your," she paused, "Lyle."

"Yes, I can see that you did. And I'm asking you to break that promise. You're worried, Leena's worried, I'm worried. You have to trust us that breaking that promise is the right thing to do given the circumstance. There's something we found in her car, well," he stumbled, "we want to make sure she isn't in *danger*." He emphasized the last word and in doing so, Eileen's next words were shaky and fueled by emotion.

"I hope she forgives me." Derek waited, quietly. His aunt started up again, with a quiet, saddened voice. "He always went by his middle name. Lyle is his middle name. His first name is Derek. I knew him as Lyle. He was always good to April, you know, they had a good relationship. But for April, he wasn't Gordon. And she and Lyle had a major falling out," she stopped. Derek's face flushed as realizations bubbled up inside of him. He was named after his father. Derek G. Densmore, he was not a true junior, but still his father's namesake. But instead of Lyle, Derek was given Gordon for a middle name. It was a lot to take in. "Derek, are you there?"

"Yes, Eileen, sorry."

Eileen continued, "The falling out part, you don't need to know any details. I'll give you his address, or at least the address I last knew." Derek's head was still spinning as he keyed the address she provided into his phone's GPS.

"Aunt Eileen, thank you. I promise we'll call you as soon as we find out more—as soon as we find her. And Aunt Eileen, you did the right thing."

Once again Eileen whispered in a dejected tone, "I hope she forgives me."

Derek walked back over to the car. Cyndi and Leena were still engaged in dialogue. "I have his address," Derek said with a stone face. "His name is Derek." The friends looked at each other with eyebrows raised and then turned back to Derek. Neither Leena nor Cyndi could find any words. "And you can probably guess where my middle name came from."

55

Without conversation, they headed to the address Eileen provided to Derek. Leena was busy in the back seat searching on her phone. The D. Densmore that she could find matched the address Eileen had given them. After more research she learned that Derek L. Densmore of Reading was a small business owner. "I found a small blurb of an article from a while ago online. It says here that he took over the business from his mother and father twenty years ago."

"What is the business?" Derek asked, nothing could surprise him anymore today.

"Insurance, auto, home, life," Leena replied. "Without paying for a background search, it looks like he's married, but I can't be sure."

They passed several desolate streets loaded with buildings in various states of needing repair. One more mile, and the scenery started to change. Sidewalks were upkept, and trees lined the streets complementing the recently renovated streetlights. One more block and they arrived at their destination. Cyndi parked across the street. They looked over at a three-story brick apartment building. On the front in large black letters, it read, 1743 Avenue E. The windows were tinted light smoke gray. They could see inside the front lobby; a large leather couch and matching chairs greeted those who entered. Beyond that, they could just make out an elevator. It was a nice building, slightly sterile, Derek thought, but clean and well kept.

"Now what?" Cyndi asked. "I hate to do this, but I'm getting hungry, and I could really use a bio break," Cyndi continued. Other than wait for their mother to arrive—if she was coming here at all—they had made no plans.

"I'm anxious, but I could use the same. I'll start with the bio break, and then I could use some hydration," Leena agreed with Cyndi. "That's three of us," Derek admitted.

"Let's go find somewhere quick and then circle back. What if your mom doesn't come tonight? I'm not looking forward to spending the night here." Cyndi paused and started again, "April said she would be back home Sunday, she might come tomorrow. Afterall, it's not a long drive back to Edwardsville."

"We don't know what's fact and what's fiction right now," Leena answered. Derek's mind swirled with thoughts; *body found, three names on a list, Derek L. Densmore, agitation, knife, gravestones, death.*

They found a delicatessen less than five minutes away and ordered sandwiches and two bottles of water each. The idea that Cyndi planted in their minds about staying in the car overnight inspired them to stay hydrated at the very least. Derek stretched his legs one more time. The stiffness in his ankle wasn't relenting, and the dog bite was tender. He wondered what the cashier thought of him with his red welted cheek when he paid with a bent and bruised credit card.

56

This time, April found better lodging than she had the night before. The hotel was no doubt part of a national chain, and it afforded a pool and a small, unpretentious restaurant. She was grateful to be able to order room service here. Before heading to her room, she retrieved her overnight bag from the hatch of her Escape, proceeded to the passenger's side and tucked her journal and the knife under her left arm. April felt compelled to clean the knife again before her next visit.

Entering her room, she placed all that she carried on the second queen bed that she planned not to sleep in. April wished for more time with Gordon. Initially, she had the entire cemetery to herself, until she spied a woman who was acting peculiarly. April wasn't suspicious because no one knew she was there. Still, the woman she spotted acted odd, and it was off-putting. *People will be people and you can't control them*, April thought as she took off her shoes and threw herself down on the bed she planned on sleeping in.

Despite the visit being cut short by the strange acting, intrusive woman, April felt relieved. In all of the time since Gordon's death, she had never visited his final resting place. In fact, there was a time many years ago that she had made a commitment to never visit his grave. That commitment now seemed so senseless, so reckless. She thought about how passionately we stand on the convictions we have when we're young, so adamant that we are right, and everything or everyone else is wrong. For a moment, April felt embarrassed by her younger self.

While today was easier than it was a few nights ago, it was certainly much easier than what she had to do tomorrow. Nevertheless, her visit to Gordon's grave was a significant emotional drain.

April found the number for room service and ordered a chicken salad and a glass of Cabernet Sauvignon. Yes, she thought, tomorrow was the greatest test. Finding the courage to confront and banish this demon would take all of her strength and willpower. Her strategy wasn't complicated; ensure he was home alone, to take the knife, and to go in strong and finish it, quickly. No matter how many times she relived this plan, it caused her hands to tremble and her palms to sweat. April wished she had ordered two glasses of wine. She was grateful to have brought a sleeping aid. Tonight, her hyperactive mind would require chemical assistance if she were to find rest in any capacity.

57

Night was approaching. Cyndi parked in the best viewing location she could find, across from Lyle's apartment. The three felt slightly better after having eaten but they were apprehensive about what was to come. The streetlights, activated by sensors, snapped on.

"Will she come tonight or tomorrow?" Cyndi asked the question no one could answer.

"I can only guess," Derek responded. They aligned on taking three-hour shifts; the driver's seat, having the best view, was to be the lookout spot. When your shift was done, they agreed, you would wake up the next shift taking person, if asleep, and they would take over in the driver's seat.

No one felt like talking. Once again, Derek's mind raced to the purpose of a list and the act of striking out the prior item when it was accomplished, or in some cases, eliminated.

Time does many things. Time flies, it goes, it creeps,

it ticks, it wakes us, it schedules our days, it dictates how long we work, or how long a game should be played. Every second on a clock has the same interval between the prior second and the future second. Seconds pass without fail and are always the same. Tonight though, they were not watching a game, or a movie, or engulfed in a good book. And while they were with each other, as close-knit friends, when time usually passes by rapidly, the situation they found themselves in took full command over the hyper slow passage of time.

The shifts started at midnight. Cyndi was adamant about taking the first shift. Leena and Derek flipped a coin for the second and third. Landing on heads, the quarter dictated that Leena's shift would be from 3AM-6AM. Derek would finish up in the morning or whenever they were all awake.

Spending a night in a car is indicative that something, somewhere, isn't right for three people who had beds to go to. That was Derek's thought after his first attempt to go to sleep next to Cyndi. Nothing about this felt right—nothing about it. Leena was in the back seat and took advantage of the extra space to uncoil herself into whatever the most comfortable position was given the space confines.

"I can't sleep," Derek whispered to Cyndi.

"You just barely shut your eyes," Cyndi returned the whisper without turning to him. Her eyes were peeled on the apartment building and then from time to time, they shifted to her side view mirror and then scanned the building's surrounding area. She was taking her role as surveillance officer seriously.

"Are you cold?" Derek asked with more whispers.

"Yeah, but it will keep me awake. My nose and toes are in that numb place."

"Same here, and I've never been able to fall asleep with cold feet," Derek answered. "Seriously, what are we doing here?" Derek's doubts surfaced repeatedly, more so when the darkness surrounded them. Several cars an hour would drive by, parallel to them. It wasn't a busy street and there wasn't enough traffic where you had a rhythm of mechanical swishing; you were unable to predict when the next car would pass. This also was impacting Derek's ability to find sleep.

"We're here to stop your mother from doing something she will regret. And hopefully bring her home, or to the hospital, somewhere safe," Cyndi paused her whisper for a moment. "Or whatever it takes to get her in a good place again." Another car passed them, this time going in the opposite direction as they were pointed. The headlights from these oncoming vehicles were another strike against sleep.

"I'm praying that she hasn't *already* done something. You can't kill a man that's dead," Derek referenced their trip to the cemetery, "but with Annie or Anika, whatever her name is, well…" His whisper ceased without finishing his thoughts. He began again, "I'm sorry you have to spend your weekend like this." Cyndi continued with her vigilance, staring out the windshield.

"Don't apologize. I'm where I want to be, with my friends." Derek couldn't tell if Cyndi was calmer than he and Leena because it wasn't her mother, or if she was just naturally more even keeled at all times. Until last Wednesday, it had been many years since he had seen her. He leaned towards her being calmer because that was her essence. She was the diffuser of tension, and fantastic at handling difficult people and conflict. Perhaps, Derek thought, her soul was tensionless and that made her be able to personify an aura of serenity.

He stole a few more glances of her right profile. *What an amazing woman, what an amazing person,* he thought. She had strengths and depth he had not seen in his prior relationships. Her sense of compassion alone, being in this car, sacrificing her bed and the amenities of her apartment, was overwhelming to him. Without realizing it, he placed his left hand upon her leg above the knee and squeezed a few times in a loving fashion. Derek realized at that moment, with that action, he had just told Cyndi that he loved her—without saying it. Her right hand topped his and she duplicated the gentle squeeze back unto his hand. He pondered the magnificence of what he was experiencing and how much his heart wanted this. For so many years he pushed Cyndi aside in his mind, after all, she was too good for him. And she had moved away and set a new life course. He also marveled at the dichotomy that was at play. At the same time, he felt the most distraught he had ever felt, and it collided with feeling the depths of love for Cynthia Vaughn. The realization was overwhelming and because of it, in addition to the cold feet, and the oncoming headlights, and the random traffic pattern, his dog bite, sore cheek, and throbbing ankle robbed any chance of him falling asleep. Derek moved his hand and massaged Cyndi's neck. "Oh, my goodness," Cyndi whispered, "how can I keep watch when you're making me that relaxed?"

"You'll find a way," Derek replied. He wanted to demonstrate to her how much it meant for her to be here now, with them, with him.

Leena took over for Cyndi at 3AM as planned. "Who wants the back seat?"

"I just got comfortable," Derek said, not having to

whisper with all of them being awake. Cyndi found her way into the back seat and positioned herself into the same contorted ball as Leena had.

58

Derek tried again to fall asleep in what few positions he could find in the passenger's seat of a Toyota Prius. The traffic waned but the streetlights still pierced through the car windows. After forty minutes he whispered to Leena. "I can't sleep, it's useless."

"Back there, I think I got about an hour, but between the cold and the streetlights, I'm craving my own bed." Derek nodded in agreement.

"I was thinking how surreal this is. Here we are on a stakeout for Mom. *Mom* of all *people*. I can't remember worrying about her, not once, and we're in a car worried sick about her and what she's doing and what she's done." Leena let what he said sink in. "She's got a knife; how can this even be happening?" Derek finished.

"I can't remember a time either. Never. I'm with you. I've never worried about her, *ever*." Leena finished her thought.

Derek whispered back, "And here we are, worried sick private investigators in the middle of the night."

"Didn't see this coming," Leena agreed with the entire situation being surreal, being beyond anything they could fathom just a few days ago.

Leena changed the subject. "Is Cyndi asleep?" Derek looked back and observed her chest moving up and down in a slow regular pattern.

"I'd say so, by the looks of it." In an even quieter whisper, "Cyndi, are you asleep?" No response came from the backseat. "Yup, I'd say so," Derek repeated.

"How are you feeling? Your cheek looks nasty. How is your dog bite?"

"Believe it or not I'd trade my sprain for another BB gunshot to the other cheek. The dog bite is fine, just some irritation. Truman wasn't able to get a good hold of me, thank goodness."

"Any idea if the dog was up to date, you know, the rabies thing?"

"I should have asked him at the time," Derek responded.

"Touché," Leena forced a smile. "There is one good thing out of this."

"What's that?" Derek asked.

"You and Cyndi, it's a very good thing."

"You're not kidding. I've been living my life, in a routine. Work, eat, sleep, you know the drill. Then Cyndi appears like a genie. I haven't been looking for the L word. It's Sunday morning, and I've seen her every day since Wednesday after not seeing her for years. And now, you know what, I don't want to spend a day without her." Derek finished his confession. "Look at me, who *am* I?"

"It happens, Derek, even to the best of us. When you called Aunt Eileen at the school, Cyndi told me something, I'm pretty certain you'll find out, if you haven't already guessed." Leena performed a sweep with her eyes, performing the due diligence of her role as the lookout. In a hushed whisper, almost inaudible, she leaned towards Derek's ear, "She's here because of you, Derek. Ken wasn't a bad guy. It's just, she has always had a thing for you. Even in high school, she'd ask me if you might be interested in her. I was your sister; I didn't want to be involved in any of that. Anyway, yes, she's here because she got a great job. *But* she wanted to be near you. She said she would have kicked herself if she didn't make the effort. Worse case, she would be closer to us both and rekindle our friendship." Derek's ears heard the whispering from his sister, but the words were hard to comprehend. He found it incomprehensible that someone as amazing as Cynthia Vaughn was here now, largely because of him.

"I'm stunned," is all Derek said. "I dreamed about us, but she's always been out of my league."

"Derek," Leena paused to make sure he was paying full attention, "that's what she said of you."

More time passed and Derek tried again to fall asleep and started to bargain with his unconscious for a nap. "If I can just have fifteen minutes," he asked for sleep to take him away. No sleep came and 6AM was upon them, and dawn began to take shape. Derek yawned and watched the streetlights kick off from the driver's side, while performing what was now his task. He scanned the apartment building to his left and the streets ahead of him and from time to time, he checked the side mirror for activity. The minutes passed slowly; slower than when he tried to find a few minutes of the sleep that evaded him.

fter so much time passes in utter silence and the loudest sound that is made is a whisper, Derek's first thought upon waking was how incredibly loud shouting can be when done at the top of one's lungs. It was Cyndi, and she repeated her last exclamation as if Leena and Derek didn't hear her the first time. "*Derek, you fell asleep*! Your mom, I just saw her —she went into the building, *knife, she had a knife!*" She paused and started to lower her voice, "She had the knife, not even concealing it and she was walking really fast." The amount of adrenaline that was now circulating throughout the small cabin of Cyndi's Prius was palpable.

Derek finally found sleep in the early morning while seated in the driver's seat. It came at the expense of the responsibility of being an effective lookout. The goal had been to spot her in enough time so that they could prevent her from entering the building where their father lived. Leena, Cyndi, and Derek all looked around dumbfounded at each other. They had no plan if she went inside the apartment building before they could stop her.

"I must have just nodded off, I'm so sorry," Derek apologized. His face showed Leena and Cyndi how disappointed he was with himself.

"It's fine," Leena said, "but what do we do now?" There was more silence. "Should we go in?" Leena asked.

"We don't know what floor he lives on. Your mom has got to be there already—the way she was moving," Cyndi said. "Do we call 911?" They all thought on this. Their mother, who they observed had been in a highly agitated state, was carrying a knife and going into their estranged father's home with haste. The disbelief of what was happening collided with what they knew they should do. They weighed it all again. Their mom lied about being at their aunt's. Her demeanor was not herself. The list of names they found. A knife. Her babysitter, her old boyfriend's grave, her ex-husband, a dead woman found.

Cyndi described again how fast she was moving towards the building, as if on a mission. "I think we need to call 911. If we don't, and the unthinkable happens, we're complicit, too," Leena stated. Derek and Cyndi thought it over. A murder might be happening right now, and there they were, paralyzed with their next move. Derek's guilt crept into his mind. His failure to stay awake was costly. If he had stayed awake, fulfilling his duty as a lookout, they would have accosted his mother in time, and all of this could have been avoided. Derek started to feel physically ill.

Leena reached for her phone. She had never called 911 before. She looked into the eyes of Derek and turned her head to Cyndi. After finding alignment in their eyes, she began to dial 9... 1... and before her finger found the final number, the glass door of the apartment building opened. April Densmore exited the building and was running hastily to her blue SUV—she no longer carried the knife. It was hard to get a good visual read because of the distance, but it looked like she was sobbing as she fled the building. Leena put down her phone.

April Densmore found her vehicle. The drive would be good, she thought. It would calm her down as much as anything could after what she just did. The last few days were some of the most emotional in her life. What she just did to Lyle was freeing, but it came at a significant emotional toll. It was over. She did what she had come to do, and she finished it. She allowed the tears to flow. Everyone drives and cries at one time of their life, she thought. She sped towards home. Her children were expecting her back today.

60

"We have to follow her," Derek turned the car's ignition. For the next hour and ten minutes, Leena, Cyndi, and Derek followed their mother back in the direction of her home in Edwardsville. Derek did his best to keep enough distance so that his mother wouldn't suspect being followed. They agreed that they would call 911 after confronting her. Derek's stomach was a mess. He forced his thoughts away from what his mother just did, it was too much for him to deal with.

Leena called Eli and filled him in with some of the details. She didn't want to get him too roused. The important thing, she told him, was that they were headed back home and were following Mom. Just after she hung up, Derek saw the fuel gauge light turn on. As far as a Prius goes on a tank of gas, it still needs replenishment. They would lose their mother in their pursuit.

As fast as she could, Cyndi filled her car up at the first convenience store they could find. Leena retrieved three coffees while Cyndi pumped the gas. It had been a long night and they needed the warmth and caffeine that piping hot coffee afforded. This time Cyndi drove. "We're not really very good at this private investigator thing," Cyndi said after finishing her coffee. It wasn't an attempt at humor, rather it was her acknowledgement of failing them. It was her car and she felt horrible about not filling it up when they had time yesterday. While it seemed humorous, her statement was as the truth. Not only had Derek failed as an effective sentry, but she also overlooked filling the tank of the Prius.

"She's got to be going home, right?" Leena asked. "I have no idea where else she would go." They had just under thirty minutes left on the drive before arriving at 23 Clover Drive. Their thoughts went to the unthinkable, and they began picturing their mother being taken away by the police, escorted to incarceration, to be arrested and then tried. Trial for murder, or murders. The enormity of it all, Derek thought. Not only would he lose his mother today, he and Leena would have to handle the publicity of this. He wondered how he could deal with the awkwardness of work when this was all out in the public. There was shame and embarrassment, without a doubt, but the real discomfort would be watching others watch him—forever keeping him at arm's length. Even his friends would distance themselves from a friend whose mother went crazy one April, just as the weather began to turn away from winter and the hyacinths emerged from their hibernation. Moving away from here was the only tolerable thing, Derek thought. Running, hiding, changing his name. And then there was Cyndi; she just arrived back. She would be forced to keep her distance from the Densmores. Just as Derek started to see a path to Cyndi, it was now gone. He would lose his mother. And he would lose Cyndi for the second time.

Their family—how would they react? He thought of Aunt Eileen and Uncle Bo getting drawn into this affair. The forever daily mental anguish of your own sister doing something as heinous as these acts. Poor Aunt Eileen, Derek thought. And then there was the house, where so many childhood memories were born, with Leena and with Cyndi. If their mom went to prison, what were they to do with the house? *How can something good turn itself upside down in such a blink of an eye?* he thought.

The silence continued within the car. Their thoughts had no escape from the ugliest Sunday they had ever known. The longer the silence lasted, the more there was no desire to break it. Derek placed his hand on his abdomen. There were no benign butterflies there today, only menacing, wretched, foreboding ones. The wrenching feeling culminated when they took a left onto Clover Drive. Derek thought of the thousands of times he returned to the family home, to this very house. He had never known the feeling of not wanting to be here, until now.

Fifteen more seconds lapsed, Cyndi obeyed the neighborhood speed limit. There, parked in the driveway of the sage green cape of 23 Clover Drive, with a moss-covered roof, and two large unique budding trees, was a blue Ford Escape. Their mom had returned home. At the back of her vehicle was a black and white police car. Its roof rack lights spun indignantly, announcing the spectacle that was the Densmore family home to the rest of Clover Drive.

61

"We don't have to call the police," Cyndi said, being the first words in over twenty minutes.

"How could they be here already?" Derek asked.

"Annie Morello, that was days ago now," Leena responded from the back seat with dread in her voice. It started to downpour. A strong April rain opened from the sky, just days before May.

Being bit by a dog and shot by a BB gun didn't feel all that strange now to Derek. Getting out of the car with neighbors already watching, pretending to rake their lawns in the rain, this was the weirdest, most unorthodox thing he had ever done. There was nothing left to do but go in and deal with whatever was happening inside his childhood home. Derek's stomach continued to cramp, and the pain radiated to his feet. Slowly, with a limp, he got out of the car. The three of them somberly found their way to the front door. All of the smells of spring hit them, made stronger by the many springs they had experienced together in this very location, together as children.

62

Just as they approached the front door, two police officers, by the first names of Lucinda and Isaac, judging by their name tags, were leaving and waved their thankful goodbyes to April Densmore. Cyndi, Derek, and Leena stared shockingly at one other. "Hello," Officer Lucinda said, "we were just leaving."

After more staring, Cyndi was able to find a few words, "Hi. Have a good one." Both officers looked at Derek suspiciously, spending considerable time examining his face. Then, in the car they went, shutting off their lights and they proceeded to leave Clover Drive.

"What in the living *Hell* is going on?" Leena said, she was the first to enter the house. Derek and Cyndi followed and stood within the entrance. "Mom?" A door closed from the downstairs bathroom and out walked April Densmore.

"Leena. Derek. Cyndi, what on earth, Cynthia Vaughn? What are you all doing here? Derek, what happened to your face?" April's face expressed complete shock.

"Mom, we came for you. We know about your trip, we followed you home from… Lyle's this morning. We're so worried for you."

"You followed me? How long? What do you know?"

Derek chimed in, "We think we know you visited Anika Morello, we know you visited Gordon McKnight's grave, and we know this morning, that you went to see your ex-husband, our biological father."

April's face expressed many emotions in a brief amount of time. At first, seeing the three of them there together put a smile on her face. Then, at the mention of being followed, her expression soured. When Derek mentioned that they knew about her visiting Lyle, and that they knew who Lyle was, her face turned despondent.

"Mom, we got so worried about you. You've been acting *off*, for way too long," Leena started, and couldn't hold back her question any longer. "Are Lyle and Annie, are they OK?"

April's face remained grim. Her mind was calculating many different things. She sighed. "Let's go sit down," April said in a low, soft voice. She sat upon her armchair. Derek and Leena sat down on either side of the couch facing her; Cyndi found the middle cushion. April was silent. She looked at each one of them, stalling for time, as if looking for the right way to deliver what she had to say.

"It seems that you know too much about everything," April began, "things that, if I had my way, would have remained secret." She paused again. The three on the couch sat mystified, waiting eagerly for whatever she had to say next. "All well and good, I suppose, for it falls into the spirit of this." Derek had no idea where she was going. His mother sounded like someone he never knew, this person had to be an imposter—hidden keys to knives to old love letters. He glanced at Leena and Cyndi; they were equally as perplexed by her words.

"Annie and Lyle are fine," April answered their question. "Aging, like we all are, but fine. I can see you being intrigued by your father, curious at least. However, I'm not sure why you asked about Annie."

"We thought you may have hurt them," Derek said, "based on how strange you have been acting. And we know you weren't at Eileen's for the last few days."

April started to nod her head and found a half-smile. "I see," she started again. "I am many things, but I'm not one to inflict harm on anyone."

Leena interrupted, "But the police were here."

"Yes, they were. They were asking questions about a couple of break-ins where I store something of value."

Cyndi and Derek locked eyes. "I think we can probably clear that one up for you," Derek gave his confession.

"So, you know about my Jetta, too?" April shook her head. "I guess it's all out in the open. This might take a little while, let me make some tea." The intensity and horror that they felt just a few minutes ago started to dissipate.

Cyndi hugged Leena, and then she hugged Derek. "Your mom is not a killer," she whispered. The slow release of a gripping terror, started to make Derek feel light, as if the earth's gravity shifted, allowing him to move more easily and fight less against its power.

Ten minutes later, April returned with four cups of green tea. "You deserve the truth," April was the first to take a sip of the hot soothing liquid. "I have been, how do I say, not myself as of late. I admit, I've been agitated, borderline distraught. I have been working myself up a lot recently. I also was working myself up to find the nerve to attend to my journey that I was just on—after visiting Eileen's."

"Journey?" Leena asked.

"I guess. It's the best word I can find. My journey of forgiveness; to give and to ask for." All four of them sipped on their tea, needing a moment to reflect. "You see, Anika, Annie as she went by and she still does today, was my babysitter. Eileen was much younger than I, she doesn't know much. All you need to know is she wasn't a good babysitter. She would make me do things, would force me to do things that no little girl—child—should have been forced to do."

Leena and Derek had never heard their mother speak at this level to them. She was letting them in, along with Cyndi, into her past and revealed more of herself than they had ever known.

"Anyway," April continued, "I found out just a little while ago that something bad happened to her when she was young. It doesn't matter what it was. Good or bad, I felt sorry for her. I wanted, no, I needed to forgive her. I wanted to be free of holding on to hating her for all these years. She went through a lot I learned. Time keeps moving, life is short. I *needed* to tell her. I *needed* the peace of issuing forgiveness. It was one of the hardest things I've done." The house was still. The three on the couch continued to take in every word.

"Gordon, well, that's where your middle name came from, Derek. We were young. But he was my everything. Gordon died in a car accident just after high school. He caught a ride and was heading to basic training. He always wanted to be in the Navy. We had plans of him coming back and having money to attend college. I found a job right after graduation, I wanted to be established and have a steady income for him to come back to. It was all cut short." With a hint of sadness, she took another sip of tea. Her voice shrank. "I have never been to that cemetery. I couldn't bear the pain, way back then. Time went by and it still hurt too much. More time passed, and then I swore I would never go. I was angry at him for leaving me. And so yesterday, I visited his headstone and left him some purple hyacinths—the flower of forgiveness. I begged for his understanding and asked for his forgiveness for being angry for so long. And I told him I would visit him every year. I plan to go again this year, on the day—the day when the accident took him from me. I think it will be good for me, this time, to say goodbye on that day."

Cyndi placed her hand upon Derek's left knee. Derek's hand found hers. April saw it and smiled. "As for Lyle, your father—this was my hardest visit. I held onto the most animosity for Lyle—for so much of my life. Where do I start?" she finished her tea and sat her cup down beside her on the nearby stand. She was having a hard time finding the words. "Your father, he was the one that Gordon rode with, that night." Leena, Derek, and Cyndi were riveted, all of these years and they had no idea the depth and tragedy of her life's experiences. Up until now, their mom was their mom, a constant; punctual, wise, and always caring, but just mom. She was now something, someone, so much more. A deeper person full of life's greatest joys and deepest sorrows.

"I forgave him today—Lyle," April began again, her voice started to crack from emotion, "see, he and Gordon were good friends back in the day. Lyle, after the accident watched out for me. I could tell he genuinely cared for me. In time, I needed someone, I wanted someone. Lyle was there for me and so we began a life together, about five years after Gordon's death, we married." She sighed and her back began to tense. Her eyes reddened.

"You don't have to if you don't want, Mom," Leena said quietly sensing how difficult it was for her. It was exactly what April needed to mount the courage to finish.

"You know, I forgave him back then, for the crash that took Gordon. Until, while pregnant for you, Leena, I stumbled upon something. It was his journal. I found it in the garden shed of all places, he was obviously hiding it. But I did find it, by accident." April placed both hands upon her face and starting at the forehead, let her hands slide down to her chin. She then put her hands together and folded them on her lap. After a long sigh, she started again. "Lyle had been drinking the night Gordon died, the night he crashed the car, when the telephone pole decimated the passenger's side of the vehicle." A tear descended down her cheek and dripped on the floor. "He held this secret from me, but his journal told the confession. I was so angry. So angry. The next day I went to find an attorney to start the divorce proceedings. And just like that, I took his children away from him because of the emotional pain I was in. I wanted him to hurt. His parents owned a business. I traded him. I let go of any rights or claims to the business if he gave up full parental rights of you two, once more, never to see you. And the deal became our decree."

"We saw it, Mom," Derek said quietly.

"In my VW, my safe deposit box," April finished. The dialogue stalled. Leena, Derek, and Cyndi just let the words soak in; it was a lot to take in all at once.

"And so," April began once more, "I needed to fully forgive him, after all these years. I wanted to be free of everything. I've been tormented by this for too long, I needed to let it *all* go."

"But the knife," Leena interrupted.

"The knife was your father's. I kept it in my Jetta up until last month. If I was going to forgive him, I wanted to give back the only thing I had remaining of his—a final release of everything, the emotional and the physical. This morning, I gave him my forgiveness, handed him his knife, and turned before he could say anything. I drove home and here I am talking with you. The last few days have been so hard. But I am feeling lighter already," she paused, "Forgiveness, you see— granting it and asking for it, and truly meaning it—is no easy task. I held on to so much animosity for so long. Hating someone takes a toll on you; what started as rage migrated to active loathing. There were times I wished he would die. I prayed at night to go back in time, for the roles to be reversed. For Gordon to be alive, and for Lyle to be dead. That's no way to feel about the father of my wonderful children, is it? Here I am at my age, I finally chose to let it all go. You must know," April looked intensely into the eyes of each of them. "Leena, Derek, Cyndi, you're all adults and probably already know this. Forgiveness is a tremendously difficult thing, it's one of the hardest things a human can do, to fully grant forgiveness with no strings attached. And I now believe, it's equally as hard to ask for forgiveness. And it's also one of the most important. I hope you forgive me, too. For taking away a father that you deserved." It was then that Derek and Leena, followed by Cyndi, got up, kneeled around her chair, and embraced their mother. Tears flowed like the April rain outside.

Cyndi, with Derek, drove Leena back to her car that was parked outside the bakery they had met at yesterday. The conversation went from disbelief to light-heartedness. Derek pointed out that it was not every day where you get to experience this type of thing; finally wrapping your head around your mom being a murderer one minute, and then finding out that she is everything but—and one of the best human beings on the planet—hours later.

63

When it was late Sunday afternoon, Derek started to think about work on Monday; it was also Cyndi's first day at her new job. "Are you excited for work tomorrow?" Derek asked.

"Yes, I am," Cyndi responded, "I know first days are always memorable. And sometimes a little nerve-wracking. Though, after this weekend, I don't think I can classify a first day of work as nerve-wracking anymore."

"Unless," Derek teased, "unless, our two new police friends come and haul you off in front of everyone."

"Did you see the way they looked at you, Derek?"

"It's almost as if they were looking for someone who got shot with a BB gun," Derek said, rubbing his healing cheek.

"Routine check, I would say. We broke nothing at *Twigg's*—not even the door—thanks to your credit card."

They underestimated the emotional upheaval the last week had on them. They craved water, food, and above all sleep. "I think it was incredibly brave what your mother did this past week," Cyndi said, they were almost at Derek's house.

"The bravest I would say. I told myself I wanted to be closer to her. She opened herself up to us, after all these years." They pulled into his driveway.

Cyndi unbuckled her seat belt. "I can't stay for long."

Derek didn't unbuckle his seat belt but just sat staring at his house.

Finally, after more pause, "All these years, Mom has just been Mom. She's not just my mom anymore. She's one of the greatest people I have ever known." The feelings that swept over Derek, from their recent adventure, were nothing short of mind-blowing. He had greater empathy for his mother than ever. She had gone through torment in her youth that was fully concealed to them. Thinking you know someone, and then finding this sort of depth—it humbled Derek. Finally, he unbuckled his seat belt, and they went inside. Derek poured large glasses of water and cut up a cucumber and toasted some bread to make a few sandwiches. They ate and drank together in silence, connecting all of the dots of the last several days.

"Let me change your bandage," Cyndi said after they both placed their dishes in the dishwasher.

"I won't fight it," Derek responded.

"What a hard life she had, early on. So much pain," Cyndi said as she applied some rubbing alcohol, the wound was healing well already.

"I can't blame her for the blame she assigned to any of them. To Annie, her abusive babysitter. To Gordon, her soulmate—for dying. I mean, it wasn't his fault, but I can see how Mom thought of it as a betrayal. And then, my father," his memory of that day when the man in the khaki jacket left them in silence flashed again in his mind, more vivid than ever before. "I can't blame Mom for blaming him, for despising him." Cyndi finished with the wound care. "In fact, if there's one thing that's come out of this, it is for me not to cast any blame, or judge anyone. The entire spirit of what Mom just did—letting go of it all so it doesn't consume you—it's a powerful lesson." Cyndi kissed Derek on the forehead. "Will you text me when you get to your apartment?" Derek asked.

"Of course," Cyndi replied, their lips met.

64

D erek waited until his manager arrived in the morning. When he knew she had enough time to start the morning, he visited her office and informed her that he wanted the promotion he was offered not long ago if it was still available. "I think we can make that happen," was the response he was given. He caught up on most of the last week's work, his mind drifting often to the last several days.

At lunch, Derek looked out the large windows of his office over the parking lot. Customers came and went, bringing home anything from a temporary repair to full on home improvement. It was a warm late April spring day. Winter had left for the year. He decided to take a walk outside and grabbed his phone on the way out.

His first call was to his mom. It was likely that he would call her every day this week to make sure things were OK. It was mind boggling trying to think of what she experienced so long ago. It was also unimaginable as to what she just went through, requesting and or granting forgiveness from three souls of your past. After the call, Derek remarked on how clear her voice was. The distracted tension in her voice that was there last week was now gone. As they finished the call, she thanked him for fixing her bathroom wall and for replacing her grill cover.

"I'm making dinner on Saturday at 5PM. Leena, Eli, and Everly are coming. I want you to come, too. And Cyndi. Do you want me to invite her, or will you?" Derek knew her angle.

"I think I can find a way to ask her." And for the first time in Derek's life, he ended a call with his mother with, *I love you*, and received the same in return.

He felt good. He asked for a promotion, and he told his mother he loved her. Today was a good Monday, if not the best ever. While he knew Cyndi must be busy on her first day, he decided to place a call. On any other day, he would have texted, today he needed to talk to Cyndi; he took the chance that she might be free.

"Hi," the phone did not go to voicemail and the intonation in Cyndi's voice made it clear that she was glad to hear from him.

"Hello, how goes your first day—I just needed to call."

"It's going *great*," Cyndi said with enthusiasm, "the people here are too nice. They are supportive, kind, I get to bring my full marketing plan forward in a month, to show how I want to grow things, plans on how we can make positive impacts in the community and bring in more revenue. I made the right choice." Derek could sense she was in a good place. While there is always a honeymoon in any job, he was convinced that this was the place for her. She had already convinced him the day they went out for coffee but had tea instead, on that wonderful Wednesday.

"I'm happy for you, Cyndi. I can't wait to hear all the details."

"How's your Monday treating you?" Cyndi asked, her voice still excited from being able to tell Derek about how good things were going.

"It's actually pretty good. Nothing better than a your-mom's-not-a-murderer moment to make you appreciative of everything you have." Cyndi laughed. "Speaking of being able to hear all the details about your day, even your week, do you think you could come to dinner at my mom's on Saturday evening?"

"Why Derek, is this your mom asking me as an old friend, or are you asking me out on a date to meet your family—*already*?"

Derek paused. "Yes."

"Then yes to both," Cyndi responded. "And Derek, why don't we come back to my apartment for dessert." Derek thought for a moment and pondered her statement. Double entendre or not, he was game for one, or both interpretations.

"I would love to join you for an after-dinner engagement," Derek retorted.

"I can't wait. I have to run, I'm going to meet with the veterinary technicians after lunch, I want to memorize their names ahead of time so I can impress them," Cyndi said. He knew they would be impressed no matter what.

"I miss you," Derek said without realizing.

"I miss you, too. And Derek, I'm so glad to have landed this job and to have found some random guy."

Derek worked for the rest of the day with a giant smile on his face. Several times a few of his co-workers asked what was going on as they had never seen him so happy. He wanted to tell them that his mother wasn't a killer and that he was falling head over heels—again—for his high school crush. But Derek tried to keep some distance at work. He always thought it was better for people to guess than know.

65

He arrived home after work and went for a walk. The spring brought more crocuses, more daffodils, but the most prolific flower he found in the young spring beds of his neighbors were purple hyacinths. He never paid much attention to them before, but it now had become his favorite flower. Perhaps he would create a garden full of them in his front yard, it needed some attention, and he could think of nothing else that he would look forward to as spring arrived the following year. A week ago, spring had been one of his least favorite seasons. Instantly it was now his favorite.

Derek turned on a baseball game. It didn't matter if it was a boring American league game. But it was still baseball and it brought him comfort. He reached for his phone and began a text. *Hi Leena, hope you are doing well. Can't wait to see you all at Mom's on Saturday.* He put it down and watched the next batter strike out—all the while attempting to be patient before picking up the phone yet again. As the next batter got caught looking, he picked up the phone and began a text to Cyndi. *I'm not thinking about you at all. Not one bit.* He hit send. The bubbles started—Derek's pupils widened. Cyndi replied, *I'm not thinking about you more. I can stop thinking about you all the time. In fact, I'm always not thinking about you.*

Sleep wouldn't come easily tonight, it felt as if there was too much oxygen in the air to breathe which created a buzzing feeling of being awake and alive at a new dimensional level. Saturday couldn't come soon enough. The baseball game was relaxing, and he was thankful for it. He wondered if Cyndi liked baseball, but he couldn't remember. It didn't matter if she did or didn't. She was Cynthia Vaughn, the smartest, funniest, classiest person to have ever broken into a vehicle storage facility.

66

The remainder of the week dragged for Derek. The anticipation of having his family together, with Cyndi, was too much of an exciting prospect. Through his excitement, he found a tremendous amount of energy. Derek caught up and surpassed his expectations at work; catching up with every to-do on his list, creating more organization in his email folders, even beginning to design an easier process for the store managers to submit their monthly reports. He would go to store number nine directly and show him how easy the new process was. It had been a while since he visited the likable, yet borderline curmudgeon.

The extra energy didn't stop at work. One night, Derek did a deep clean of his house. The next, he purchased more artwork for several of his walls that had screamed for décor, ever since he moved in. On Thursday night, he came home with a gallon of soft sage green paint to paint his bedroom. He had the urge to make it feel more like spring and his house, more like home. Painting called for music, and to Derek, *Holst's*

Planets provided the right mix of powerful crescendos to match his paint rolling, and it offered the soft flowing calmness to assist him while he did the edging.

On Friday evening, he decided he'd create a surprise for Cyndi and his mom that would take some time. To either side of his entrance way stairs that led up to his front door, Derek started to dig a hyacinth garden. In the fall, he'd plant the bulbs.

67

Saturday arrived. More warmth came and the color green made itself known; the deciduous trees were fully out, and the lawns were days away from asking for their first cut. Derek was so excited to see Cyndi that he invited himself over to pick her up and drive her to his mother's.

As Derek walked up the stairs to Cyndi's apartment, he was greeted by the door swinging open, "Welcome, Derek G. Densmore. How do you do?"

They embraced for a minute before Derek responded, "I do much better now." Cyndi offered Derek some iced tea and they sat while catching up on all of the week's events. On one of her windowsills stood two framed pictures—the ones she acquired while going through his mom's box of photos. To the left, in a brushed nickel frame was the photo of the three of them, smiling together, looking as happy as what worry free would look like if it could be captured in a photograph. To the right, in a lightly stained wooden frame was the photo of he and Cyndi playing tag, the depth and authenticity of their smiles almost matched. Cyndi noticed his eyes were on the photos. "I think we were pretty cute, back then. That photo is almost twenty years old."

"I remember that day," Derek responded, "and you know what, I think we're still pretty cute." They started to kiss. "Dinner, there's dinner at my mom's," Derek attempted to say in-between the brief moments that Cyndi's lips weren't on his.

"Hors d'oeuvres, Monsieur?" Cyndi countered.

After their drive, Derek gave his mother a giant squeeze when he entered 23 Clover Drive. This was new, too—as was his saying *I love you* after every time they talked or texted. "You're well, Mom?"

"I couldn't be better. I'm in a good place," his mother replied. It was evident to Derek that things were indeed better. She seemed so much more relaxed, both in her voice as well as the way she moved about. Everything was in its place within her house, and no dirty dishes hid in the sink.

Leena arrived with her family. Everly brought her toy and began to show off how good she was at it. Everly was getting big now, but Derek ran over and picked her up anyway. "How's my favorite niece?"

In a giggly voice only a happy five-year-old can make, she responded, "I'm good, Uncle Derek, I'm glad you're here."

"I'm glad you're here," Derek kissed her cheek.

"What's wrong with your cheek?" Everly asked while pointing. It was healing nicely, and he had picked up some concealer to use, though the appetizers at Cyndi's removed any trace of his attempt to hide it earlier in the morning.

"Big mosquito," Derek responded, "it's doing much better."

They sat down to feast on salad and pasta. April started to center family meals around the taste buds of Everly. During the meal, Derek glanced around the table at everyone. How simple a thing it is to enjoy a meal with people you care about so deeply. Derek reached under the table to squeeze Cyndi's knee. She responded back with a wink. Derek smiled so intensely that Leena asked him what was so funny. "Just life," Derek responded. "A toast," Derek raised his water glass; Everly became fascinated. "A toast to family. A toast to Mom. A toast to a friend returning. A toast to springtime. And a toast to forgiveness." They touched each other's glasses and drank deeply.

After dinner, Leena, Derek, and their mom were in the kitchen attending to the dishes. Leena looked perplexed. "Something on your mind, Leena?" their mom asked.

"Yes, and I didn't want to ask you at the dinner table. The other day when we—when we had our talk—you indicated that your old car was something of value to you. Derek said it looked like an old VW. I didn't know they were a sought-after classic, are they?" April shut the dishwasher door and turned to them.

"No, it was a good car, but I don't think it's a car collector's dream."

"But it's valuable?" Derek asked.

"It's valuable to me, more like precious. I brought you home in that car from the hospital. Both of you. It just made me happy to bring my healthy beautiful babies home. I couldn't part with it. And it made one heck of a good hiding place—at least until Derek and Cyndi meddled in my affairs." Derek and Leena planted kisses on her cheeks.

"You're the best mom," Derek whispered in her ear.

68

Derek drove Cyndi's Prius to her apartment. They both took a few quiet minutes to reflect on the dinner they had with family and friends. Cyndi broke the silence, "I've always wanted to go to a Phillies game, would you like to go?"

"I think we can arrange that, pretty sure of it," Derek replied.

As they drove, Cyndi softly whistled much of the way. "What are you smiling about?" she asked.

"I've never heard an unhappy person whistle," Derek responded.

"Well, maybe I am happy, Derek G. Densmore. Can you drive me home please? See, I'm kind of in a hurry. I have a date with some random guy. I promised him dessert."

"I see," Derek said. His smile and Cyndi's met; two happy souls, interlocked with the thoughts of a lifetime ahead of them, connected in a pattern of togetherness.

Cyndi continued to gently whistle. The memory of his middle school teacher popped in his head. "Well, have you ever heard an unhappy person whistle?" Derek was certain she was doing what he did when he was happy; she was making up an impromptu whistle to let the world know—*I'm happy*.

He was with Cyndi Vaughn. *The* Cyndi Vaughn. He had dreams about her, from sophomore year of high school. They were not the typical kind of male teenage dreams that you think of. Derek knew he wanted her in every way; he wanted to protect her, be there for her, love her. And then she moved, and he had only one thing he could do—let her go. We all must let go of the people we love. His mother let go of Leena and him. Luckily, he found his way back to his mom after so many years.

"You came back," Derek said after a few minutes of driving. Cyndi stopped whistling.

"True friends are true friends." This time she squeezed his knee.

It was as if he was in a movie. Just last week he was in a twisted murder mystery with his mother playing the lead role. Now he was in a romance with the used-to-be girl next door. Approaching Cyndi's apartment, Derek thanked the Universe for forgiveness. Everything about his mother's forgiveness quest, it brought him closer to Cyndi. It brought him closer to Leena, to Everly, to Eli. It brought him closer to his mother. Never had he had such a grateful point of view—finding so much joy in the breeze; consciously releasing the unrestricted thoughts of gratitude.

"Thank you," Derek said upon parking Cyndi's car, arriving at her apartment.

"For?" Cyndi asked as she unfastened her seat belt.

"Being there, being here. Last week, now. Tonight. You just have no idea how much it means."

"Derek G. Densmore," Cyndi let a few moments

pass, "I've always wanted to be part of your family. Now let's go inside and talk about our week. And remember, there's dessert."

They sat on the couch relaxing after the long week, unwinding after the prior week's intensity. "Question, should I go before your random guy comes over?" Derek asked turning and finding Cyndi's eyes.

"I think you can stay," Cyndi responded. "Besides, I like a man who gets bit by a dog and shot in the face for his mother."

Cyndi reached to turn off the light and began to straddle him. Her lips found his and time evaporated. Moments passed. "Cyndi?" Derek asked.

"Yes?" Cyndi responded, jolted, as if interrupted mid performance.

"Mom asked me tonight if you and I wanted to go and get her car from *Twigg's*. She said there was no reason to have it there anymore—she said she might like to drive it again."

"What did you say?" Cyndi asked.

"Hard pass," Derek said, and he pushed Cyndi's torso down onto the couch and delivered every ounce of every feeling of happiness, love, and appreciation and applied it to her lips.

After recovering from the kiss, Cyndi spoke. "If that random guy happens to show up, tell him to go away. I'm good."

ABOUT THE AUTHOR

David J. Hull hails from the Green Mountains of Vermont. Growing up, his father could never pass by a bookstore without bringing a book home. In doing so, David was quite literally surrounded by books in almost every room of his childhood home.

His stories shine the spotlight on the human condition and expose the true joy and real pain that comes with being human—emotional highs and lows that none of us can escape. Because he was not surrounded by musical instruments, he writes mainly because he cannot play the guitar all that well.